**Also available from Allie Therin
and Carina Press**

The Magic in Manhattan Series

Spellbound
Starcrossed
Wonderstruck

Proper Scoundrels deals with topics some readers might find difficult, including mentions of past torture and self-harm.

PROPER SCOUNDRELS

Allie Therin

carina
press

Recycling programs
for this product may
not exist in your area.

carina
press®

ISBN-13: 978-1-335-47404-9

Proper Scoundrels

Copyright © 2021 by Allie Therin

This edition published by arrangement with Harlequin Books S.A.

For questions and comments about the quality of this book, please contact us at CustomerService@Harlequin.com.

Carina Press
22 Adelaide St. West, 41st Floor
Toronto, Ontario M5H 4E3, Canada
www.CarinaPress.com

Printed in U.S.A.

For the dandelions.

Although the novels set in the Magic in Manhattan world are works of fiction, real history also runs through these stories. This series would not be possible without the hard work of historians and librarians to make the archives of the past available to the public.

PROPER SCOUNDRELS

Prologue

November 1922
Yorkshire

Parties were a wretched invention.

Wesley stood near the wall, whiskey in hand. The ballroom was brimming with guests. They clustered in endless tight circles, their clothes too modern and their laughs too loud. Men in tuxedos with too-short tails, flirting with women in sequined dresses and feathered headbands, the lot of them sipping gin cocktails under centuries-old chandeliers.

Wesley didn't follow trends. He wore the exact same style of tuxedo he would have worn ten years ago, when he was a shamefully innocent nineteen-year-old who had never heard of a trench.

The eyes of the other guests darted his way now and then. Wesley ignored it; he hadn't made the trip all the way out to Yorkshire to care what the socialites said about him. Christ, why *was* he here? His father had been the one acquainted with the Earl of Blanshard; Wesley had only been invited because he now carried the title. He'd been done with Yorkshire; had planned to go the rest of his life without seeing the green and gray moors and their frolicking lambs, or the giant cathedral in town.

But he knew why he was here. The Earl of Blanshard had implied his dinner would be a draw for military men, and Wesley craved that company like he craved his cigarettes, people who understood that the world wasn't good or fair and no amount of frivolity would bring back everything and everyone the war had taken. Wesley had come up from London because he'd let himself indulge in a pointless, pathetic moment of weakness, and he had deserved to discover that there were no other soldiers in the ballroom after all. Now all he wanted was a smoke before he crawled out of his own skin.

A baronet he knew from his club, Sir Harold Kerrigan, broke away from the closest cluster of guests and began heading toward Wesley with the puffed-out chest of a schoolboy who'd accepted a dare. Marvelous; someone, probably a pretty woman Sir Harold wanted to impress, had decided Wesley needed to be engaged in conversation.

"Lord Fine!"

Wesley didn't flinch at the new title, but it was a close thing.

"The new viscount, good to see you." Beneath thin yellow hair, Sir Harold's pale skin was flushed red through the cheeks and nose, and his hazel eyes were shiny from liquor. He'd chosen to flout traditions and go gloveless, the classless sod, and even more insulting, picked one of those modern double-breasted tuxedo jackets that mimicked military styling. If this soft prat had ever seen action, Wesley would eat the man's under-starched collar.

"I say, I was sorry to hear about your father," Sir

Harold went on, as if Wesley could possibly want to talk about this. "You're his spitting image, you know."

Wesley's brother had been too, all three of them over six feet tall with the same brown hair and gray eyes. Now only Wesley was left, and he couldn't set foot in society without people who'd sat out the war in the comfort of their homes wanting him to know how sorry they were for his losses.

"By all means, let's hear your condolences for my father, whom I know you were barely acquainted with," he said crisply. "Would you like to discuss my dead mother too? After all, this is a party."

Sir Harold gave him a wide-eyed look.

"Oh, I'm sorry, was I supposed to say something tritely polite?" Wesley turned away, and Sir Harold unsurprisingly didn't follow.

Wesley left the ground-floor ballroom, wandering down a wide hall with red carpet. The dark wood walls were lined with portraits of white men—Blanshard's ancestors, certainly, because every last one was almost eerily similar in look to the Earl of Blanshard himself: the same small pointed nose and chin, the thin lips, the pale skin and eyes. They could have been portraits of the same man, only the clothes of the past two centuries changing.

Wesley preferred landscapes to people, both in his art and his company, but then, art was a waste in the first place. Nothing but an attempt at a distraction, as if a bit of paint could camouflage the shortfalls of one's true surroundings.

At the end of the hall was a wide staircase curving up to the first floor. Wesley's feet made no noise on the carpet as he climbed, passing a dark window at the landing, rain lashing the black glass. The smoking room had to be nearby; surely he wasn't expected to make it through an evening without respite.

The stairs brought him to another wide hall, this one lined with doors along one side and an open railing that overlooked the downstairs on the other. Waist-high white pillars were spaced down the hall, topped with glass display cases. The closest one held a Spanish morion, the silver gleaming almost too bright in the hall's electric lights.

Wesley wasn't interested in art, but a helmet that might have seen battle did make him pause. As he leaned in for a closer look at the etchings that decorated the morion, a woman's shout came from somewhere to his right.

"Mr. Chester! I told you to—oh, my lord!"

Wesley looked over to see a woman in a maid's uniform, her face bright red. "Begging your pardon," she stammered, making a hurried curtsy. "We had someone's valet poking about earlier. I didn't mean to—"

"It's fine," he said tiredly, before the maid could continue her self-recrimination. She was probably around thirty, like he himself was, like many of the women downstairs. But unlike the guests, she wore no makeup, the lines visible at the corners of her mouth and eyes. His soldiers' faces had been like hers, aged too soon by too much work and uncertainty, and Wesley had a shred more patience for her accidental impudence than he had for Sir Harold's insincere sympathies. "If you could point me to the smoking room?"

She curtsied again, rag still in hand. "Of course, my lord. The next hallway, second door. I'll see that you're tended to."

The next hallway had doors on both sides, which meant it had two *second doors*. Wesley narrowed his eyes. The headache forming in his temple wasn't going to go away without a smoke, and the maid truly could have been more precise and not wasted his time.

The first door he tried was locked, but the other door was, mercifully, the smoking room. It had the dark wood walls of the rest of the manor, with leather furniture in shades of burgundy and black. At least the art was landscapes here, every last one a hunting scene. Wesley's father would have approved, and would have expected Wesley to approve as well—Wesley was a dead shot with a firearm, thanks to the man, even four years after the war. The thought only made Wesley want a cigarette more.

This early in the evening, the room was empty, the other men were likely waiting until after dinner to join each other for smokes. Exactly as Wesley wanted. He picked the chair in the deepest corner and settled into the leather. A footman appeared, a box in hand. He opened the lid, displaying a selection of fine cigars, two of them quite rare.

Wesley would have blown the man for a cheap pack of Woodbine. It was all tobacco, the doctors were saying it all rotted your lungs—what was the point in dressing it up? He'd smoked whatever he got his hands on in the army, same as his men. Giving it a fancy appearance now didn't change how Wesley's skin itched for it, how he became irritable as a bear without it, how he'd been infected with something as galling as an addiction.

But then, people did assume a cigar was a choice, not a craving. He picked one from the box at random. It would give him the peace of mind to get through dinner.

He took his time inhaling peppery tobacco, smoking the cigar down to the stub and letting it take the edge off his irritation. Eventually, however, the thought of someone looking for him made him reluctantly stand from his seat. Marginally calmer, or at least no longer itching, he left the stub in an ashtray and went back into the hall.

But as he stepped into the hall, he saw Sir Harold again, opening the door straight across.

Christ, could Wesley not even get a smoke in peace? "This one is the smoking room," Wesley said impatiently, to Sir Harold's back.

Sir Harold visibly startled. "Fine, old boy, I didn't realize you were up here," he said, a bit blustery as he quickly turned around.

Hearing *Fine* for himself, when it had always been his father, when it was always going to be his elder brother, was at least less sharp this time. "The earl has some rare cigars." Wesley could see Sir Harold had opened the door across the hall, his hand still on the knob. "Were you just in there? But that door was locked a few minutes ago."

"It wasn't locked when I arrived," Sir Harold said. "Perhaps you didn't turn the knob fully, jolly easy mistake to make."

"I didn't make a mistake," Wesley said flatly. "I turned the knob fully. The door was locked."

"Then I bet the earl himself had it unlocked!" said Sir Harold brightly. "My valet told me Lord Blanshard's main collection is in here, I simply couldn't resist taking a peek." He pushed the door open wider. "Here, come see for yourself. The earl's got all sorts of things in here I'm sure he'd love for us to admire. Jewels, weapons, a pomander from fifteenth-century Spain."

"What, those perfume balls people used to carry instead of bathing?" Wesley had as little interest in antiques as he had in art, and he rather doubted the earl would want them to admire a collection that had been behind a locked door.

But then, maybe the earl *had* unlocked the door, because what was the alternative explanation, that Sir Harold or his valet were going around picking locks on antiques collections? That seemed patently far-fetched, and regardless, it was an excuse to be late to dinner and engage in even less conversation. What more motivation did he need?

The main collection was in a library of sorts, with teeming bookshelves along the walls. Delicate carvings and gilding bordered the painted ceiling. The mural was of wolves hunting animals—and frightened peasants, a rather morbid artistic choice. Beneath the gilded ceiling, the antiques were set on glass-domed pillars every few feet: jewelry, sculptures, weapons—several weapons, in fact, and some even more sinister items.

Wesley stopped short at one display. "Christ, are those thumbscrews?"

"Terribly wicked, isn't it?" Sir Harold sounded more delighted than disturbed, like a child enjoying a scare at a carnival show, not a grown man seeing real atrocities.

Wesley eyed the screws for a moment more. Perhaps the earl fancied himself one of those carnival showmen, shocking his audience with a ceiling of wolves devouring humans and torture devices on open display, but Wesley frankly wouldn't be shocked by anything less than sorcery.

Past the screws was a collection of rings, then a small crystal bottle with a carved ivory case, perhaps eighteenth century. It reminded Wesley of the *sal volatile*, the smelling salts that he'd seen as a child in the Yorkshire country doctor's medical bag.

He quickly moved on.

The next display held a pendant on a chain, and then there was a stunning astrological clock, with dials for the Zodiac as well as time. A small display tag read *Victor de Leon, 1498*. Wesley took in the clock for several moments, grudgingly admiring it. The dials were rings of gold inlaid in circles of onyx black, accented with a bright turquoise that reminded him of the impossible blue-green of the Caribbean he'd once seen painted on a tourist advert for Puerto Rico. The poster had been fanciful nonsense, of course; how could an ocean ever be such a color?

A few more displays down was the pomander Sir Harold had mentioned. It was a sphere about the size of an orange, made of filigreed gold and silver with a delicate chain. The gold seemed exceptionally bright, shining like it had just been polished.

Wesley bent for a better look. The pomander was nestled in silk in an opened box and the glass box surrounding it seemed thicker than the other displays—leaded, perhaps. *Gascon de Ayala, 1495, its display tag read.*

"Blanshard has a lot of things from the Spanish Inquisition," Wesley observed.

"Maybe that's where the screws are from too," Sir Harold said, with relish. He clapped Wesley on the bicep. "Best get down to dinner, then."

"I don't remember employing you to manage my schedule."

Sir Harold held his hands up. "It was just a suggestion. Lady Newton is right; you'd do better with a wife, Fine."

As if Wesley would ever saddle some poor woman with his rude, curmudgeonly presence for public appearances' sake. There was no one left but him now, so that meant no one could argue if he chose to damn well stay a bachelor forever.

He heard Sir Harold's footsteps disappear, but Wesley lingered at the pomander. He might have described the item as *unpleasant*, somehow, if that wasn't a patently ridiculous thought. It was undeniably fine craftsmanship, after all. But it was just so frightfully well-preserved, seemingly untouched by age, as uncannily bright as if it had been made the day before.

"That's my favorite item."

Wesley glanced toward the doorway. It was the Earl of Blanshard himself, standing in the outline of the doorframe. As with the men in the portraits that lined his hall, Blanshard was a thoroughly unremarkable man, perhaps in his forties, particularly pale with dark blond hair and a pointed nose and chin.

He wasn't looking at the pomander, however. His gaze was on Wesley.

How long had he been watching?

Wesley straightened up. "It's an impressive collection."

"Thank you," said Lord Blanshard. "I've been working on it for longer than you would believe."

His gaze stayed on Wesley. As with the pomander, there was something unsettling about the moment, although for the life of him Wesley wasn't sure why. If Blanshard had unlocked the door for the party, then surely he did want his antiques collection admired?

The earl was also far from imposing physically, and he was only blinking calmly at Wesley now. Yet some part of Wesley's mind was screaming at him that he didn't want to be alone with Blanshard.

Then again, of course he was uncomfortable in his host's presence: Wesley was being unpardonably rude, poking about the earl's home and purposefully making himself late to dinner. He grudgingly adopted a more gracious expression. "I'm afraid it's so impressive that I've lost track of time. I was meant to be at dinner already, wasn't I?"

Blanshard only inclined his head. He moved out of the doorframe, however, making room for Wesley to join him.

"We both are," Blanshard added, lightly. "I'll just close this room behind us, shall I?"

The earl didn't seem particularly moved by Wesley's attempt at manners. Well, he could stew in it. Wesley didn't give a toss about being disliked; he frankly wouldn't know what to do with someone who *did* like him.

He followed Blanshard down the hall, leaving the room of antiques behind him.

Chapter One

The residential street in Kensington was as quiet as always, the stillness broken only by the occasional Bentley or Aston Martin puttering past the row of tall and stately homes. Sebastian stood under one of the trees that lined the street, its leaves a mix of summer greens and autumn browns. The air was chilly and damp with a misty evening rain, and he tucked his chin into his scarf under the flat cap.

Across the street was a four-story home of reddish brick with graceful front steps behind a short iron gate and large white-trimmed bay windows that curved to the street. A lovely home, and as far as he could tell, still completely hidden from magic.

Not that the home's owner, the Viscount Fine, had any idea. Lord Fine likewise had no idea Sebastian made sure to pass by every so often to check that everything was in order. But it was really the least Sebastian could do. Maybe he couldn't ever fully atone for the things he'd done to Arthur Kenzie and Rory Brodigan, but he could at least make sure that Arthur's aristocratic friend wasn't in any danger after Arthur and Rory had stayed in the Kensington house in the spring.

Not that Lord Fine *should* be in danger. Sebastian had never met or even seen Lord Fine for himself, but Arthur and Rory had said he didn't know about magic. Lord Fine hadn't known he'd had a paranormal house-guest in Rory, and he didn't know that in his basement now hung a paranormal painting by Sebastian's cousin, Isabel, a Barcelona cityscape that hid the home from magic eyes and would send most paranormals who got too close wandering in the opposite direction.

Lord Fine lived a perfectly normal life, safe and un-aware, but Sebastian still stayed careful. After all, not every paranormal who'd come after Rory Brodigan was gone. No one had seen one Jack Mercier, a paranormal with fire magic, since the spring. He knew exactly how deadly Mercier could be, and Sebastian chose not to take chances with nonmagical lives.

At least, now that he got to make choices for him-self again.

Sebastian abruptly stuck his hands in his pockets and turned to keep walking. Lord Fine was safe; maybe the bustling of the London Underground would distract him from the memories.

He took the train from the High Street Kensington station back to Liverpool Street. It was dark when he emerged out of the station onto the busy street, where more light rain fell on waiting taxis as flower girls and newsies wove between people and the occasional organ or pull cart. The meat man's cart was nowhere to be seen in the throng, but hopefully Sebastian could get some scraps for the cats from the pub later that night.

Sebastian's room was the same one he'd had since February, on the second floor—first floor, they called it in England, but he hadn't been here long enough to think of it that way—above the businesses that lined a pedestrian side street off Bishopsgate. The business directly below his room held the appearance of a shuttered art gallery. In the spring, they'd used it as a front for Isabel's paranormal art. Now her paintings had all been shipped back to his family in Spain—well, all except two, the painting of Barcelona in Kensington, which would stay where it was, and the painting that hung over Sebastian's table, of the blue San Juan Bay, the beach and palm trees, the bright sun and El Morro on the hill.

That one, he hadn't been ready to give back.

Sebastian went in through the gallery's front door to grab any mail that had been stuffed through the slot, usually nothing but flyers. He locked up behind him and scooped up the good-sized pile of papers from the gallery floor before heading up the internal staircase.

His room at the top of the stairs held only a narrow bed on one wall and a tiny table with two chairs on the other. It did, however, have its own potbellied iron stove with gas instead of coal, and September in London was already cool enough that he was grateful for it.

He lit the stove's pilot light, and it began to glow welcomingly warm at Sebastian's back as he sorted through the mail. Flyer for a chemist. Flyer for a grocer. Flyer for a dance show.

Letter from Jade Robbins.

Sebastian's eyebrows went up. He set everything else to the side and spread the envelope's contents across his tiny wooden table: a handwritten note and three newspaper clippings, one each from Paris, France; Frankfurt, Germany; and York, England.

June 18, 1925, *Meurtre non résolu à Paris.*

July 29, 1925, *Mord ohne Erklärung.*
September 2, 1925, *Body found, police stumped.*

Sebastian frowned. He spoke only the most basic French and German, but he was pretty sure the three headlines implied more or less the same thing.

Unexplainable murder.

He took a seat without taking the time to shed his coat, flat cap or scarf. He wasn't particularly tall or broad, but the rickety chair still protested beneath him as he picked up the letter. He hadn't seen Jade since May, when she had appeared in London with Rory and Arthur. They'd all gone off to Paris to recover the de Leon family's stolen siphon clock—the thing Sebastian himself absolutely could not do. Last he'd heard from any of them, they'd been successful, and the siphon was on its way to New York City.

There had been an invitation to America, but Sebastian's history with Jade and the others was—complicated. Complicated enough that Sebastian didn't like revisiting those memories, but then, did he have any memories from the past three years he ever wanted to see again?

He glanced up at the painting of San Juan over his table. It brought the good memories; if only they came more often than the bad ones.

Pushing all memories aside, he read Jade's letter.

Dear Sebastian,
I hope this letter finds you well since our eventful May—at the very least, that the recent months have been an improvement on those that came before. I'm sorry to pull you in again, but we believe the headlines we've sent you are connected, and that the killer is like us.

Can we speak with you? We will be at the pub
by Liverpool Street Station at 6pm on Friday.

A killer like us.
In other words, a paranormal murderer.
Sebastian glanced at his watch and swore quietly. It
was Friday, and he'd be five minutes late—if he'd arrived ten minutes ago.
He swept everything back into the envelope and took
the stairs back down as quickly as he could.

Besides its main door, the shuttered art gallery also
had a back door, into a dirty, claustrophobic alley overlooked by boarded-up windows. The pub was down at
the corner, where the alley had a narrow opening to
Bishopsgate. There were two half-grown cats in the
alley with him, maybe six or seven months old, probably siblings with matched orange-and-white coloring.
They were nosing in the trash cans outside the fish and
chips shop, but saw Sebastian and froze.
Even though he was in a hurry, Sebastian automatically slowed his pace and tried to look nonthreaten-
ing. "Están bien, gatitos," he said, softening his voice.
"You're okay."
The rangy kittens watched him warily from behind
their cans. The garbage had probably been picked over
by bigger strays, but maybe he could still get something for them.
He bypassed the pub's back kitchen door in the alley
for the main door along Bishopsgate. The flyers Isabel
had painted were still in the windows, and as he stepped
through the door, Sebastian felt the telltale tingle of
magic in his wrist, in the tattoo Isabel had given him.
Like Sebastian—like all of the de Leon family—Isa-

bel's paranormal talents worked on other paranormals, and her flyers protected the pub the way her painting protected Lord Fine's home in Kensington: they kept the pub hidden from magical detection, and would send most paranormals who laid eyes on the flyers immediately heading in the opposite direction with no memory of why they'd come.

Hopefully Jade and Zhang had remembered to avert their eyes, or he might find them wandering lost down Bishopsgate.

He pulled off his flat cap and held it in one hand as he entered. The pub was bustling and warm, every barstool full and most of the booths beside. Almost immediately he had to sidestep out of Calum the busboy's path, and nearly bumped into a group of men watching darts.

"Molly's Spanish prince!" Calum said, imitating Sebastian's Spanish accent as he breezed past with a tub of dirty dishes. He added, in his regular Scottish brogue, "Come on in, lad, Moll'll see to you. She always does," he added, with a lewd wink.

Sebastian didn't protest, because Molly had asked him to let people think they were *shagging*, as she called it. Molly liked princesses, not princes, and furthermore, was happily *seeing to* Sebastian's cousin every time Isabel was in town.

Sebastian was happy to be their cover. Maybe no one of any gender would be eager to cozy up to a man with a past like his, but at least he could help Isabel and Molly be together.

Molly herself was behind the bar, fighting with a stuck beer tap, green eyes narrowed in concentration and her bobbed black hair pinned out of her face. She'd pushed up the sleeves of her dress, some of Isabel's tattoo artistry just visible on Molly's right forearm. There were four impatient-looking men on barstools, but she spotted Sebastian as he came in, and gave him an eye roll that clearly said what she thought of work that day.

As Molly turned to deal with one of the customers, Sebastian caught a tiny movement—the beer tap unsticking itself, so subtly he almost could have been imagining it. Except, of course, he was meeting a telekinetic in this pub and he hadn't imagined a thing, because there Jade was, across the pub in one of the wooden side booths, cozied up to her man, Mr. Zhang.

Their heads were bent close together, but when they looked up, Zhang's glowing astral projection suddenly appeared floating to Sebastian's right. The projection would have been invisible to anyone who wasn't a paranormal, and was studying Sebastian so intently that he didn't seem to notice as Rosie, one of the waitresses, walked obliviously right through him.

"Molly'll get right with you, handsome," Rosie said to Sebastian, balancing her full tray of drinks.

"She is busy, I can wait—" Sebastian started, but Rosie had already disappeared.

In the booth, Zhang's physical body put an arm around Jade's shoulders, while to Sebastian's right, Zhang's astral projection frowned and said, "It's so annoying I can't find you on the astral plane until I know where you are with my physical eyes."

Sebastian's lips quirked. It was genuinely nice to see the two of them again, and perversely the spark of pleasure made him aware of how deeply alone he was now. He pushed away the thought. They needed him, and he owed them. They weren't here for his friendship, and considering his history with them, he was going to count himself lucky that they were here at all.

"The tattoo only hides me from magic," Sebastian

said to Zhang's projection, as he approached the edge of the table. He inclined his head politely at Jade and at Zhang's physical body. "Miss Robbins, that was very kind of you to help Molly."

"She's so terribly busy tonight," said Jade. "Least I can do is make sure she can pour her draughts."

Sebastian slid into the booth across from Jade. She was a particularly beautiful woman, her bright brown eyes and russet-brown skin luminous in the pub's yellowish light. She wore a well-tailored houndstooth man's suit and a cloche hat over her bobbed black curls, and her pink lipstick matched her scarf.

He offered her a rueful apology as he balanced his cap on his knee. "I'm sorry I'm late."

"And here we gave you so much notice."

Jade's self-deprecating smile was so charming that Sebastian found himself smiling back. "It is not a problem," he said, his voice warming. "I am always at your service."

"Are you?" Zhang said dryly, his arm still around Jade's shoulders.

Sebastian hid a wince. He never meant to put anyone on their guard around their partner, but he still managed to stumble into it regular as clockwork. Then again, Zhang could have simply been worried Sebastian was going to do something villainous, like kidnap them. In fairness, there was precedent.

"And at your service as well, of course," he said to Zhang, as sincerely as he'd addressed Jade. "You found my family's missing siphon clock. You will always have my gratitude."

"Hmph." Zhang didn't seem mollified, but he did let it go. "The siphon is still in New York. My mother has it." He was as handsome as Jade was lovely, with high cheekbones and deep brown eyes that popped against his pale skin. His jet-black hair shone when it caught the light. He was a scholar too, Sebastian remembered, and despite Sebastian's magic, didn't seem the least bit nervous.

Handsome, smart, and unintimidated.

Sebastian cleared his throat, forcing his thoughts to move on. "Did you learn anything more about the man who stole the siphon clock and tried to auction it?"

"Perhaps," Jade said meaningfully. "The Earl of Blanshard, known in his English social circles for his collection of continental antiques. I had a run-in with him at the world's fair in Paris in May, but we haven't found any trace of him since."

"We presume he only put the siphon up for sale because he was forced to by the Puppeteer," Zhang added.

Sebastian didn't quite hide his flinch. This was exactly what he hadn't wanted to talk about.

Jade's voice was gentle with pity as she asked, "Did you meet Lord Blanshard when you were under that same blood magic?"

Sebastian shook his head. "Perhaps he came to Baron Zeppler and the Puppeteer's attention after I was sent to New York." *Oh, perfect, Sebastian, why not bring up New York, where you kidnapped one of their friends and had a standoff at gunpoint with another?*

Jade hesitated. "How are you, by the way?" she said seriously.

Sebastian shrugged, trying for a lightness he hadn't felt in years. "Oh, you know," he said, possibly too quickly. "Keeping busy, moving on."

But Zhang shook his head. "No one simply *moves on* from blood magic," he said. "Are you actually going to claim you're fine, that you don't even have blood terrors?"

Wake up, de Leon. I need your magic—

Sebastian shoved away the echo in his head, and tried to smile reassuringly. "I am grateful for your concern," he said, which was true, and then he added the lie. "But I really am fine. My magic weakens other magic; why would the Puppeteer's blood magic be able to keep its hold on me?"

Like that question didn't haunt him with every nightmarish waking.

"But the newspaper clippings you sent are not about the siphon or the Earl of Blanshard, are they?" he said hurriedly moving the subject off himself. "Three bodies with no known cause of death?"

The couple exchanged a look, seeming to have a silent conversation. Then Jade leaned in. "You're probably wondering why we think the deaths are connected, and the killer one of us." She lowered her voice. "We did some more digging into the deaths. Jianwei went into the police stations and morgues on the astral plane."

Zhang had leaned in as well. "There's no known cause of death because there's no explanation for three shriveled bodies."

Sebastian's eyes widened. *"Shriveled?"*

"Like someone put a straw to their jugular and sucked them dry," said Zhang. "Skin translucent, muscles atrophied, bones thin and brittle."

"Neither of us have ever heard of magic like that," said Jade. "Have you?"

Sebastian chewed his lip. "It does remind me of a story, yes," he said. "Of an eighteenth-century paranormal. In English, they would have called him the Vampire."

"Family legend?" Zhang correctly guessed, because he was from a many-generations paranormal family too, Sebastian remembered. "What does a paranormal have to do to get a moniker like the Vampire?"

Sebastian winced. "Eat auras."

Jade and Zhang stared at him.

"That is the story," Sebastian said weakly. "He was a paranormal who could drain the auras of the nonmagical, and their life forces along with them."

Jade and Zhang exchanged a look. "Magical abilities always come back around," said Zhang. "We could be dealing with a paranormal with vampire magic."

Jade looked back at Sebastian. "What happened in your family story?"

"Supposedly one of my ancestors stopped him," said Sebastian. "But we don't know exactly what happened because my great-great-great-grandfather had written her out of the family. Apparently tía Casilda was something of a gray sheep."

"*Black* sheep," Zhang said reflexively.

"Oh, right." Sebastian made a face. "Idioms."

Zhang's expression seemed to grudgingly thaw, just a little.

Molly appeared at that moment, balancing three tonic waters and a basket of french fried potatoes.

"Wasn't expecting you, luv," she said to Sebastian, setting the potatoes in the middle of the table. Her pushed-up sleeve revealed the golden Celtic harp Isabel had tattooed on her forearm—not magic, like Sebastian's tattoo, because Molly wasn't a paranormal, but still so real you almost believed you could hear its angelic notes. Her mouth was uncharacteristically downturned and sad, enough that Sebastian would have hugged her if she wasn't carrying a tray.

"Dulcita, you did not have to bring me anything," he said to her.

"Rather see your handsome face then any of the louts at the bar." Molly set Jade and Zhang's drinks down first, casting a subtle, appreciative look at Jade in her man's suit. "Warm welcome to London, lovebirds." Molly's voice was friendly, but her smile still didn't appear. "We'll be seeing you tomorrow, then, won't we?" she said, again to Sebastian as she put his drink in front of him. "Me and Isa?"

And maybe that was why Molly was sad. Isabel was leaving again tomorrow, heading back to the world's fair in Paris. Isabel had gone several times over the summer, an artist in her element at the modern decorative and industrial arts exhibition. A handful of paranormals from different countries were showcasing paranormal tapestries and weavings together, using one of the department store pavilions as a front.

Sebastian nodded and leaned forward. "If I promise to bring lunch tomorrow, do you have any scraps I can take tonight?" he said, quiet and hopeful.

That got an almost-smile out of her. "Don't tell me how many cats are skulking in the alley, I don't want to know."

"Only two," Sebastian said, "but they're kittens."

"You know, most blokes come in here and bother the girls, not politely ask if we have food waste you can give the strays." Someone at the bar called Molly's name. She sighed, loud and put-upon. "I'll make Calum throw the scraps out now."

"Oy, Molly!" someone yelled again, and she left with another conspiratorial eye roll at Sebastian.

Jade looked amused, but she didn't comment on the cats. "Speaking of the world's fair," she said, "that's where we met Lord Blanshard. It was at a magic show, but I didn't learn what his magic is."

"And whatever Blanshard's magic, he's vanished," said Zhang. "So that's two problems. A murderer, likely a paranormal, who can drain life from bodies. A missing earl, definitely a paranormal, and definitely a thief."

Sebastian sat back in his seat. "Do you think these problems could be related? That the murderer could be the missing Earl of Blanshard, perhaps with this same vampire magic?"

"That's just what Jianwei and I have been wondering," Jade said grimly. "I'm certain Blanshard would have killed me at the magic show in May, if he could have. But now, he's not under blood magic anymore, we haven't found him, and the last murder was in York, where Blanshard has a manor."

Zhang reached into the breast pocket of his suit jacket and produced a folded piece of paper. "We have a copy of the guest list from his last-known party at that manor, about three years ago." He unfolded the paper, set it on the table, and pushed it over to Sebastian.

"There are three people of particular interest." Zhang tapped a name at the top of the list. "Sir Harold Kerrigan, a baronet. Found murdered in his London home in January of this year. Sir Harold's valet, Benedict Chester, made his way to New York this past February. He was the one in possession of the notorious pomander relic."

Sebastian remembered.

While under the Puppeteer's blood magic, he had been sent to New York by Baron Zeppler. There had been two other paranormals with him, including an Englishman known as Mr. Hyde who could transform into a monster. Mr. Hyde had gutted the valet and stolen the pomander relic—and then Sebastian had kid-napped Jade and Zhang's friend Rory and held Arthur at gunpoint.

He ran a hand through his hair. He wanted to ask if the siphon had worked, if they had succeeded in destroying a relic, but he was the one who owed them help and answers. He owed Jade and Zhang and their friends. He owed everyone for the things he'd done under blood magic.

"You mentioned Blanshard is known for his collection of continental antiques," Sebastian said. "Perhaps many of them are paranormal? Perhaps Blanshard stole the pomander and then this baronet, Sir Harold, stole it from him—only for Sir Harold's valet to turn around and murder his employer, and steal it for himself?"

"We think so," said Jade. "But look who else was at that party."

Zhang tapped a name farther down the list, one that had been circled.

Wesley Collins, the Viscount Fine.

Sebastian tilted his head. "Lord Fine? As in, the viscount who lives in Kensington and has one of my cousin's paintings?"

Jade nodded. "I will swear on a stack of Bibles that Lord Fine knows nothing of magic. But Sir Harold's valet hitched his ride to America by insinuating himself into *Fine*'s life as a valet. We may not know if Blanshard is a murderer, but I can vouch that he's a nasty piece of work. If he connects the stolen pomander to Chester and then to Lord Fine…" She made a face. "It's a lot of ifs."

"But also far too interwoven to be a coincidence." Sebastian bit his thumb. "I was in Kensington today," he said. "I stop by every now and then to be sure the magic is still protecting him, and it is. He should be safe."

Jade and Zhang both looked slightly surprised. "That's decent of you," Jade said. "You don't owe Lord Fine that."

"But I do owe it to Arthur and Rory, after what I put them through in America," Sebastian said. "But if Lord Fine might be a target of a paranormal murderer, I would help even if I did not feel the debt—well. If, ah." He swallowed. "If you want my help."

Jade picked up her tonic water, considering him. "Did you meet Lord Fine in the spring?"

Sebastian shook his head. "He was out when I arrived. I gave the painting of Barcelona to the footman and said it was a gift." The footman had seemed confused but pleased, and had agreed to hang it by the back door. "Lord Fine is your friend too, no?"

Zhang snorted. "*Friend* is such a strong word," he muttered, picking up his own drink.

Jade smiled ruefully again. "Fine has a reputation for being an ass—a deserved one, if I'm being perfectly honest—but I can't seem to help but like him. I'm sending a telegram this evening." Her smile turned more speculating. "And with that warning, if he agrees to meet with me, could I convince you to talk to him at some point?"

"Of course," Sebastian said. "How bad could he be?"

Chapter Two

It was eight o'clock on the dot. Wesley's tea was the proper temperature, steeped for exactly four minutes and served with freshly sliced lemon. His toast was satisfactorily golden. His newspaper had been unfolded and placed in its correct spot to the side of his tea, and the morning room's fire was adequately warm to offset the chill of a September day.

It would have been an acceptable breakfast, if not for the *ceaseless fucking yipping*.

"Christ, does that mongrel ever shut up?" Wesley raised his voice. "Dog! Cease this racket!"

His footman, Ned, lifted the teapot from the table. Wesley's staff was small these days—his footman, his driver, the cook, and two maids. Once upon a time, he'd also had a butler, and briefly, a valet, but the butler had retired and the valet had gotten himself offed in America—*mauled by an escaped zoo tiger*, the police reports had said, what were the fucking odds—and Wesley hadn't replaced them. Plenty of the aristocracy were reducing their staff, and he was, after all, quite alone and likely to stay that way forever.

"Begging your pardon, my lord," Ned said, as he poured tea into Wesley's china cup, "but Powderpuff probably can't hear you from Lady Pennington's yard."

Wesley gritted his teeth. His elderly neighbor, the one with whom he shared the back garden wall, had gone and adopted a Maltese, because she claimed the ridiculous creature's affections eased her rheumatoid pains. What a load of sentimental rot. Everyone was miserable; it was no excuse to dote on a yappy speck of fluff.

"I demand silence with my breakfast," said Wesley. "No music. No speaking. No *barking*." He raised his voice again. "Dog! Quiet!"

The yipping continued.

Wesley was going to end up with a headache. "Ned," he snapped at his footman. "Bring me a cigarette."

"I'm afraid I can't, sir," said Ned. "You're trying to quit."

"Don't nag me," said Wesley. "Do as I say."

"Sir, you specifically told me that if you requested smokes, I was *not to acquiesce*—those were your words. You said you'd read the latest medical reports, that your American friend, Mr. Kenzie, was *sodding right*—apologies, sir, but again, your words—and that you intended to quit for your health. You said you would dock my pay if I ever brought you your cigarettes again."

In actuality Wesley intended to quit because having an addiction was intolerable, but he would not show weakness in front of his staff or anyone else. Let them think it was only for health—as long as they still brought him the bloody things. "I'll dock your pay if you don't bring them."

"I'm sorry, sir," Ned said loftily. "But I'm a man of my word."

Wesley huffed. He had never once docked any member of his staff's pay, for any reason. Clearly he should start, if they felt entitled to be cheeky. "Bring me my revolver, then."

"My lord."

"Don't take that tone with me. I'll only fire a warning shot above the dog's minuscule head. I could do it with a cigarette in my mouth, if the man I pay to do my bidding would ever bring me one."

"I've brought your *messages*." Ned set a silver tray down near Wesley's plate. There were two letters and a telegram stacked upon it, along with his monocle.

Wesley fit the monocle between his eyebrow and cheekbone. In his most private spaces, he opted for reading glasses, which were more comfortable and better served his vision. But for even his own ground-floor rooms, he used the monocle. Monocles were mistaken for an affectation, not a necessity, the way a man smoking cigars was considered cultured, not an addict.

It was obnoxious, to be a champion sharpshooter who needed a reading aid at thirty-two, but then, life was obnoxious, as Powderpuff was intent on proving.

He picked up the first letter, glanced at it, then held it out to Ned with a curl of his lip. "Dispose of this one. I have no intentions of selling any properties at this time and no amount of thinly veiled wheedling will guilt me into marriage. I have my own solicitor I'm already ignoring; I don't require advising from Geoffrey's."

"Yes sir," said Ned, without any sass for once, because Wesley suspected his footman didn't care for Cousin Geoffrey any more than Wesley himself did. His living relatives were few and distant, but to a one they all wanted the same thing—for Wesley to either marry and produce an heir, or for him to give them all his money and properties. Wesley hoped they enjoyed disappointment.

The second letter was no better—an invitation to

a gala of decorative arts, apparently inspired by the world's fair still carrying on in Paris.

"Ugh." Wesley held it out without looking at Ned. "Who on earth believes I would willingly choose to spend my time around art and bohemians?"

"Art's lovely, sir," Ned said, as he took it. "We've got that painting from your American friend, Mr. Kenzie, downstairs by the room where he stayed with us. Brightens the whole basement up, it does. Makes little Elsie smile every time she sees it."

Wesley's ex-lover Arthur had stayed with them in the spring, and because he was a sentimental sot he'd gone and gifted Wesley's staff for having him as a guest. Some kind of art, apparently, that had left the cook's eleven-year-old daughter Elsie squealing.

Wesley had let the staff hang it up, but he'd never bothered to go down to the basement to see it. Why torture himself? He didn't need the reminder that he hadn't had a regular lover since Arthur—hadn't taken anyone to bed at all in a frustratingly long time.

And he most certainly did not need a reminder that Arthur had thrown him over for a surly twenty-year-old antiquarian who looked and spoke like a guttersnipe.

One who made Arthur happier than Wesley would ever be capable of making another person.

As Ned put the two letters into the morning room's fire, Wesley picked up the telegram. It was sent from a London office.

And it was from Jade Robbins.

Seeing her name was like catching the scent of spring flowers in winter. Wesley had met Jade only a handful of times, but he enjoyed her company—a surprise in and of itself, as he could count tolerable companions on one hand. A spy during wartime, she now ran a Harlem speakeasy with her siblings, where he'd spent a remarkably excellent night drinking bootlegged Canadian gin and listening to her sister sing like an angel. He'd been a pathetic fool to make that trip to America, but the Magnolia had been an unexpected delight, and the men who'd been with him still reminisced about that night like giddy schoolboys.

MY DEAR LORD FINE STOP IN LONDON NOW AT GREAT EASTERN STOP MAY I SEE YOU STOP

Wesley read the telegram again, but the words didn't change. Jade was in town and wanted a visit. "Ned," he said slowly. "I need you to send a message to the Great Eastern Hotel, and to make a reservation for dinner tonight."

Ned's eyebrows flew up, but he gave a short bow. "Of course, my lord," he said, and left the morning room.

Wesley's gaze stayed on the telegram. It was also something of a surprise that things weren't unbearably awkward around Jade, considering she was his ex-lover's best friend. But instead, Jade was lovely company: warm and interesting, and always giving him the sense there was even more to her than it seemed on the surface.

But then, he got that same sense from Arthur's new lover Rory. It seemed patently ridiculous that a scruffy, penniless antiques dealer like Rory could have enemies, but Wesley had heard the man get kidnapped out of his own antiques shop by bootleggers.

Wesley hadn't seen the kidnappers' faces, but his too-sharp memory had snapped up their names and voices in perfect detail: Hyde, an Englishman with a feral edge to his words; Shelley, an American woman with a dreamlike voice; and a man with a honey-sweet Spanish accent who the others had called Sebastian. They had spoken in strange code that night, using non-sensical phrases like *subordinate paranormal* to describe Rory—bootlegging code, that's what Arthur had said it was.

So yes, Rory was more interesting than he appeared, and Jade the ex-spy turned bootlegger was certainly one of the most interesting people Wesley had ever met.

Maybe Jade would know another interesting man.

A fresh burst of yaps cut through Wesley's thoughts. He gave the garden wall a scorching look through the morning room's window and went back to his breakfast.

Rise and shine, de Leon.

Sebastian's eyes wouldn't open.

His body continued to breathe, calm and slow, in a terrible contrast to his heart, which raced like a frightened mouse in a cage. The air was icy on bare skin he wanted to cover, and he itched to see the morning light he could sense on his still-closed eyelids. But his limbs refused to move, as if bound by an invisible straitjacket, and despite his frantic heart, his blood moved too slow, like oily magic still clogged his veins.

Wake up, de Leon. This isn't your tropical paradise, and I need your magic.

The paralysis dragged on—maybe seconds, maybe an hour, Sebastian couldn't tell. Sweat beaded on his skin and his brain frizzled like an electric circuit shorting out. At some point, his eyes would open themselves, and the Puppeteer would be standing in front of him—

Sebastian's eyes did open. But instead of the Puppeteer, there was Isabel's painting, directly across from his bed on the wall over his table, the brilliant colors of tropical San Juan brighter than ever in the gray morning.

He was in London.

He was free.

The ghost-hold on his limbs vanished. Sebastian's breath left him in a rush and he began to tremble. He stared at the painting, his pulse in his throat, and took deep breaths, willing the shaking to pass.

Libre, he reminded himself. *Free*.

Maybe someday he'd believe it.

Rain was dotting his window, not the pelting of a tropical downpour but a lighter, misty cold rain that came with fog. He concentrated on the soft sound of droplets against glass as he ran a hand over his face, finding his skin clammy and soaked with sweat despite the chill.

He'd been free for four months. He should be over this by now.

But the blood terrors still came, seizing him on random nights with no warning. If anything, they were getting worse as autumn came in, when the stove went out overnight and his drafty room turned cold. The night there'd been frost on his window had been the worst of all.

Rise and shine, de Leon.

The slithering memories coiled around his brain like tentacles from the deep, nowhere he wanted to revisit. Forget going back to sleep anytime soon.

Sebastian relit the stove's pilot light, and then pulled on a shirt to slip into the hall and fill his kettle from the tap in the bathroom. He boiled the water on his stove to make instant coffee with powdered milk. He overdid the sugar, and the coffee was cloyingly sweet, but it was hot, and it would keep him from drifting back into sleep.

He left the stove on to warm the room and sat back on his bed with his mug, tugging the blanket around his shoulders. He stared at the painting of San Juan and willed the early memories to come. Not the years with Baron Zeppler—definitely not those—and not the war years in Europe, but the childhood before that. Sun on his skin and wind in his hair as he sprinted through ocean waves and sand to launch a kite for his little brother. The soft coos of pigeons, tame enough to hand-feed at the little courtyard park by the beautiful old stone church. The flash of metal in light filtered by palm leaves as his tío let him tinker with the engine of the new Model T.

The hand holding the mug was trembling. Sebastian's magic literally weakened other magic. Auras too. He could stop almost any other paranormal, could send the nonmagical crashing uselessly to the ground. Before the Puppeteer, there'd been no one he thought he needed to fear.

Now, to be betrayed by his own blood that couldn't remember it was free—that woke him up in dread and panic, night after night—

I should be over this by now.

But the blood terrors disagreed.

Sebastian let himself stare at the painting only until his mug was empty, then he forced himself to his feet and went to shower and dress. There was a paranormal killer loose, and Zhang and Jade's friend, Lord Fine, could be in danger. After he got Molly and Isabel to the train, he'd need to find a way to help.

After breakfast and several increasingly tiresome telephone calls, Wesley had Marcus, his driver, bring the car around front to take him to his first appointment.

As Wesley strode down the front steps, he glanced each way down the quiet street.

An absolutely foolish moment of weakness, and Wesley ought to know better. But yesterday, he'd been in the backseat of his Bentley, and he'd caught a glimpse of someone walking on the street across from his house. Not one of his neighbors—old-fashioned, upper-class English like himself, top hats and crisp suits paired with walking sticks—but a younger man, his well-tailored clothes stylishly casual in the modern trend, bundled in a coat and scarf despite it only being September.

Wesley hadn't been able to see most of his face—far-sightedness didn't let him see beneath a flat cap—and he'd blinked and the man had gone. But the fleeting impression of *handsome man* had stuck in Wesley's head, the glimpse fusing itself to his memories and refusing to be shaken like one of those American jazz tunes one heard everywhere nowadays.

Granted, Wesley was cursed with remembering things *too* well; he'd never been able to live in cushiony forgetfulness the way others did. The man probably hadn't been anything special. More likely, Wesley hadn't bedded a man in so long that his flytrap mind was cataloging mirages as if they were memories worth keeping.

Ugh, this was exactly why he didn't like handsome men. Hadn't he learned anything from the travesty he'd made of things with Arthur? Six months he'd slept with the man and he'd barely known who Arthur really was, because every time they tried to talk they fought like bucks on a proving ground. But Arthur was outrageously beautiful, and Wesley had convinced himself that maybe, with enough time, he could learn to like him, that his own unfeeling heart might have hidden a single soft spot that could belong to another person.

More the fool him, then. It turned out Wesley was just another shallow idiot who thought with his cock. His heart of stone was impregnable, and he'd discovered he was an inattentive and self-absorbed partner, to boot. The handsome mirage had good sense to keep his distance.

The Bentley rolled up to the curb. Wesley kept his eyes resolutely on the car and didn't indulge in another glance down the street. He was putting the man out of his mind. The world was what it was, as cold and colorless as it seemed; there was no point wishing it was more.

He would focus on the decisions ahead and the charity appointment he had today. Nuns this time, Christ.

After the train ride to Kilburn, Sebastian stopped at an A.B.C. tea shop on the way to Molly's boarding house. He awkwardly clutched the paper bag in one hand as he started up the fire escape to her window.

The room under Molly's belonged to a friendly scullery maid who worked for a lord's household. Sebastian clearly hadn't been climbing as quietly as he'd hoped, because Olive the maid leaned her head out the open window as he passed.

"No boys, house rules," she teased.

A house rule apparently made by someone blithely unaware that some girls liked girls, but Sebastian played his cover role. "Our secret?" he said innocently.

Olive grinned. "Only if you find me a man who looks and sounds like you."

One more floor up, and rain dotted the back of Sebastian's neck as he knocked on the glass of Molly's window. It was Isabel who swept the curtain aside. Only three years his elder, Isabel was often mistaken for Sebastian's sister instead of his cousin—a similar accent, same olive skin and brown hair, although hers was long and swept into a center-parted bun accented with a hair comb, and her eyes were hazel-green instead of brown.

"Sebi's here," she called over her shoulder, pushing up the window. She leaned out to kiss Sebastian's cheek, taking the paper bag from him as she asked, "Nos trajiste el almuerzo—oh yes, Molly, he brought us lunch!"

Moments later, Sebastian was sitting on Molly's rug, his back against one of the two beds. The women of Molly's house always kept at least four cats roaming the floors, and Clover, an elderly calico, was currently curled in a ball on the bed. She lifted her head to eye Sebastian speculatively, and he reached up to stroke her soft fur.

"Hola, gatita linda, como va tu día?" he said, pitching his voice low so none of the other tenants would hear him.

"Hello, pretty cat, how's your day going?" Molly grinned. "You're so soft, Sebastian."

He raised his eyebrows. "Are you learning Spanish?" he said, impressed.

"Got a phrase book and everything," she said proudly. Molly didn't have a stove, but she'd put a kettle on a hot plate, and she was humming as she moved around the room, a sharp contrast to the lines of sadness around her mouth and eyes at the pub the night before.

It was so good to see her happy again; what had caused the change?

"Olive saw me climbing up," he said.

"She's a doll, she won't tell the matron," said Molly, as Isabel unpacked the sandwiches and queen cakes Sebastian had brought. "Olive didn't get home from Kensington until nearly midnight—bet it made her morning, seeing you."

"The lord she works for lives in Kensington?" Sebastian said in surprise, as Clover leaned her face into his hand and he scritched behind her ears. "Do you know his name?"

"I don't," Molly said. "Just that he's a demanding arsehole and the staff quarters are squalor, apparently. Bad enough that she'd rather be here, and only stays at their house when she has to."

Could it be Lord Fine? Sebastian hoped not. Jade had said Lord Fine was an ass, but she'd also said she liked him, and Sebastian didn't think Jade would like someone who was terrible to his staff. The glimpse Sebastian had caught of the staff quarters in Lord Fine's basement in May, when he'd delivered Isabel's painting, had been clean and nicely furnished.

"I'd rather work at a pub than a lord's house," Molly said, with feeling. "But then—I suppose I'm not going to have to work at the pub anymore either."

Wait—what? But Sebastian belatedly realized that while the one chair in the room was taken by Isabel's suitcase there was a second suitcase on the bed by Sebastian's head. "Is that yours?" he asked Molly, pointing to it.

Molly's face lit up as she glanced at Isabel, who was smiling brightly back.

"Molly's coming to Paris with me," said Isabel, and Sebastian's eyebrows flew right back up.

"All the way to Wonderland," Molly said, beaming. "Magic and all."

Isabel plopped down on the other bed, across from Sebastian. Like him, she was bundled up against London's chill, all her own tattoos hidden. "She sold all her jewelry to buy a train ticket to Paris, can you believe her?" Isabel was lit up like the sun, looking more than a little smitten as she handed Sebastian a sandwich. "I told her that if she wanted to come with me, she didn't have to sell anything, she just had to say so."

The kettle whistled on its hot plate, and Molly went to it. "She's so perfect for you," Sebastian said to Isabel.

"The tattoo knew it first," Isabel confided, like she was confessing to a priest.

"Molly's harp?"

Isabel nodded. "My art is too tied to my magic, and my magic likes her. You know what Teo says, that if your magic likes someone, the rest of you falls like dominoes."

Sebastian rolled his eyes good-naturedly. Sebastian's brother, Mateo, was a seer, but that didn't make everything he said true. "That is superstition, not one of Teo's visions."

"That's what you think," Isabel said, grinning. "But wait until it happens to you."

It never would. Molly might call him soft, but his magic was hard. He could weaken other magic, rendering other paranormals useless, and he could weaken auras, knocking the nonmagical to the ground with his mind. He was grateful to have an ability that had let him protect others, but even he wasn't fanciful enough to think his magic could ever be soft enough to do something as romantic as fall for someone.

Clover hopped down from the bed to sit next to Sebastian, pointedly eying the sandwich. "Don't feed her, you softie, she'll just keep begging," Molly said over her shoulder.

She was right. Sebastian tore off a small piece of ham and gave it to Clover anyway.

Isabel pulled her sandwich out from the wrapper. "The world's fair is nearly over—why don't you come too? You can tell Teo you got to see it after all. He hated it, but he hates everything."

Mateo had been in Paris in July, at the world's fair with Isabel. He'd sent Sebastian a long letter of complaint, telling Sebastian to come and reminding him that they hadn't seen each other in three years. But how was Sebastian supposed to face Mateo after the things he'd done?

"There was a lot of magic in the paranormal pavilion, though," Isabel went on. "I don't blame him for not liking it. I told him he should spend some time at my house before he went back to America and university."

Isabel and Mateo had what English speakers called *subordinate* magic. Where Sebastian could wield his magic like a weapon, Isabel and Mateo's magic came to them like they were radios receiving a signal, whether they wanted it or not. Their magic was far more powerful than Sebastian's—and a far greater risk to their minds.

When they'd all been younger, Sebastian had used his power to weaken magic to keep Isabel's and Mateo's powers at bay. But with Sebastian gone, Isabel had found a new solution: taking the home she'd inherited on the sea near Barcelona and using her painting talents to turn it into a refuge from the magic that threatened her sanity.

"You haven't seen the house since I finished," Isabel said. "I painted murals on the walls, the azotea, all of it. Any time the magic gets too much, I go, and it helps. You should come. Your parents are in Madrid; you could go see them after."

For a moment, Sebastian could almost see it: the warm wood and polished tiles complemented by Isabel's bright art, the boardwalk and golden beach out front, the rooftop terrace with its view of the Mediterranean stretching out endlessly.

The Puppeteer's blood magic had been able to bypass the protective tattoo Isabel had inked on Sebastian's wrist, going straight to his blood. But maybe, in Isabel's townhouse, the echoes of blood magic still plaguing him would ease.

"Mateo said he would stay in Barcelona, but I never heard if he did," she said, pronouncing the city with a soft *th*. "He has sent no messages, not to me, not to your parents."

Sebastian frowned. "No one has heard from him since he got back to America?"

"No. Perhaps he's so deep in his science he's forgotten people with magic, but he should tell us. He makes everyone worry." Isabel clucked her tongue. "They worry about you too, Sebi."

"But I do send messages," he protested.

"Cryptic messages saying you're fine but you can't leave London yet. Family still worries."

He didn't meet her eyes. Clover had settled at his side on the rug, and he stroked her nose. He'd always had a house full of pets, whether in San Juan or Spain. He missed them. He missed his family. He wanted to go.

But if the rest of them saw him now, a shadow of himself, fractured into someone he barely recognized— they'd only worry more.

"I can't come to Paris, or Barcelona," he said, throat tight. "We have a mystery here," he quickly added, because it was much easier than admitting how the Puppeteer still controlled his life, even from death.

He told Isabel about the newspaper articles and her eyes grew concerned. "Should I stay?"

He shook his head. There was no need to put non-magical Molly in danger. "Take Molly to the fair. If we need you, I'll send a telegram. And we should check on Mateo."

"Your parents sent telegrams," she said wryly. "Teo's going to be very sorry he forgot to send messages when he has your dad's American friends knocking on his door to check up on him in the middle of the night."

Sebastian winced in shared sympathy. Molly sat down on the bed, a mug of tea in her hand.

"I think that's everything packed," said Molly. "We can head for the train when you two are ready."

Isabel kissed Molly's smile. "I can't wait to show you Paris."

"You two could pretend to be less blissfully happy in front of the always-single man," Sebastian said wryly.

"There's nice girls you could meet on every floor of this house." Molly's smile turned mischievous, and she leaned forward and said knowingly, "And nice *boys* in the house next door."

Sebastian covered his face as Isabel's laughter rang around the room.

Chapter Three

The Great Eastern Hotel at Liverpool Street Station was several stories of red brick with arched windows and peaked roofs. It was bustling with activity, a thick throng of cars and taxis in front, people milling about despite the evening's chill.

Wesley's driver, Marcus, pulled the Bentley up to the main entrance.

"What time shall I be here waiting, my lord?" he asked, as one of the doormen hurried over.

Wesley considered this. Normally, he wouldn't allow a dinner to last longer than ninety minutes. But he was actually looking forward to seeing Jade.

"No need to wait," he finally said. "I'll have the concierge call me a car when we're finished."

Marcus's eyebrows went up the barest hint. "Very good, sir," he said, as the doorman opened the door to the backseat so Wesley could get out.

The Great Eastern was a railway hotel in the middle of the city, its clientele as diverse as London itself. Wesley was shown to the restaurant, where dozens of square tables with white tablecloths were set amongst large carved pillars. Tuxedoed waiters glided between full tables before disappearing through gilded archways, and the warm light of the many chandeliers reflected off the green and gold adorning the walls.

Wesley was seated at a prominent center table beneath a large stained-glass dome set into the ceiling, and given a drink menu. He'd only had time to glance at it when a host was approaching with his companion.

Wesley stood and offered his hand. "Miss Robbins. What an unexpected pleasure to see you again," he said, and even meant it.

Jade, looking more Parisian than American in a man's suit and high heels, took his hand with a smile. "Lord Fine, I am so pleased to see you safe," which seemed a bit unusual to say. It wasn't as if he was in any danger.

He waited for the host to get Jade's chair before taking his own seat. A waiter appeared almost instantly at their table. "Drinks tonight?" the waiter asked, starting with Jade.

"Just tonic water, thank you," she said.

That also seemed a bit odd. Wesley ordered a whiskey neat for himself, and as the waiter disappeared, he said, "Just soda? There's no Prohibition here, you know. Don't you run a speakeasy?"

"Yes, but I'm afraid I'm a bit of a problem after a drink," Jade said, as if confessing a secret.

"Are you really?" Wesley had a hard time picturing her as anything but composed. "Then you're a teetotaler?" He snorted. "Christ, next you're going to tell me you don't eat meat or some other rubbish."

Jade raised an eyebrow. She looked amused, rather than annoyed, but Wesley still wanted to wince. Surely he wasn't yet such a lout that he couldn't manage to be civil to an immensely interesting person for one sodding evening?

"Then again, your choices are none of my business," he said, trying to sound more gracious. "If you do eat meat, the lamb here is very nice, and if you don't, I'm certain they can provide a suitable alternative."

"Lamb sounds lovely, thank you." Jade, unlike his thorny rudeness, was effortlessly warm and gracious.

The waiter reappeared and set their drinks on the table. He took their orders, and as soon as he'd vanished again, Jade leaned forward. "How are you, Lord Fine?"

She sounded sincerely concerned. How curious. "I'm hale enough. Why wouldn't I be?"

She shrugged delicately. "I didn't know if perhaps anyone was bothering you as of late."

"Bothering me?" He snorted again. "No one *bothers* me, Miss Robbins. Or rather, everyone bothers me, the world itself bothers me, but no particular individual is bothering me at present. Why do you ask?"

"Just wondering," she said lightly.

"Well, that's clearly bollocks." Wesley picked up his whiskey. "You know, the stories Arthur told me about your time as a spy during the war—they made you sound practically supernatural."

"Did they?" Jade said, a little weakly.

"They did," said Wesley. "So you see, I don't believe anyone *just wonders* something like that, but I particularly don't believe *you* would ever just wonder anything without a good reason."

Their first courses were dropped off, oysters and consommé, and when they had privacy again, she finally spoke. "I met an Englishman in May that I believe you might know. The Earl of Blanshard."

It was Wesley's turn to raise his eyebrow. "Yes, I've met Blanshard, went to a party of his once. What of him?"

Her eyes darted to the side, her head tilted almost

as if she were listening to the air, except that would be quite strange. "Will you tell me about him? About that party?"

Curiouser and curiouser, as Alice had said in Wonderland. "I don't have much to say, I'm afraid. Blanshard would be utterly forgettable if he weren't completely unlikeable."

"That's certainly something," she said. "May I ask why you don't like him?"

"I'm not sure I can say why," Wesley admitted. "There's simply something off-putting about him, but then everyone is off-putting, so even that is hardly noteworthy."

Jade steepled her hands in front of her mouth, pretty pink nails to match her scarf and lipstick. "Have you ever heard or noticed anything odd about Lord Blanshard?"

"Odd." Wesley sipped his whiskey. "No, I don't believe I have. He hoards antiques like a magpie, but that's a fairly harmless hobby, isn't it?"

"Depends on the antique," she said, "and where you got it, and how you got it. Do you happen to remember any of the items you saw?"

Wesley recounted what he'd seen over their fish course and then their lamb with mint jelly. Jade listened intently. "Your memory is excellent," she said, when he'd finished.

It was, for all the good it did him when so few of his memories were ones he wanted to revisit. "So I've been told," he said instead. "Apparently as a small child, I could sing entire songs for my mother after hearing them once."

Jade smiled. "How sweet. Can you still?"

"No," he said crisply, because he didn't want to say *she's dead now and I don't sing anymore.* "Are you going to tell me why you're asking about Blanshard? Has something happened?"

"I don't know," Jade said, rueful and honest. "But I think Lord Blanshard may be more dangerous than he appears. At the very least, the clock you described from his collection was stolen from a friend of mine."

Wesley's eyes widened. "What, really? The earl is a thief?"

"At a minimum." She pursed her lips thoughtfully, then said, "My friend he stole from is here in London now and might recognize more of the items you described. Do you mind if I tell him of our conversation?"

"I don't see why not," said Wesley. "What's your friend like? An angry antiquarian prodigy, like Rory Brodigan, or an unlikeable pillock like Blanshard?"

"I don't think he's either." Jade looked thoughtful. "He's a tough one to read. He's quiet. A bit mysterious. Has a terribly complicated past and is one of the more dangerous men I've met, and yet I'm starting to suspect he might actually be soft as a marshmallow."

Wesley raised one eyebrow. Exactly how *dangerous* did a man have to be to reach Jade the ex-spy's standards? That was almost intriguing.

Except softness in men was a foolish character flaw, a liability in a hard world of scoundrels and knaves. Wesley had no patience for it.

Still.

Not the kind of man one heard about every day.

Wesley pursed his lips. "Anything else to say about your *dangerous marshmallow*?" he asked, before he could stop himself.

Jade grinned. "He's got a charming accent," she said. "And—" She hesitated.

"And what?" he prodded.

"Well." Her grin turned mischievous. "Arthur thinks he's handsome."

Wesley narrowed his eyes. "I'm sorry, but in that case, you can't tell him one whit of what I've said. Handsome men are trouble."

"They're the worst," Jade said, her eyes darting almost playfully to the air at Wesley's side. "And this particular fellow doesn't even seem to realize he's foxy."

"Bullshit," Wesley said flatly. "Pardon my language, but they always know."

"I really don't think he does," said Jade. "Maddening, isn't it?"

"Hmph." That was rubbish, of course. Handsome men always knew just how handsome they were. They weren't worth it. Wesley, luckily, knew better than to get anywhere near one. "And when were you going to see this *foxy* fellow of yours?"

"Tonight, if I can," Jade said. "He's living in London, for the time being, right here by Liverpool Station. I thought I might pop round after our dinner to tell him what you've told me."

A friend of Jade's. She was interesting; this friend of hers was likely interesting too. Mysterious, she'd said. Apparently a *dangerous marshmallow*.

And a *handsome* one.

Wesley would later blame it on his second whiskey, because he heard himself say, "Do you think, perhaps, he'd like to hear my account in person?"

After the excellent dinner followed by a port wine paired with vanilla custard, Wesley and Jade got their coats and walked from Liverpool Street to Bishopsgate. A light rain fell on his hat and Jade's flowered umbrella, the droplets speckling the puddles that dotted their path.

"It's just up here," she said, after they'd gone only blocks. She glanced down a narrow side street near the Liverpool Street tube station. The street was lined with multistory buildings with businesses at the bottom, a jeweler, a fish and chips shop, a pub at the corner.

Jade's gaze seemed to be on a shop with darkened windows across from a chemist. "Lights are out," she said. "Let's try the alley door."

Wesley followed her farther down Bishopsgate. "They've certainly papered that over, haven't they?" he observed, glancing at the many flyers in the pub's window as they passed.

"Have they?" Jade seemed to be looking very fixedly forward. "What are they of?"

Wesley furrowed his brow. Surely she could see the flyers for herself? "Holidays," he said anyway. "Every last one seems to be advertising for some kind of getaway in Spain or the Caribbean."

The corner of Jade's mouth curled up in a small grin. But she still didn't look at the pub.

The alley was easy to miss, a barely noticeable opening on Bishopsgate just past the pub. It was far narrower than even the side street, hemmed in tightly by the tall buildings on both sides. It was unpleasantly dark as well, as the windows facing the alley were mostly boarded, and everything smelled of stale ale and piss. Wesley wrinkled his nose.

Jade stopped in front of a door partway down the alley, and knocked. After a long moment, she knocked again. "I wonder if he's not home. It's terribly frustrating not to be able to tell ahead of time, isn't it?"

"Is there a way to know ahead of time without calling?" Wesley liked this plan less and less. She said this man was her friend, but what sort of riffraff would haunt an alley like this?

But as he stepped behind her protectively, his foot connected with something.

"What the *devil*—" Wesley scrambled backward. "Something wet just spilt all over my ankle!"

"Oh dear." Jade craned her neck. "Well, if it's any consolation, I think it was just the cats' water."

"*What* cats?"

"The strays."

"The *strays*."

"My friend feeds the animals." There was just enough light to see Jade's face and her apologetic smile. "I did say I suspect he's a marshmallow."

Wesley's sock was drenched because of *stray cats*? "Feeding strays is how you catch disease. What on earth is wrong with your Mr.—you know, I don't believe you've told me his name."

"Mr. de Leon," she said. "Sebastian."

She pronounced Sebastian not as he would have, but with an elegant roll of the tongue at the end, like she was speaking French or Spanish, like a hint of a Mediterranean breeze to warm a cold English alley.

But no warm name would change Wesley's cold, wet ankle. He folded his arms. "You know, the last man I met named Sebastian was a bootlegger and a kidnapper."

Jade blinked. "What, really?"

"Oh yes," said Wesley. "To be fair, I didn't actually meet him *per se*. I was in the backroom office of a New York antiques shop when a group of three people came in after Rory Brodigan—bootleggers, apparently, that's what Arthur said. One of them was named Sebastian and he had a Spanish accent."

Jade looked like she'd had a shock. "You're—you're certain?"

"I told you I have an excellent memory, and frankly who would forget an experience like that? They used ridiculous code words like *subordinate paranormal*. I'd recognize any of the three kidnappers by their voices alone." Wesley frowned. Jade really had gone awfully still. "I'm sorry, was that not a story I should tell a woman?"

He heard footsteps then, coming into the alley.

Jade's gaze went to the side, and she said, a little desperately, "Wait—"

The new voice that floated down the alley was like velvet in Wesley's ears, an exquisite tenor made even more honeyed by a soft Spanish accent. "Oh, I'm so sorry! I didn't know you were waiting."

Wesley knew that voice.

"I was at the train," that very same bootlegging, kidnapping Sebastian de Leon from New York was saying. "But please, come in—"

In one sharp move, Wesley had his arm around de Leon's neck and slammed him face-first into the alley wall.

"How the hell can you be the same man?" he hissed into de Leon's ear. The gasp of pain was barely audible as Wesley wrenched de Leon's arm behind his back and used his full weight and strength to hold him pinned to the bricks. "How the fuck can you be in London?"

Jade's hand was suddenly on Wesley's arm. "Lord Fine, let him go."

"Miss Robbins, you don't understand," said Wesley. "He's a kidnapper."

De Leon stiffened. Wesley tightened his grip, but the other man seemed to have abruptly stopped moving.

"Sebastian, get free," Jade said, almost impatiently, and some distant part of Wesley's mind registered that she seemed completely certain de Leon could easily do such a thing even though Wesley was taller and broader.

The man pinned under Wesley only gave a tiny shake of his head.

Jade tugged again on Wesley's arm. "You're hurting my friend."

"He's a criminal!" Wesley snapped. "This is Sebastian the bootlegger, who kidnapped Rory Brodigan." He kept a tight grip on de Leon. "I don't know how you're here now, but I was there," he said, again into de Leon's ear. "I was in the back office of the antiques shop in New York and I heard everything you said and did, you and your two friends, Mr. Hyde and Miss Shelley. I will never forget your voice."

He raised his voice. "Miss Robbins, please call the police."

"I'm not calling the police—this is all a mistake." Jade sounded exasperated. "Lord Fine, let him *go*."

The small, feminine hand on Wesley's arm pulled. Jade was petite, a head shorter than Wesley himself even in her heels. She should never have been able to move him.

But this time, it was almost as if invisible hands were with her, yanking at Wesley's clothes, and he stumbled backward with the unexpected force.

De Leon's coughs filled the air as he caught his breath. Wesley shook his head to clear it, and would have lunged forward again, except at that moment de Leon rolled so his back was against the alley wall, and as he lifted his head his face caught the light coming from one of the partially boarded windows.

Oh hell.

De Leon *was* handsome. He was *stupidly* handsome, the sharp masculine lines of his cheekbones and jaw contrasting with giant doe eyes and soft olive skin. Pink lips were parted as he panted against the bricks, cradling the arm Wesley had been wrenching.

Wesley stood, frozen. *What are you doing?* the rational part of his mind screeched. *You can't let a criminal escape because he's fit!*

Of course we're not going to let him escape, Wesley's starved and reprehensible libido answered. *We're going to lock him up. In our bedroom.*

Oh, for fuck's sake. Wesley scrambled to regain control. "I am not mistaken," he snapped, stepping forward again.

But Sebastian raised his hands, a gesture of surrender. "You're right, you're not."

"It's not that simple," Jade said.

"Isn't it?" De Leon's words were quiet. "This is Lord Fine, yes? He is right. I did exactly what he said I did."

Christ, that *voice,* so lush and lovely. Wesley ought to grab him again, but de Leon's hands were still in the air, the perfect picture of complete surrender. His eyes were guileless and he was so infuriatingly *pretty.*

"There were extenuating circumstances," Jade was saying.

"I don't care if he was tortured," Wesley said bluntly. How dare attraction rear its head at this moment? So the fellow was handsome—it changed nothing. "He can't be your friend, Miss Robbins. There are no extenuating circumstances that would excuse what he did."

De Leon winced. "I'm sorry. I will leave."

"It's your home—" Jade started.

But de Leon had taken off down the alley in the opposite direction from Bishopsgate.

Wesley started after him, but again, he felt the sensation of invisible hands stopping him. He jumped back, brushing forcefully at his clothes but finding nothing but fabric. "What is going on tonight?"

"I'm sorry, but I won't let you hurt him," Jade said, like she could somehow be responsible for that sensation.

This was lunacy, all of it. "We can't just let him go. We need to call the police."

"Absolutely not." She seemed distracted; her attention focused on a patch of empty air.

Wesley huffed. "That man is a bootlegger—"

"*I'm* a bootlegger."

"And a kidnapper—"

"*Was* a kidnapper, like I *was* a spy."

Wesley threw up his hands. "Arthur is your best friend! Isn't Rory Brodigan your friend too? How can you not want his kidnapper locked up?"

"Because I know the whole story," said Jade. "Which you don't."

"I don't need the whole story—"

"Sometimes things are not what they seem." She finally turned to face him fully. "Lord Fine, please. I know everything Sebastian did. I know more than you. I've forgiven him, and so has Arthur."

"Impossible," Wesley said flatly. "Arthur would beat someone bloody for touching a hair on Brodigan's tiny and angry head."

"You can cable Arthur and ask him yourself," Jade said.

Had she lost all reason? "You said yourself, at dinner, that de Leon was one of the most dangerous men you'd ever met—"

"He is," said Jade. "And did that dangerous man fight

back tonight? Or would he have let you snap his arm before he took the chance of hurting you?"

Wesley tightened his jaw. He was bigger and stronger than de Leon; she was mistaken if she thought that de Leon had been *choosing* not to hurt him. "I had the upper hand the entire time."

But she shook her head. "I swear to you that things are not what you think," she said earnestly. "Six months ago, in the antiques shop, you were in terrible danger, yes. But now, the most danger you face from Sebastian is getting mange from one of his strays."

She took a step in the direction de Leon had gone. "I'm going to try and find him. To *talk* only—I can't let you call the police." She hesitated, then said, "Maybe you deserve to know more. Do you want to come with me?"

Wesley pursed his lips. Whatever Jade, and de Leon, and apparently even Arthur and Rory Brodigan were involved in, it was bigger than he had realized, a transatlantic lunacy of bootleggers and invisible hands on his clothes and outrageously handsome kidnappers with velvet accents. It beckoned for a moment, mysterious and unknown as Alice's storybook rabbit hole.

Wesley wasn't going to Wonderland.

"No, thank you," he said crisply, and turned away.

Out of respect for her, he would not call the police, but he would take no further part in this madness. He set off in the opposite direction, returning to Bishopsgate and Liverpool Street Station, alone.

Chapter Four

Sebastian walked with his hands in his pockets, steps a little too fast, no real destination, just trying to give Lord Fine the distance he needed.

The air next to him flickered, and then Zhang's astral projection materialized. "Jade talked Lord Fine down," he said, floating through the air backward in front of Sebastian. "He isn't calling the police."

Jade was a better friend than Sebastian deserved. "How can you see me right now?"

"I was waiting for Jade and saw you walk past the pub with my physical eyes," said Zhang. "She was planning to stop by your place after dinner, and I just thought I'd—you know. Go with her."

Ah. Of course. "You are worried I would have hurt her."

"That's not exactly—"

"It's okay," Sebastian said. "I don't blame you, and I don't blame Lord Fine."

Zhang frowned. "All right, yes, your magic makes you dangerous to us, but—well. You're also—I mean. You're also probably popular with women, right?"

Sebastian furrowed his eyebrows.

"Never mind. Look, I'm sorry I didn't get to the alley in time to pull Fine off you, I was trying." Zhang huffed.

"And slow down already. With that tattoo of yours, I'm going to lose you if you don't."

That was probably for the best. Poor Lord Fine, thrown into the paranormal world with no knowledge of magic. Poor Jade and Zhang, stuck cleaning up more mess from Sebastian's past.

Zhang's projection flickered again, unsteadily, like a light bulb when the train roared by. "I really am going to lose you. Stop running away."

"I'm not running away," Sebastian lied.

"Sure you're not." Zhang hesitated. "I guess you didn't know Rory had hidden Fine in the backroom of the antiques shop in New York."

Sebastian shook his head.

Zhang sighed. "Jade and I hadn't put it together either. Even if I'd remembered, I never would have thought he'd recognize you by your voice."

"It is not your fault." Sebastian was coming up on High Street, and another underground station with lit shops at the sidewalk level. "And I am glad that Rory hid him. The other two paranormals with me would have slaughtered Lord Fine without a second thought. And I can't be sure what I might have done."

Zhang was quiet for a moment. "It must be hard for you," he finally said. "To live in the aftermath."

Every time Sebastian thought he'd found the edge of his actions, he discovered more damage he'd done while under blood magic. The consequences rippled across the world, poisoning everything. He could still hear the contempt in Lord Fine's voice, see the anger and fear in his face as he laid out Sebastian's crimes.

I don't care if he was tortured. There are no extenuating circumstances that would excuse what he did.

Lord Fine was right: nothing ever would.

Sebastian swallowed. "You are kind. But I am not one of the heroes anymore. It is simply smart business not to trust me." He tried to shrug, like that didn't hurt. "I will still do whatever I can to solve the murders."

"Sebastian—"

"And Lord Fine has been too close to magic too many times," Sebastian said. "I will still help you protect him. I'll just also stay out of his way."

He reached the stairs of the underground as Zhang's projection flickered again, and then went all the way out, like a light turned off.

Sebastian stood for a moment, looking at the space where Zhang had been.

You're a villain and *a coward,* the little voice in his mind said. *No wonder you can't fight off the blood terrors. You can't even face your own past; you just run.*

Sebastian swallowed. Then he took the steps down. He could ride the trains for a bit, give Jade and Lord Fine time to leave his home.

Wesley had a car called for him at Liverpool Street Station. He had the driver take him straight home, where he went straight to his smoking room and poured a shot of straight whiskey.

He sat with his whiskey in one of his leather club chairs. On the small side table, his reading glasses were balanced on Wells's *The Outline of History,* and his illicit pack of Woodbine sat next to the ashtray.

He was in no mood to read, and he wasn't reaching for the cigarettes either for a change. He was distracted—by Sebastian de Leon.

The man was a bootlegging kidnapper. A handsome one, fine, but that only made him more dangerous. After all, Jade Robbins was a lovely and levelheaded woman, and even she'd been suckered in. Perhaps he'd told Jade some sob story and she'd fallen for it, because a man that gorgeous probably enthralled every skirt he met.

Jade had told him to cable Arthur, had seemed to think Arthur had also forgiven de Leon, but that was preposterous; he would never have fallen for such an act. Arthur was immune to beautiful people because the bastard was one, that exact kind of man so handsome he made other people behave irrationally.

Wesley should know. After all, the heart in his own chest was cut from the same stone as the statues in his garden, and yet he'd once taken a ship all the way to America in an attempt to win Arthur back, like the bloody Greeks sailing after Helen of Troy.

Because Wesley had actually fooled himself into thinking he could learn to have feelings for a man he only ever fought with, instead of admitting he was a shallow prat who just liked the way Arthur looked in his bed. He had behaved no better than all those frivolous idiots who were everywhere now, who clung to pretty clothes and baubles because they were too soft to bear the memories of the war.

No, Wesley had learned his lesson about handsome men. They made other people stupid, and Wesley would not be stupid. He would stick to company like himself, unpleasant in every aspect, and not trust so easily as Jade.

He sat back in his chair and raised the whiskey to his lips.

And remembered de Leon's ridiculously handsome face, panting against the wall, no fear or anger, only sorrow in those big eyes.

Six months ago, in the antiques shop, you were in

terrible danger, yes. But now, the most danger you face from Sebastian is getting mange from one of his strays.

Oh, for fuck's sake.

Wesley set his glass down on the side table so hard whiskey splashed over the side, and stood.

One single fucking cable, he told himself, as he thundered down the staff stairs. *And Arthur will tell you that Jade is mistaken and of course he didn't forgive that de Leon bastard, what was he, born yesterday, and you can put this entire sodding night behind you.*

Wesley reached the basement, and knocked on Ned's door.

The door opened, his footman blinking at him. "Something wrong, sir?"

His confusion was fair. Wesley rarely broke his routines, and even more rarely came down to the basement. "I need a telegram sent first thing."

"All right, sir." Ned hid a yawn behind his hand. "Begging your pardon, but if you'll give me a moment to dress, I'll come upstairs and—"

"No need," Wesley said brusquely. His father would be turning in his grave, but Wesley had lost his taste for perfect social etiquette on the battlefield. He didn't want to take a bloody half hour for a two-line telegram; he wanted to get this done, then go back upstairs and have his drink alone and be done thinking about Sebastian de Leon.

Because here he was. Still thinking about him.

Wesley gritted his teeth. "Have you paper and pen? It's a short message, I'll write it out now."

"Yes, sir," Ned said again, and disappeared into his room.

Wesley took the opportunity to glance around the basement. No one would ever have made the mistake of calling Wesley *soft*, but he preferred his staff to be discreet, and a comfortable man was a loyal man. Wesley made sure his staff were better paid, and had better quarters, than most, and in return, not a one of them said anything when he had men stay overnight in the guest room that was very close to his own.

The basement appeared clean and well-kept, and looked as it always did.

Except.

Except also hanging on the wall was a large, Impressionist-style painting of exceptional quality. Church steeples rose out of the tightly packed city, rooftops under a bright sun and the blue ocean in the distance. In the foreground, a couple, hand in hand, walked away from the viewer, toward the edge of the painting.

It was mesmerizing, drawing even Wesley in. As Ned reappeared in the doorway, Wesley said in surprise, "Is *this* the painting from Arthur?"

"Lovely, innit?" Ned said, with real pleasure. "Bloke delivered it on behalf of your American friend in May, same day Mr. Kenzie and his friend Mr. Brodigan left. Real gentlemanly gift of Mr. Kenzie, we all said."

Ned added, in a confiding tone, "That's a painting of Barcelona, that is. Would be a nice place to visit, eh? That golden beach along the sea?"

Wesley furrowed his brow. Arthur had never seemed to have much more than the polite interest in art required by society and their parents. Wesley had not expected a genuinely lovely work delivered in an odd and clandestine manner to his staff.

But come to think of it, Arthur had behaved terribly strangely the day he had left. He and his boyfriend, Rory, had never come back to the townhouse that night, leaving behind all of their bags. A telegram from Arthur had arrived the next morning, explaining they had gone to Paris by boat and that Wesley needed to get the hell out of London for a few weeks.

With a reminder that Rory had enemies and a strong implication that Wesley could be in danger too.

Wesley stared at the painting.

Barcelona.

A strange thought curled in Wesley's mind, the memory of a younger man on his street, attractive enough to stir Wesley's blood with nothing more than a fleeting glimpse. "Tell me about the man who delivered it."

Ned snorted. "Begging your pardon, sir, but you ought to be asking Elsie. Every time she passes by on her way to the kitchens with her mum, she giggles about the handsome man with the Spanish accent who brought the painting."

Wesley's eyes narrowed. "Have the painting brought to the study at once, I need to examine it," he said crisply. "And a second telegram must be sent, to the Earl of Blanshard."

At 5am, Wesley was still awake, and now seething.

Both of his telegrams had gone for delivery. Arthur was back in America and Wesley might not hear from him for an age, and he hadn't heard hide nor hair from the Earl of Blanshard for nearly three years.

But Jade had asked about Blanshard last night, and she had planned to tell Sebastian de Leon of their conversation. Jade was so convinced de Leon was a reformed criminal, but did she know the man had been to Wesley's home in May? That the man had been on Wesley's street mere days ago?

Lord Blanshard needed to know de Leon was interested in him.

Wesley had pored over every inch of the painting—removed the canvas from its frame and gone over that too. He didn't know what he was looking for, exactly—code, perhaps. De Leon had spoken in code with the other bootleggers in New York, referring to Rory Brodigan as a *paranormal*. Perhaps the painting held a clue or a cipher.

Maybe you deserve to know more, Jade had said. *Do you want to come with me?*

Wesley had walked away from the lunacy, only to find it in his home. Now, he damn well wanted to know more.

At 4am, Wesley had finally stuck the canvas in the tub in his bathroom and upended a can of turpentine over it.

As the paint dissolved, he watched, expecting to see a cipher or figures or something else entirely.

But there was nothing. Just the beautiful Mediterranean city leeching away into a blur of bright colors that washed down the drain, leaving only gray behind.

And now here he was, alone and angry, no closer to understanding the mystery, no closer to understanding Sebastian de Leon, and nothing to show for it except Ned's shocked and hurt expression when he'd checked on Wesley and seen the ruined canvas of the staff's treasured painting.

With an angry huff, Wesley gave up and went to bed.

The morning light through his window was pale and fog-filtered as Sebastian woke, thankfully not to another blood terror, but to knocking on his door—and not the door to the hallway, either, but the interior door that led down to the former art gallery.

He opened his eyes, and Zhang's astral projection was in the middle of the room.

"I can't see if you're actually here," Zhang's projection said. "But if you are, open your damn door already."

Sebastian blinked. He scrubbed a hand over his face, but Zhang's projection was still there, and someone was still knocking.

He shook himself all the way awake. He grabbed his shirt and yanked it over his head, then hastily pulled Isabel's painting of San Juan off the wall and slid it underneath the bed, face down, before going to the door.

Jade was there, her arms folded, and Zhang's physical body on the step behind her, a paper bag in hand.

"And *now* I can see you from the astral plane," said Zhang's astral projection, behind him.

"If you're going to use your magic tattoo to disappear where we can't find you," Jade said, "then I reserve the right to telekinetically pick your outside locks so I can knock on your door."

That was fair. "I upset Lord Fine last night, I had to leave," he said, as he held open the door wide enough for them to come in.

"Even though you were leaving your own home." Zhang followed Jade in and handed Sebastian a thermos. "Here. Coffee."

Sebastian unscrewed the lid and brought the thermos to his nose, inhaling the welcome scent. "You are a gentleman," he said to Zhang, as he gave the couple the table, and went to the shelf above the stove. "But I apologize that I'm not dressed to receive a lady."

"Mmm, true, and no couch for me to faint on," Jade said dryly.

Zhang set his paper bag on the table. "Is that an army-issue T-shirt?"

Sebastian nodded as he took a half-full can of powdered milk off the shelf. The T-shirts were comfortable and he'd kept them after his service, preferring them to the union suits most men still chose.

"American army, right?" Zhang sat back in the rickety chair, which creaked. He was about the same size as Sebastian, and the chair apparently didn't like Zhang any more than it liked him. "How old were you when you enlisted?"

"Eighteen—why?" Sebastian said, as he stirred powdered milk and sugar into the thermos.

Zhang gestured at Sebastian. "Have you considered you might need to size up?"

Sebastian furrowed his brow. But then, he had filled out in the arms and shoulders over the past several years, and Zhang was probably right. "Maybe I should," he said, trying to sound casual, and not like he'd never thought about the fit of his T-shirts because it had been an embarrassingly long time since anyone had seen him even partially undressed.

Zhang looked at Jade. "Okay, you're right," he said, like they'd been having some kind of disagreement. "He's not trying to seduce anyone. I'll relax."

"Thank you," said Jade, as she accepted the currant bun Zhang offered her from the paper bag. "I'm afraid we're here with terrible news," she said to Sebastian. "There was another murder last night, near a woman's boarding house in Kilburn."

"What?" Sebastian said in alarm.

"Kilburn was where your cousin was staying, wasn't it?" Jade said. "With Molly, from the pub? But you said you took them to the train."

"Yes." Sebastian ran a hand through his hair, which was already standing up every which way from sleep. "I will send a telegram to be sure they arrived in Paris, but I saw their train pull away from the station. They were not in Kilburn last night."

But someone in Kilburn had still lost their life. "Do we know who the victim was?" he asked, stomach churning.

"Not a name yet," said Zhang. "She was a maid who worked for a Lord Thornton in Kensington."

Sebastian sat down hard on the edge of the bed. Molly's friendly downstairs neighbor, Olive, had been a maid for a lord in Kensington.

Zhang looked as unsettled as Sebastian felt. "The article in today's paper said the cause of death was unknown. I haven't been able to see the body yet, but we need to find out if it's the same method of murder."

"A paranormal murderer stalking the nonmagical." Sebastian set his jaw. "Is there any connection between the victims that also makes this seem related?"

Jade and Zhang exchanged a look. "A tentative one, maybe," Jade said. "Magic."

"The body found in Germany was one of the guards who was under the Puppeteer's thrall, with Baron Zeppler," said Zhang. "The body in Paris was a barber, found in the shop where Arthur got a shave from the Puppeteer. And the body in York—we know Lord Blanshard is a paranormal with a Yorkshire manor."

"And now someone is dead in Kilburn," Sebastian said, jaw still tight, "near the boarding home where Isabel stayed."

"Certainly lends credence to our theory that these are paranormal murders." Jade shook her head slowly. "Also, there have been no witnesses to any of these crimes, and I'm not naive enough to think that's a co-incidence."

"Let's say we continue the theory that Lord Blan-shard is one of these vampire paranormals, like your family legend," said Zhang. "Was that paranormal able to turn invisible, or into a dog or bat like Dracula?"

Sebastian shook his head. "I do not think so. But there are so many magical means to avoid detection. Charms and trinkets, powders and potions."

"Tattoos," Zhang said pointedly.

"But I can only hide from magic," said Sebastian. "And no de Leon would be killing the nonmagical."

"Because you all have the legacy of magic that thwarts other magic—is that really true?" Jade asked, as she pulled off a piece of her currant bun.

Sebastian probably owed them the story. "Yes," he admitted. "It's a blood curse."

Zhang's eyebrows went up.

Sebastian sighed. "It goes back to the relics. Every-thing always goes back to the relics."

"The same story of the nobles who tried to hide their magic from an inquisitor during the Spanish Inquisi-tion?" Jade asked. "By siphoning their magic out of their bodies and into objects, like a ring, a brooch, a pomander?"

Sebastian nodded and took a bracing sip of sweet, milky coffee. "The story I know is that the inquisitor found all seven nobles, but he didn't know how to put their magic back or destroy the relics. So he locked the relics up with the siphon and enchanted his own blood, so his descendants would have magic that works on other magic." He shrugged helplessly. "And we do."

"He used blood magic on his own descendants," Zhang mused.

"Cursing us was probably the least awful thing he did," Sebastian said. "He was part of the Spanish Inquisition; I'm sure he wasn't a good guy."

"I understand the nobles made all the relics with murder, so it sounds like unpleasantness all around," said Jade. "At least your family has tried to turn it into something better. How many of you have enervation magic that weakens other magic?" she asked, as she and Zhang shared their food with practiced ease.

"Just me," Sebastian admitted. "I might be the first in my family to have it, or at least, we don't have a record of any others. Isabel can create her art that traps magic, and my brother is telegnostic."

Zhang's eyebrows went up. "Your brother's a *seer*?"

Sebastian nodded. "But still a de Leon. Mateo can see the future of magic—he sees how a paranormal will use their magic or how magic will be used on them. Well," he amended, and held up his wrist so his tattoo was visible. "Almost any paranormal. Obviously, he cannot see my future."

Jade's eyebrows were up too. "Seeing of any kind is quite a powerful subordinate ability. How is he doing?"

I don't know. I haven't seen him in three years, and I wasn't brave enough to face him this summer.

Sebastian stared unseeing into the thermos Zhang had brought. "Teo is at Oberlin in America now. He's never liked his magic, so now he just wants to study science."

"Another scholar. Maybe you can make a friend," Jade said to Zhang, with a smile.

Zhang rolled his eyes good-naturedly. "We also think Blanshard is avoiding witnesses with some kind of magical object," he said to Sebastian. "After all, Lord Fine described an entire collection that could be paranormal. Hopefully we can find out more in Kilburn today."

"I could come?" Sebastian blurted. "If there was an object, or if there are traces of magic, my magic could be very useful. And it was Molly's boarding house. I might have met the victim—I should help—"

"We'd be glad to have you," Jade said, but then she made a face. "There is one other problem we should tell you about, though. It's about Lord Fine again."

Oh boy.

"I was able to find his townhouse on the astral plane just before dawn," said Zhang. "Lord Fine destroyed your cousin's painting."

"Destroyed?" Sebastian repeated.

"Turpentine." Zhang sighed. "We think he figured out it was from you."

"Oh no." Sebastian winced. "Poor Barcelona." He'd loved that painting, his second favorite of Isabel's.

"Still want to help him?" Zhang said ruefully.

Sebastian sighed. What a needless loss of Isabel's beautiful art, but was it really a surprise Lord Fine had destroyed the painting? Lord Fine had been yet one more victim of Sebastian's history and had every reason to think of Sebastian as dangerous. "We can't leave Lord Fine unprotected. Blanshard could still connect Fine to everything that happened in New York. And a maid for an English aristocrat was murdered—you said her employer, Lord Thornton, is in Kensington, where Lord Fine also lives. Too many innocents have already died."

Jade frowned. "I tried to call Lord Fine this morning, but he wasn't available."

"Lord Fine is safe right now and hasn't left his house,

at least," said Zhang. "I've been keeping an eye on the him through the astral plane."

"I suppose I'll call again later." Jade sighed. "And here your cousin has left, and all her paintings have been returned to Spain."

Sebastian bit his lip, then said, "Not all of them." He ignored the near-painful tightening of his own throat as he gestured under the bed. "I kept the one of San Juan."

Because it pulls me out of the blood terrors. Because it's the only thing that helps.

He swallowed. "I have the protection of my tattoo," he said, striving to keep his voice casual. "We can give the last painting to Lord Fine."

Zhang started to crane his neck, but Sebastian quickly said, "I can look because I have Isa's art in my magic, but no other paranormals should look at it. It will take you awhile to come back to your senses. It would have kept you from ever finding me, if you didn't already know where I lived."

The wall above his table was so unsettlingly bare without the painting, as blank as his walls had been when he was a prisoner with Baron Zeppler. No brilliant colors and happy memories to trigger the blood terrors into remembering he was free. Sebastian forced an easy tone of voice. "The painting will help protect Lord Fine. Maybe he will tolerate the Caribbean more than the Mediterranean."

"That's kind of you," Jade said, her gaze searching his face as if she sensed he was hiding something. "After all, he could have listened to me last night and not done something so barbaric as destroy art."

Sebastian shrugged lightly. If Lord Fine destroyed the painting of San Juan too—permanently leaving Sebastian no way out of his blood terrors—

Well, he had no one to blame but himself, and the villainous past that had nearly ensnared Lord Fine. The blood terrors couldn't kill Sebastian; he would survive.

"Lord Fine could be in danger," he said, as if his throat wasn't tight. "He needs the painting more."

Chapter Five

Wesley didn't rise from bed again until 10am, when he put his dressing gown over his pajamas and went back to the morning room. No one had made a fire in the grate, and the room was unpleasantly chilled.

Ned was late bringing in breakfast. When the table was finally set, Wesley picked up his china cup, sipped, then set it straight back down. "The tea is cold."

"Is it, my lord?" Ned said, not looking at him.

"Yes it is," Wesley said, with an edge. "The tea is cold and the toast is burnt and the fire unbanked and I don't have my newspaper."

"I'm sorry to hear that, my lord. Perhaps we're all a bit distracted on account of little Elsie being so upset."

Wesley was not actually tolerating this sass from his footman, was he? "It was just a painting," he said sharply. "Nothing but oil and pigment on canvas. So what if it's gone? Why would my house rally around Miss Elsie's oversentimentality?"

Ned raised his chin. "She's still crying, my lord."

Oh hell. He'd made his cook's eleven-year-old daughter cry. *Well done, Wesley.*

"I'll buy a new painting for the basement," he said, instead of firing the man, which he should have done on the spot.

Ned finally glanced at him out of the side of his eyes. "Will it be of Barcelona, sir?"

"I'll buy ten paintings of anywhere you lot bloody want if you'll take this inedible tripe away and bring me a proper cup of tea."

Ned seemed to be considering that. "Will it be by the same painter and delivered by the same handsome fellow with the accent?"

"Christ, no," said Wesley, with feeling.

Ned's gaze set itself forward again. "Begging your pardon then, sir, but if I may speak plainly, that might not be enough."

"Might not be enough?" Wesley sputtered. "Get me my paper and get out."

"But I haven't given you your messages—"

"Out!"

Ned gave a half bow with a frankly impertinent edge and disappeared. The staff was staging a revolution as if he employed a gaggle of French peasants. This was also Sebastian de Leon's fault, and Wesley needed a fucking cigarette.

A few minutes later, his tea was still cold but he had the *London Times* on a silver tray—damp from being passive-aggressively left too long on the step in the morning's rain. Wesley took a breath through his nose, ignored the tea, and picked up the newspaper.

An envelope fell out.

Wesley furrowed his brow. He set the *Times* to the side and considered the letter. It was addressed to him, but with no stamp, like it had been slipped into the newspaper by hand. There was no return address, but the wax seal was of the highest quality and bore the letter *B*.

Highly abnormal way to receive mail, but then, nothing had been normal in Wesley's life since the moment he heard the name *Sebastian de Leon*. He opened the envelope.

Your telegram was most welcome, the letter read. *You are right to be concerned about Mr. de Leon; his family has a history of brutish tactics and interfering where they shouldn't. Tell him nothing of me. You and I must speak in person. Tonight, at 8pm. I will send a car for you.*

It was signed by the Earl of Blanshard.

Wesley pursed his lips. Well, that was patently obnoxious of the earl, to think he got to decide who Wesley got to tell what, where Wesley would or would not be at 8pm, and how Wesley might arrive.

But de Leon was apparently worse than Wesley had even imagined. Jade thought the earl had stolen from de Leon but surely it was more likely de Leon had robbed Blanshard. Jade likely had no idea the kind of criminal she'd aligned herself with.

"Sir?"

Wesley looked up to see Ned had returned to the morning room. "I said out."

"I still have your messages." Ned cleared his throat. "It is rather later in the morning than you usually rise."

Wesley narrowed his eyes. "Lady Tabitha sent a letter," said Ned. "Apparently she's met another lovely young woman—"

Wesley cut Ned off with a dismissive hand gesture. His third cousin thrice removed met new women for Wesley every other month. The language and the tactics sometimes varied, but everything his distant family and solicitors had ever said to Wesley boiled down to the same thing: *you're sitting on piles of money with no heir; it makes the landed gentry restless.* "Do I have one single message that isn't a request for funds, marriage, future bequeathments, or the presence of a viscount at some useless social?"

"Just the one, in that case," said Ned. "You had a call early this morning from the American lady, Miss Robbins. She'd like you to call her hotel as soon as you can."

Wesley looked down at the letter on the table. Blanshard had warned Wesley to tell de Leon nothing of him. Jade could be in danger herself. He should call her back immediately—

Except she'd been firmly on de Leon's side last night. She seemed to think she knew everything de Leon had done, implied there was much more to the story than Wesley knew. Would she listen to him, if he called her now?

Wesley frowned.

"Sir?" said Ned. "Will you be calling Miss Robbins back?"

"Not yet." Wesley would talk to Blanshard first, learn the truth, and gather facts. Jade did know de Leon was dangerous; Wesley would present her with an irrefutable case of the *brutish tactics* Blanshard had mentioned in his letter.

Unbidden, another snippet of his conversation with Jade flitted through his mind.

You said yourself, at dinner, that de Leon was one of the most dangerous men you'd ever met.

He is. And did that dangerous man fight back tonight? Or would he have let you snap his arm before he took the chance of hurting you?

Wesley's fingers tightened around Blanshard's letter, just shy of crumpling it. More lunacy, that's all it was. Everyone, apparently even Jade, assumed Wesley's title meant he was a useless incompetent, forgetting his war record, his medal, his sharpshooting trophies. Wesley was bigger, stronger than de Leon, and a former British Army captain to boot. Unless de Leon was secretly capable of sorcery, the man had simply been outmatched.

"Sorcery." Wesley scoffed the word out loud, for good measure. As if anyone was capable of something that wasn't real.

Even if de Leon had used the word *paranormal* in New York, to describe Rory Brodigan.

Wesley paused.

And then he shook his head. Christ, now he was having *flights of fancy.* All that rot about *paranormals* was all bootlegger code, that's what Arthur had said, and why would it be anything else?

Wesley did not believe in fairy tales, true love, or other childish nonsense. He most certainly did not believe in *magic.* The only thing bewitching about Sebastian de Leon was his supernaturally handsome face, and Wesley would not be so easily enchanted.

The murder had happened behind Molly's boarding house. A crowd had gathered, kept back by several policemen.

Sebastian hovered on the edge of the crowd, just behind Jade and Zhang's physical body. "We may have to rethink the plan of using my magic," he said reluctantly.

"How would it normally work?" asked Jade.

"My magic is enervation, yes?" Sebastian tilted his head back to look from under the brim of his flat cap. He was tall enough to see over part of the crowd, but two officers still blocked his view of the alley. "I cannot tell you what kind of magic was used, but if I sweep out with my magic, I will feel if there is residual magic that gets cleared away."

"Cleared?" Jade looked fully over her shoulder. "I thought you could only *weaken* magic and then it eventually comes back."

"Yes, living magic, in people," he admitted. "This would be sweeping away the effects of magic, like traces left by alchemy."

"Or an astral projection?" asked Zhang, on his other side. "So if you use your magic here, Jade won't be able to use her telekinesis, and my astral projection will vanish."

"And every person without magic will crash to the ground when my magic hits their aura." Sebastian winced. "I don't think I can risk it. I could hurt all of these people here."

"Agreed, but I feel certain there are magical traces that you would find," said Jade. "This alley is off a central street in the middle of Kilburn. How is the murderer moving unseen and unheard?"

Under his eyelids, Zhang's eyes moved like he was dreaming. "There are ashes in the street."

Sebastian's eyes widened. "Ashes?"

"In a perfect circle," said Zhang. "As if someone made a ring of fire and let it burn to the stones."

Sebastian exchanged a look with Jade. "We know at least one paranormal with fire magic," she said grimly.

Jack Mercier. Sebastian knew him too, another paranormal who'd been enslaved alongside Sebastian by the Puppeteer's blood magic under Baron Zeppler. Only where Sebastian had hated the things he'd been forced to do, Mercier had enjoyed the violence, and only ever hated being under someone else's thumb.

"It means nothing good if Jack Mercier is in town," said Jade.

"No," Sebastian said quietly. "Nothing good at all. Could it actually be him behind these murders?"

Zhang made a doubtful *hmm*. "The body's been moved to the morgue already, but there's a pair of policemen talking about it. One of them just said *she was shriveled like an ancient raisin*. I think it's a good bet this is the same murderer, but I don't know if it could have been done with fire."

He opened his eyes for a moment. "The body was scheduled for an autopsy this afternoon. I'm going to take a look."

"We'll cover for you," Jade said.

"What does that mean?" Sebastian asked, as Zhang closed his eyes again.

"The farther he projects, the more effort it takes, and the less he can act normally here on the street with us." Jade threaded her arm through Zhang's. "Let's find a quiet corner."

Sebastian nodded in understanding. "I have limits too," he said, as they walked, Jade guiding Zhang's physical body with an ease that spoke of their comfort with each other. "If I have to keep my magic tightly controlled, it's tiring, and the stronger the magic, the more effort it takes for me to weaken it. And with a paranormal like Rory, with a relic, it's like running face-first into a lead wall. I can't touch or weaken their magic at all."

There was a park bench across the street, and the three of them sat. "You know far more about the relics than Jianwei and I," said Jade. "Baron Zeppler had a relic, a brooch. Do you know anything you can share about it?"

Sebastian bit his lip. He wasn't supposed to talk about the relics, but this was the fourth nonmagical victim in the past few months. He needed to work with Jade and Zhang if they were going to stop these killings. "The brooch makes a paranormal's magic work on other paranormals."

"What, it turns them into a de Leon?" she said, with a ghost of a smile.

"That is…sort of accurate, yes," he admitted ruefully. "The records are unusually messy, with no names noted, but we know it was sunk off the coast of Puerto Rico generations ago in the hope it could not be unlocked."

"But then Jianwei found it by astral walking on the ocean floor," Jade said.

"He did not unlock it that way," Sebastian said. "The relics all have their keys, yes? The brooch's key is theft and murder together—it must be stolen while someone is dying at someone else's hand."

"Charming," Jade said dryly. "But then, it seems all the relics were made with murder, so none of them are exactly charming trinkets. So someone sank the brooch to the bottom of the ocean in the hopes that no one would be murdered near it?"

"And that the brooch could not be stolen if no one owned it."

"But then Baron Zeppler stole it from Zhang, and murdered one of their family friends while doing it. So that's how he unlocked it by accident." Jade looked pensive. "There was more than one murder at that French country estate where Baron Zeppler was in May. Could Mercier have been there and somehow stolen the brooch from Zeppler, and be using its magic to commit these murders?"

"The brooch would make Mercier's fire magic much stronger, but I don't see how it could give him the power to kill like this," said Sebastian. "What if Lord Blanshard was the one who stole the brooch?"

"Then which one of them was in the alley last night?"

Zhang suddenly opened his eyes. "I saw the body." He'd gone too pale. "It's hard to tell, but there may have been burns on her arms. Everything is shriveled, including the heart."

What a terrible crime. "Did you get her name?" Sebastian asked.

"Olive Reilly," said Zhang.

Oh no. Sebastian buried his face in his hands.

"Did you know her?" Jade said gently.

He nodded into his hands. "She had the room under Molly. We only spoke a few times, but she was very sweet. She did not deserve to meet an end like this." He'd need to send a telegram to Molly and Isabel; they were going to be crushed.

"The poor thing." Jade sighed, a frustrated sound. "What do we do now?"

"My mother has a friend in Limehouse," said Zhang. "Not a paranormal, but used to be married to one, and still trades sometimes in paranormal books. We could pop in, see if they have any ideas."

Jade and Zhang looked at Sebastian expectantly.

"Considering how things went with Lord Fine, it is probably best I do not meet any more of your friends, yes?" Sebastian said, trying for a lightness none of them felt. "I am going to go into the boarding house, see if I can learn anything more. A few of Molly's friends think I'm her boyfriend. They might talk to me."

"I'm sure they'll be glad to see you," Jade said sincerely.

Lord Fine wasn't, Sebastian's mind pointed out. *Lord Fine wanted to call the police. And if Molly's friends knew the truth about your past, they'd be as scared of you as he was. Your history will never rewrite itself, Sebastian; nothing you do will make you one of the heroes again.*

Sebastian swallowed. There was a paranormal killer in London. Whatever his past, he had to do what he could to stop them.

Wesley spent the day chain-smoking in the study, trying and failing to distract himself with the newspaper and his own business. A useless effort; he couldn't focus in the slightest on the registry of charities he'd requested from his solicitor, and the newspaper was full of sensationalized shouting about the ghastly murder of Lord Thornton's scullery maid in Kilburn.

He didn't return Jade's call either, and it needled at him like a splinter, dismissing a lady's request like that, especially a woman like Jade. He'd apologize when he had a case to present to her. Surely keeping her out of danger was more important than manners.

I know everything Sebastian did, Jade had said. *I know more than you. I forgave him, and so did Arthur.*

Balderdash. Of course Arthur hadn't forgiven him. Jade must have been mistaken.

I swear to you that things are not what you think.

Of course it was what he thought. Everything was always exactly as bleak, and people as villainous and self-serving, as Wesley thought they were, and the only time he got it wrong was when he wasn't pessimistic enough.

He glanced back down at the newspaper on his desk, and saw not black-and-white print, but shades of soft brown like the rolling hills of the Yorkshire moors, eyes the color of the autumn leaves of the ash trees on the dales.

Case in point: he had not been nearly pessimistic enough about how much his own libido would try to thwart his reasoned mind.

"My lord?"

Wesley looked up from his desk, over the reading glasses perched on his nose.

"The earl's car has arrived," said Ned. "I've readied your coat."

"A light fall one?" Wesley said dryly. "Or are you still angry about the painting, and chose something heavy and stifling so I'll be sweating like a pig?"

"That would be beneath your footman," Ned said, lofty and probably lying.

A few minutes and much snapping later, Wesley had an appropriate coat and was approaching the Rolls Royce idling at his curb.

Blanshard's driver opened the backseat door for Wesley. "The name's Mercier, sir." The man was shorter than Wesley, with dark brown hair and pale skin, a French surname but an English accent. "Jack, if you prefer. At your service."

"I just want quiet," Wesley snapped, climbing into the backseat, which was unusually warm.

"Of course, sir—"

"It's not quiet if you're speaking, is it?"

Mercier opened his mouth, then closed it with a snap and shut the door, mercifully without saying anything more.

Wesley stretched his legs out behind the passenger seat and folded his arms, watching as the driver walked around the car. A moment later, Mercier was behind the wheel, and the car glided away from the curb and headed out of Kensington.

* * *

Sebastian spent several hours at Molly's boarding house. The matron had relaxed the *no men* house rule for the day to allow the police officers in, giving him a chance to talk quietly to Winnie, Ada, Nellie, and Violet, the women who rented the rooms near the victim. None of them had much to add, unfortunately. It seemed Olive was often forced to work late for Lord and Lady Thornton, and sometimes grudgingly stayed overnight in the servants' quarters. No one had realized anything was amiss when she didn't return—at least, until her body was found in the alley after midnight.

It was fully dark by the time Sebastian took the train back to Liverpool Street Station. He hunched his shoulders against the night's already-dropping temperatures as he bought some scraps for the strays from the meat man's cart.

The two young orange-and-white cats were sniffing the pub's trash cans when he arrived. This time, they followed him down to the gallery's back door. Sebastian put the food out and lingered in the alley, talking soft Spanish to the half-grown strays until they came over to eat. The bolder kitten even wove between his calves, letting Sebastian pet her as he voiced his grief and frustration that a paranormal killer was still loose and he didn't know where to find them.

Finally, Sebastian straightened. He'd eat something himself, then go back out, maybe back to Kilburn, to sweep the alley with magic if it was finally empty in the night, or to the train stations to investigate, but at least he'd go out somewhere to do something.

Upstairs, he lit his stove to warm the room, and began heating the contents of a can of spaghetti in a pan that needed a better scrubbing than he could give in a bathroom sink.

He'd just gotten it bubbling when he heard Zhang's voice. "Sebastian, are you here? Please be here, I have no idea where else you might be if you're not."

Sebastian looked over his shoulder. Zhang's glowing astral projection was in the middle of the room, and he was addressing Sebastian's table, a few feet over.

"I'm here," Sebastian said, even though it was pointless and Zhang's astral projection couldn't see or hear him.

"It's that idiot, Lord Fine." Zhang was still talking to the table. "He just got in a car with Jack Mercier."

Sebastian's eyes went wide.

"They're in a Rolls Royce passing Fenchurch Street Station, and the car is slowing," Zhang continued. "Jade and I are on our way, but there's too much traffic. You can get there in minutes, if you leave now. If you run. If you're even here," he added mournfully.

Sebastian swore. He set the hot pan to the side—there would be enough fire when he got to Mercier, he thought, slightly hysterically—and thundered down the stairs on his way to Fenchurch.

The Rolls Royce was far too hot. Sweat had beaded on Wesley's forehead and between his shoulder blades. "Christ, turn down the heat. It's roasting in here."

"My apologies," said the driver, Mercier, almost mockingly. "I forget I like things hotter than other people."

Wesley narrowed his eyes. The Rolls had passed Fenchurch and turned down a narrow side street that seemed oddly deserted for central London. "Where are we going?"

The car slowed to a crawl. "We're nearly there," said Mercier.

Wesley leaned forward. "That wasn't an answer to my question."

"Where did you expect we were going, the Ritz?"

"I haven't been told what to expect," Wesley said testily.

"Then you're hardly in a position to be asking questions, are you, your lordship?"

Wesley's eyes narrowed further. It meant nothing good if his driver had suddenly decided to become impertinent. "Tell me exactly what's going on."

"I'm sorry, sir, I don't know what you mean," said Mercier pleasantly. "We're in the Earl of Blanshard's very nice car, going exactly where he wants you."

"Are we?" Wesley said dangerously, as his mind quickly ran through his options. "Because I'm beginning to suspect you're not the earl's driver."

"I'm afraid I am," Mercier said, with unsettling sincerity.

The car turned a corner, under an archway, then abruptly stopped. Wesley glanced to the right, and found the brick wall so close he couldn't have opened his door. On the car's left was the ominous empty dark of the alley, and ahead, through the windshield, the headlight beams illuminated more bricks in the darkness, a bend at the far end where the alley seemed to trail away beneath a building.

"Oh, look at that, you've taken me to a deserted alley. How original." Wesley began to work the cufflink free from his shirt. First chance he got, he was jamming it into a neck, or perhaps an eye socket. "Whatever you have planned, it won't work. I have no friends to speak of and my only family is distant and would love to see me dead. There's no one to extort if you kidnap me, and I make a particularly unsuitable victim."

He palmed the cufflink and waited. He was prepared to be yanked from the car. He was prepared for someone to have a gun.

He was not prepared for Mercier to burst into flames.

Chapter Six

A cry escaped Wesley as the man behind the driver's wheel lit up like a human match. Fire erupted along Mercier's arms, up his shoulders, enveloping his entire head. *Real* fire, its sudden heat almost unbearable in the enclosed space.

And then Mercier turned to look over the backseat at Wesley, his face unburnt within an aura of flame. "Get out of the car, Lord Fine."

Wesley bolted.

He threw open the backseat door that wasn't hemmed in by bricks and rolled out, hitting the stones of the alley. Cold wet air slapped him in the face, a pungent burst of piss and wet ashtray that was downright welcome after the heat of the car—a heat that Wesley still couldn't explain.

He scrambled up to his feet. They were in something that was half alley, half underground car park. The path ahead was dark beyond the headlights—did it lead back to Fenchurch and safety? Was it a dead end?

Behind Wesley, a car door slammed. "I didn't say leave," said Mercier.

The alley was suddenly bright as a bonfire as flames burst into life at Wesley's feet like Mercier had touched a lit match to invisible gasoline. The flames rose up and out, curving like serpents until Wesley was standing in a ring of fire as high as his thighs.

He raised his head in shock.

Christ, Mercier himself was *still on fire*.

Right. He'd been kidnapped by—by a magician. A street performer. A criminal capable of tricks. Wesley balled his hands in fists and raised his chin. "What are you playing at?"

Mercier's lips quirked in an unpleasant smile. "Do you really still think I'm playing?" He had a small glass bottle in his hand, and as he spoke he uncorked it. "Are you telling yourself I'm a circus performer or some other rot?"

Something poured out of the bottle—like fog, but moving too fast, spilling out like an ethereal cage around him. More tricks, more illusions, literal smoke and mirrors, that was all this was.

"What else would you be?" Wesley snapped.

Mercier popped the cork back into the bottle. "I'm not with the circus."

The flames encircling Wesley rose higher, nearly to his waist. The heat was intense enough to hurt, as sweat drenched Wesley's brow and his heart pounded in his chest.

"You're mad," he said tightly. "I don't care for plays or performances and I have no desire to be in one. I demand you stop your tricks and let me go. We're a stone's throw from Fenchurch—you won't get away with this."

"I do, in fact, get away with this," Mercier said. "But go ahead and call for help if you'd like." He gestured at the insubstantial cage around them. "For all the good it will do you. These flames won't go out with water, and no one can hear you now."

Mercier took a step closer. Wesley instinctively tried

to move back, but there was nowhere to go unless he went through the flames. Flames Mercier had somehow lit—that he was somehow controlling—

No, no no, that was all impossible. "What do you want from me?"

"Nothing," said Mercier. "I'm just the opening act."

"Opening for what?"

"For *whom*," Mercier corrected. "And you already know. I'm his driver, and you're the one who sent him a telegram."

So Mercier *was* doing this at the behest of the Earl of Blanshard. Jade had warned Wesley the earl might be more dangerous than he seemed—that Blanshard was, at the very least, a thief. Wesley should have listened.

"I don't recall telegramming the earl to send his pet reprobate to threaten me," Wesley said, like he wasn't cursing himself. "If he wanted an apology for my behavior at a three-years-past soiree, he could have simply fucking asked."

"You brought this on yourself, my lord," Mercier said, with heavy sarcasm on the title. "You shouldn't have whined to the earl about your run-in with Sebastian de Leon."

For fuck's sake. De Leon was involved in this too? "Friend of yours?" Wesley said bitingly.

"Hell no," Mercier said, with feeling. "Sebastian's always got to be special, doesn't he? Special family, special legacy, special magic."

"Special *what*?" Wesley could not have heard right. "Are you also a bootlegger? Is this more of your code?"

Mercier rolled his eyes, like he was very tired of Wesley. The flames rose another inch higher, and Wesley understood with sudden, bone-deep certainty that Mercier intended to kill him.

"The earl will have questions for you, but that's not my job," Mercier went on. "My job is to get as much magic as I can in your aura."

He was talking complete gibberish, every single word out of his mouth was nonsense, but the cage still shimmered around them, and the flames ringing Wesley burned infernally hot.

"Of course, that means using my pyrokinesis on you." Mercier smiled one of the most horrible smiles Wesley had ever seen. "And you're not fireproof like I am. Don't worry; no one comes when you scream."

Wesley tried to process what that could possibly mean, his brain refusing to accept *aura* or *pyrokinesis* but very much understanding *scream*.

And then Wesley was on fire too.

His leather gloves were suddenly enveloped in flames, shooting up his forearms like he'd reached into a stove. It burned straight through his coat, too fast and too hot, fabric blistering his skin in a shock of pain so sudden a cry tore itself from his throat—

"Let him go!"

Wesley knew that voice.

Relief swept through him just as something swept down the alley like a tidal wave. The glimmering cage burst into shimmering dust, the flames went out like they'd been doused with water, and Wesley's legs collapsed under him like jelly.

He fell to the alley floor. His body wouldn't move, his muscles heavy as lead. The dust of the cage fell like glittery rain around him, vanishing before it hit the cobblestones, as Wesley tried to force his leaden eyelids to stay open. Mercier was staggering like a drunk, just flesh and blood again with his flames gone like Wesley's prison.

I'm not on fire anymore either, some distant part of Wesley realized.

"And of course it's the spanner in the works." Mercier straightened up, and the alley was suddenly lit as he burst back into flame. "I didn't realize you were still in London until Lord Jackass here told us. You're going to regret showing yourself, Sebastian."

Wesley tried to lift his head, but he could only make out a man's silhouette in the archway at the mouth of the alley, leaning hard on the wall.

Sebastian's voice came again. "Get away from the viscount."

And the inexplicable sensation of a toppling flood came harder. Wesley's head hit the pavement, but Mercier's aura of flames disappeared again like a match shaken out. "Fuck," he bit out, sounding genuinely unsettled. He raised his voice. "I know your limit! I can wait you out. This is all your magic and you can't keep this up."

Except Mercier didn't sound at all certain anymore.

"I *will* keep this up," came Sebastian's voice, strained like he was carrying a huge weight, "until Lord Fine is safe. And I cannot promise *your* magic will survive our battle."

Magic, Wesley mouthed to himself. He was so very tired, his limbs utterly useless, his body glued to the ground.

"Bluffing, you're bluffing, you don't have that power!" But Mercier had gone paler, and was backing away from Sebastian.

Sebastian's silhouette lifted one shaky hand. Mercier squawked and bolted in the opposite direction, disappearing beyond the bend where the headlight beams couldn't reach.

As Sebastian stumbled down the alley, the lethargy vanished from Wesley so suddenly he reeled. His eyes popped open, his limbs strong and body hale again. He pushed himself up to sitting just as Sebastian fell to his hands and knees on the pavement next to him.

Sebastian raised his head to look at Wesley, breathing so hard Wesley could hear him pant. "Are you all right, Lord Fine?"

Wesley had some bruises, some scrapes, and blisters on his arms. But he was alive, and free, and most importantly, *not on fucking fire anymore*, so what came out was, "Yes."

"Oh good," said Sebastian.

And then he toppled over.

"De Leon!" Wesley leaned forward, hurriedly shoving at de Leon's shoulder. "De Leon, what the devil is going on?"

But as he forced de Leon over to his back, Wesley saw his eyes were closed. In a panic, he put his fingers on the other man's neck. He let out a breath of relief as he found a pulse.

Unconscious. But alive.

Wesley sat back, his fingers still on the soft, warm skin of de Leon's neck.

"Well...fuck," he said inelegantly, to the alley.

Discomfort was the first thing Sebastian became aware of, his mouth parched and his head pounding. He ignored both, struggling to recall what had happened.

Mercier—the ring of fire—

Lord Fine.

Sebastian's eyes flew open and he sat up.

Or tried to.

He swore as metal bit into his wrists. His arms were

stretched up and out to either side, cuffed to—he craned his neck with difficulty, following the line of his right arm—cuffed to—

Bedposts?

Tall mahogany bedposts, exquisitely carved, and above them stretched a deep green canopy, embroidered with gold. His head rested on something soft, and the fabric against his cheek was like silk.

A twitch of his legs confirmed they were free, and there was no bite of lead against his skin. So someone with significant money had cuffed him to a bed, but they hadn't taken his magic into account—

"Finally awake, are you?"

Sebastian turned his head to the left, toward the sound of Lord Fine's voice.

The viscount was only a few feet away, sitting in a chair of dark wood and green velvet. He had removed his jacket, his shirtsleeves rolled up to his elbows above bandaged forearms, and on his lap was a revolver.

Sebastian swallowed around his scratchy throat. "Good...evening?" he tried.

"It's morning," Lord Fine said dryly. "You've been unconscious for six hours."

Oh, Sebastian's mouth formed. He eyed the uncomfortable straight back of the chair. If Lord Fine had been sitting there the whole time, he was likely stiff, sore, and even more on edge. "I'm not going to hurt you."

If anything, that made Lord Fine's expression even more suspicious. "You're the one in handcuffs. I'm the one holding a gun." He leaned forward, and in a dangerous voice said, "Tell me, why exactly do you think *I* should be the worried one?"

Uh-oh. Sebastian wet his lips. "Is there a reason I'm here?" he asked, instead of answering.

"Because I have questions."

Lord Fine's gaze had traveled from Sebastian's face to his outstretched arms, and was lingering. Was he straining against the handcuffs? That would only make poor Lord Fine even more nervous.

Sebastian forced his muscles to stop flexing. "I meant, is there a reason I'm *here*, in this bedroom?"

"Was I supposed to leave you passed out on the street?"

"It's what I would have expected," Sebastian said honestly.

Lord Fine smiled thinly. "Well, then we both need to examine our expectations, because I wasn't expecting a man to set me on fire."

Sebastian opened his mouth—

Lord Fine held up the revolver. "Don't give me whatever lie you're about to spin," he said curtly. "Mercier lit up that alley—lit up *me*—like a match. Then *you* showed up, and all the fire was gone, and I want an explanation or you can spend the rest of your days handcuffed to my bed."

Sebastian considered that. "It's a nice bed."

Lord Fine cocked the revolver.

Sebastian let his head fall back against the pillow with a sigh. How was he going to explain this?

There was a loud scrape of wood against wood as Lord Fine stood so abruptly the chair slid on the floor. Then Lord Fine's face filled Sebastian's vision, narrowed eyes of cool gray-blue, a thin, straight nose, morning stubble on a sharp jaw.

Nice view, some wildly untimely part of Sebastian's mind decided to observe.

The revolver was still in Lord Fine's hand, and he lifted it to point between Sebastian's eyes.

Sebastian raised his eyebrows. "What are you doing now?" he asked curiously.

"Conducting an experiment." Lord Fine held the revolver steady for several moments, then his eyes narrowed further. "Look at you. You're not remotely scared of this gun. You're not even nervous."

"Should I be?"

Lord Fine looked at him like he was stupid. "I'm pointing a gun between your eyes, Mr. de Leon. Most men would be." He lowered the gun, only an inch. "But you're not most men, are you?"

Sebastian winced. "Maybe I believe you won't use it."

"I most certainly would," Lord Fine said. "I would shoot you as easily as I would a fox."

Sebastian frowned. "Why would you shoot a fox?"

"It's an analogy," Lord Fine said testily. "You don't actually shoot the fox, you sic the dogs on it, but the point is—"

"You make your *dogs* kill it?"

"It's a fucking fox—"

"But they're so cute," said Sebastian. "They've got those little noses, and those big ears."

"Are you serious right now?" said Lord Fine incredulously. "You're handcuffed to my bed at gunpoint and you're more upset that the English hunt foxes?"

"No," Sebastian lied. He held his tongue for a moment, then couldn't help adding, "But you shouldn't."

Lord Fine tilted his head back, appraising. "You have no fear of me at all. Can this bullet even hurt you?"

"Oh yes," Sebastian admitted. "You could kill me if you shot me right now."

"But you're not defenseless, are you?"

Sebastian hesitated.

Lord Fine clenched his jaw and steadied the gun. "What happened last night?"

"Perhaps you had a lot to drink?" Sebastian tried.

"And there's the lie I told you not to tell," Lord Fine said. "I don't know what kind of imbeciles you're used to dealing with, but I was not drunk, or touched in the head, or any of that other rot people say when they want you to doubt yourself. I know what I saw. More to the point, I still have blisters on my bloody arms."

Sebastian opened his mouth to suggest opium—

"Lie to my face again and I will kill a fox, just for you."

Sebastian snapped his mouth shut to glower instead.

"I was on fire. And then I wasn't—" Lord Fine pointed at him "—and that was your doing. You will not lie there and pretend you're harmless. I want to know how I was nearly immolated near Fenchurch Station and I expect an answer *now*."

It was an impressive command, said in the rigid and forceful tone of a man accustomed to instant obedience. Lord Fine was standing ramrod straight, still holding his revolver, and his glare dared Sebastian to cross him.

And then, from somewhere down below, came a yip.

"Oh!" Sebastian tried to sit up, only to jerk against his handcuffs and flop back to the bed. "You have a dog!"

"I most certainly do not," Lord Fine snapped.

"Then your neighbor has one?" Charming, enthusiastic little yips could still be heard. "She sounds cute. What's her name?"

"My neighbor?"

"The doggie."

"The *doggie*." Lord Fine's lips had gone very thin. "Powderpuff."

"Oh, that is very cute, yes? I bet she is a sweet companion for someone—"

"Enough." Lord Fine whirled away from the bed. He began pacing the floor, gun still in his hand. "What the devil is going on?" he said, as if to himself. "There was fire; he stopped it. He's in handcuffs, I have a gun, yet he cares only for the dog. Is he a fae? It would explain why he's not afraid, and preternaturally handsome."

Sebastian nearly choked.

"But I've caught him, so shouldn't I get a wish?" Lord Fine went on. "Or must I offer breakfast? Isn't there some myth about fairies eating human food and then they're your captive, or is it the other way around? Christ, I hate fairy tales."

Sebastian would very much have liked some breakfast, or at least some water, but what he said was, "I wouldn't take you captive."

Lord Fine gestured at the handcuffs with the gun. "Can't say I return the sentiment," he said dryly. "Mr. de Leon—"

"You can call me Sebastian," he interrupted. "I'm handcuffed to your bed."

"Believe me, I am *well* aware of you in my bed right now," Lord Fine said, extra testy as he put a knee on the edge of the mattress. "Sebastian."

His name rolled off Lord Fine's tongue not with a perfect Spanish accent but not completely Anglicized either, as if Lord Fine couldn't quite get there but had given his best effort to pronounce it correctly. His clothes were tailored for a close fit, trousers tight to his hips, and with no jacket it was easy to see how his shirt and vest molded to broad shoulders and a flat abdomen. The bandages were clear on his forearms, but his movements were controlled, and there was no fear on his face.

"I was caged in a circle of fire. I was set aflame by a man who didn't touch me. And Mercier used the word *paranormal*, the same word you used to describe Rory Brodigan in New York," said Lord Fine. "So I don't believe you're a bootlegger, Sebastian, because Mercier also used the word *magic*."

The word hung between them for a moment.

Sebastian glanced up, meeting his eyes. "Surely you don't believe in magic, Lord Fine?"

They stared at each other for a long moment, the only sound the distant, happy yips of the little dog, Powderpuff.

"You're not going to talk?" Lord Fine finally said, harsh and biting.

Sebastian blew out a breath. "You are too nice to get mixed up in my world," he said softly. "You have been right about me all along. I am a villain, a rogue, a— what is the word—a scoundrel. I am a dangerous man with a bad past and you an innocent."

He tried a pleading tone, anything to convince Lord Fine to turn away from this. "Show me the door," he said, "and forget what you saw. Forget you ever met me. It is how you will stay safe."

Lord Fine stood several moments more, the hand not holding the gun clenched in a fist.

Then he said, "Very well. We'll do this the hard way."

"What?" But Lord Fine had turned on his heel and was striding away. Sebastian tried to sit up, only to jerk against the cuffs again. "Lord Fine, what are you doing?"

Lord Fine ignored him, instead crossing the room to the large window framed with velvet drapes. He set the gun on the ledge and then opened the window, deliberately, so there was no question as to his movements.

Powderpuff's little yips became louder.

Lord Fine picked the gun back up and leaned on the wall, eyes on the outside.

Sebastian furrowed his eyebrows. "What are you doing?" he asked again.

"Waiting," said Lord Fine.

"For what?"

"For Powderpuff to come into view," said Lord Fine. "She's barely half a stone, you know, nothing but white fluff and barks."

"But why are you waiting for Powderpuff?"

"The racket this mongrel makes has been the bane of my mornings." He sighted down the barrel of his gun. "Not for much longer."

Sebastian drew back in horror. "You wouldn't."

"I just told you I indulge in the monstrous English pastime of hunting foxes for sport. What do I care for a Maltese?"

Sebastian tried to sit up. The handcuffs bit into him, and held him down. "Lord Fine—"

"Tell me the truth about what happened last night."

"You're not taking your neighbor's dog hostage!"

"I believe that's exactly what I'm doing," Lord Fine said, without taking his eyes off the window. "I am not *nice* nor an *innocent*. I want answers and you will give them to me if I have to point this gun at every overindulged pet in Kensington."

Sebastian's temper was rising. Lord Fine wouldn't. He *wouldn't*. Would he? "You can't make that shot."

"I served for four years in the British Army, three as captain, and have won five marksman trophies since. I could make this shot in my sleep." Lord Fine steadied the gun. "And there's little Powderpuff now. Lady Pennington is going to be so sad when her precious puppy is gone—"

Sebastian's magic swept out before his brain could stop it.

Lord Fine toppled like a felled tree.

A strangled "*fucking hell*" escaped as he collapsed, missing the wall and falling out of Sebastian's line of sight. Then there was a loud thump, like a body smacking solid wood planks.

Sebastian scrambled to rein his magic in, but it was too late.

"And there it was," Lord Fine's voice came, from the floor.

A moment later, two hands came into view at the side of the bed. One of the hands set the gun to the side. Then Lord Fine's head emerged over the edge of the mattress, his hair sticking up strangely and the side of his face red, like he'd hit the floor with some force.

Sebastian winced.

Lord Fine crossed his arms, still kneeling at the side of the bed so their eyes were level.

"I believe in magic *now*," he said.

Chapter Seven

The last of that strange watery sensation was leaving Wesley's limbs as he watched the guilt and sheepishness play out over Sebastian's face. For a man who claimed to be a dangerous scoundrel, he wasn't very good at hiding his feelings. Frankly, the sheepishness was a good look on him.

Everything was a good look on him, the bastard.

Sebastian's chained arms had to be bothering him by now. Wesley didn't owe the man comfort, and he hadn't taken the chance of keeping him free. Sebastian had, after all, once kidnapped a man, and he was apparently capable of instantly flattening any opponent by using—Wesley almost couldn't think the word—what might have been *magic*.

But Sebastian had also saved Wesley's life.

He'd looked so helpless in the alley, unconscious and unresponsive, and despite the possible danger, Wesley hadn't been able to leave him behind. Carrying Sebastian into a taxi and then up the stairs to his bedroom had been difficult—he wasn't that much smaller than Wesley himself, with sleek muscles and obnoxiously perfect proportions—

Not that those actually had anything to do with carrying him. Just an observation his brain had insisted on making.

At any rate, Sebastian hadn't woken while Wesley was carrying him, not even when Ned had appeared in wide-eyed surprise at Wesley's singed appearance and arms full of unconscious man. Now, awake, Sebastian would occasionally reflexively flex against the handcuffs, his biceps filling out his shirtsleeves. His shirts had come untucked, and had rucked up to his ribs on one side, showing golden skin and part of a flat abdomen. Wesley hadn't pushed the shirt or undershirt up on purpose when he'd been putting the cuffs on, but he hadn't pulled them down either. They were now high enough to tease what the man would look like with the handcuffs but without the shirts, and combined with the memory of carrying Sebastian in his arms, Wesley's unhelpful mind was only too happy to fill in the details.

Wesley put his elbow on the mattress and his chin in his hand. "So, Sebastian," he said, in a conversational tone with a knife's edge, "are you a faery or a witch?"

Sebastian made a face. It was cute, damn him. "English speakers call us paranormals," he said, with obvious reluctance.

"You don't look like a ghost," Wesley pointed out. "You look like flesh and blood. And muscle." *And muscle? Christ, Wesley.* "But you use magic," he hurriedly added.

"Yes," Sebastian admitted. "And I am very sorry I used it on you. Um. Twice."

The sheepish look was back, and for fuck's sake, it was distracting. The bloody accent was distracting. And his shirts had just ridden up another distracting inch—

Wesley forced himself up to his feet before his mind went down that path again. He picked up the gun. "You're a paranormal, then," he said, opening the nightstand drawer, "and I suppose since we've established you can hurt me regardless, then there's no point in keeping you chained to my bed. Well." His gaze stole back to Sebastian out of the corner of his eye. "No safety-related point, at any rate," he muttered to himself.

He plucked the handcuff key out of the drawer and shut the gun away. "I assume you'd like out of those cuffs."

Sebastian furrowed his eyebrows. "You just saw my magic. I had actually assumed you'd keep me here forever."

"You didn't use your magic to stop me from waving my gun in your face." Wesley coughed. "In a manner of speaking." He sat on the edge of the bed. "And the night before, in the alley, you could have stopped me at any moment, but you didn't."

"I don't like to use my magic on the nonmagical," Sebastian said quietly. "I don't like to hurt anyone."

Sebastian's magic did not actually hurt. Wesley kept that to himself as he reached for the closest wrist, the one without a tattoo.

"I'm not a fool, Sebastian," he said sharply, as he turned the key in the cuff. "You can't move me with pretty words. But the undeniable fact is that you have had reasons to defend yourself, but didn't use your magic until I threatened something else. Ergo, I believe that, at least for now, you don't intend me harm."

"Oh." Sebastian shook out his arm with an almost imperceptible wince. He probably had downright vicious pins and needles, and no, Wesley did not owe him comfort, but it was uncomfortable to realize he'd caused Sebastian pain. How old was he? Surely someone with a criminal history, with magic like his, was at least as old if not older than Wesley himself? But in that moment he seemed younger, too innocent for the past Wesley knew he had. "I, um. I don't think you're a fool at all. You seem very smart."

And you seem like an injured lamb lost far from home, despite having the magic to knock me on my arse with a thought.

Wesley pushed the unhelpful thought away; Sebastian might not be an immediate threat, but he was even more dangerous than Wesley could have ever imagined, and it would not do to forget that. He leaned over for the other wrist.

But as he caught sight of the tattoo, he paused. He'd noticed it earlier, of course, when he'd put the handcuffs on the unconscious Sebastian, a stunning swirl of colors that seemed almost alive. And now, with more light filling the room, he wanted a better look. He put his hand on Sebastian's wrist, the skin chilled under Wesley's fingers—

Sebastian took a sharp breath.

Wesley cut his eyes down.

He was stretched across Sebastian's chest, the two of them closer than Wesley had been to another man in quite some time. Close enough to feel the anticipation of touch, to appreciate how the morning light lit the golden-brown of Sebastian's eyes to a warm glow.

There was a polite knock on the door.

"My lord?" Ned's voice came through the door.

Wesley hastily pulled back, yanking his hand off Sebastian's wrist like he was a sodding schoolboy afraid of being caught, not a grown man in his own home.

"Ned," he hissed, because his staff knew to never disturb him in his room. "You had best not have knocked for anything less than another war—"

"Begging your pardon, sir," Ned said hurriedly, "but the American woman you went to dinner with is here for you. Miss Robbins hoped I would ask you if we've seen her friend. A Mr. de Leon?" he finished awkwardly, mercifully not adding, *is that the unconscious bloke you carried in here last night and took into your room?* "I didn't want to disappoint her," he added. "She's...well, she's very pretty, sir."

Oh, for fuck's sake. The revolution-prone French peasants Wesley employed were also weak for beautiful women.

Then Wesley blinked. "Hang on," he said suspiciously, to Sebastian. "Is Jade—"

"I would not tell a lady's business," Sebastian said, not meeting his eyes.

The man couldn't prevaricate worth a damn. And apparently Jade was even more interesting than Wesley had guessed.

He raised his voice. "Tell Miss Robbins I'm coming," he called back to Ned, and dropped the key on the mattress by Sebastian's free hand. "I assume a dangerous rogue like yourself can handle it from here," he said dryly.

Sebastian nodded once, his eyes guarded. He was shifting more, his muscles certainly sore. He didn't look dangerous; he looked wary, and tired, and worst of all, utterly unsurprised, like he hadn't expected anything better than to wake up in handcuffs and now be told to get himself free.

Wesley shoved any softness away. The man was still a criminal, and apparently a paranormal one at that. "You still have mud on your face from the alley. There's a bathroom on this floor if you wish to clean up. Have the staff show you to the morning room after; I want answers."

* * *

In Lord Fine's bathroom, Sebastian took big gulps of cold water from the sink. When he'd finally slaked his thirst, he straightened up to face his own reflection. The man looking back at him was in desperate need of a shave, with mud smeared on his cheek, bags beneath his eyes and hair sticking every which way like a sucked mango pit. He didn't wear the unraveling look nearly so well as Lord Fine; he just looked a mess.

Captain in the British Army, he reminded himself, as he splashed the cold water on his face. *Lord Fine is not a man you can look at.*

There was a footman waiting for him in the hall, the one Lord Fine had called Ned. Sebastian vaguely recognized him from May and the day he'd delivered the painting of Barcelona. "Um, good morning," Sebastian said awkwardly.

Ned had to be aware he'd just spent the night in Lord Fine's room. He didn't know about Sebastian's magic; how would Lord Fine have explained the situation?

But Ned just said, "Nice to see you again, sir." If he had opinions about his employer keeping a man in his room for the night, he didn't let it show on his face. "His lordship requested you be brought downstairs."

Ned took him down two flights to a room at the back of the home, away from the street. Sebastian left Ned in the hall and slipped quietly inside to find Lord Fine and Jade sharing a table by the large curved window that overlooked a garden.

Lord Fine's tea was pouring itself, and the viscount was watching with an expression of genuine delight, in a way that took years off his normally cold face.

Zhang's astral projection was hovering over by the bookshelf. He wouldn't have been able to see Sebastian, but Jade looked up from the table at that moment and smiled. "There you are," she said, and Zhang's projection turned in her direction. "Jianwei, he's all right."

"She keeps talking to her fellow but I can't see him." Lord Fine pointed at the tea set. "De Leon, did you know about this? She's telekinetic!"

Sebastian leaned on the wall, a soft smile crossing his face unbidden. "Yes. She's the only one with that magic I've ever met. It's very impressive."

Lord Fine snorted. "Certainly more impressive than whatever that brutishness you do is."

Sebastian's smile slipped off his face.

"And she says her fellow, Mr. Zhang, walks on the astral plane," continued Lord Fine, "and apparently Arthur's friend Rory Brodigan can see history and control the wind. Can you do anything incredible like that?"

Sebastian swallowed and shook his head. "You've seen all I can do already."

Lord Fine snorted again. He leaned back in his chair at the table, his eyes now the same cool gray as his suit. "Well, you lost out when it comes to abilities, didn't you? You're basically a paranormal bully."

Ouch.

Lord Fine's delight had vanished, as if Sebastian's presence had sucked it away. But then, Lord Fine had heard him commit a kidnapping, had been knocked to the floor just that morning by Sebastian's magic. How could Sebastian ever make him anything but afraid?

Just past the table, propped up on a settee near the bookshelf, was a rectangular outline covered by heavy cloth, exactly the right size to be Isabel's painting of San Juan.

Sebastian ignored the pang of loss in his chest. It was good that Jade and Zhang were here; maybe they could show Lord Fine that not all magic was bad. Sebastian could give the painting, the one helpful thing he could do, and then get out of the way before he kept making things worse.

Lord Fine had turned back to Jade. As quietly as he could, Sebastian stepped back into the hall. He followed the length of the hall until it brought him to the front door, where his flat cap and coat had been hung—much cleaner than they should have been, after his collapse in a muddy alley—on a coatrack.

You're running again, the voice in his head said, as Sebastian hurriedly pulled on his coat.

He gritted his teeth. He had to leave; all he did was put Lord Fine even more on edge.

There was a time when a man without magic would have felt safer around you.

Sebastian jammed the cap on his head. Those days were gone. Lord Fine now knew about magic, but it didn't mean he was going to magically forgive Sebastian or want his company. There was no point in thinking about it further.

There were footsteps in the hall, and he looked up to find Ned approaching. "It was kind of you to clean my things," he started.

But Ned waved the thanks away. "You're not leaving yet, are you, sir? Mrs. Harrick—that's our cook, see?—is making breakfast. Her daughter, Elsie, was there when you brought us that painting, in the spring. She'd like to see you again."

The painting of Barcelona that Lord Fine had destroyed, because Sebastian made him so afraid.

Sebastian swallowed. "Thank you, but it's best if I go. Please give my thanks to Miss Elsie and the others, yes?"

He stepped out into the drizzly London morning and quickened his steps, leaving the townhouse behind as he went to find a taxi or tube station.

The next time Wesley looked up, the wall where Sebastian had stood was empty.

He frowned. He hadn't heard the departing steps, and the wall seemed blank without the handsome man.

That made him frown harder. Christ, could he not even look at his own walls now without wanting to see Sebastian?

"Where has Sebastian gone?" he said to Jade.

Jade cocked her head, and wasn't that sodding bizarre, now that he knew she was listening to her lover's astral projection. "I'm not sure. Jianwei can't actually see Sebastian at the moment."

"Why not?"

"Did you see the tattoo on Sebastian's wrist?"

Of course I did, I can't take my bleeding eyes off the man. "I might have," Wesley said cagily.

"The tattoo is also magic," she said. "It hides him from magical detection. Jianwei can't see him from the astral plane unless he's seen him from the physical plane as well."

Magic men with magic tattoos. Wesley really was in Wonderland.

He glanced at the empty wall again. There had been a moment of softness on Sebastian's face when he'd first stepped into the morning room, and it had disappeared as soon as Wesley had insulted his magic.

And so what? Wesley had no cause to feel defensive. *Handsome men are just bleeding touchy,* he reminded himself. *Sebastian is likely so used to admirers he can't handle a few hard truths.*

But another voice in his head pricked at him. Don't lie to yourself, Wesley. His magic saved your life; you think he's perfectly incredible. The only hard truth here is that you insulted him because he makes your cock hard without your permission and your ego can't handle it.

Wesley's frown became pinched. Sebastian is still a criminal, just apparently a sulky one. Ignore him, he instructed himself.

Ignore him.

Hilarious.

Wesley resolutely looked away from the empty wall, gesturing at the covered painting on the floor instead. "You haven't yet explained your *gift*," he said, using the word Jade had used.

"Not actually *my* gift at all," Jade said. "It's from Sebastian. His cousin, the paranormal who created his tattoo, also paints. This is the last of her art he has in this country, and as you don't have the Barcelona painting anymore, he's offering this one to protect your home."

Wesley opened his mouth, then closed it.

He had many of his own *hard truths*, and he prided himself on being able to face them like a man. And at the top of Wesley's truths was that no one would ever seek his company unless they wanted what he had. It might be his money, his status, or possibly sex, but to a one, his social circle, his family, even his lovers only tolerated his near-intolerable presence because Wesley had the things that everyone else wanted.

Except apparently magic was real.

And Wesley didn't have it.

As he stared at the covered gift, the memory of the brilliant colors of Barcelona swirling down the drain replayed itself in Wesley's mind. Sebastian had magic.

And even though Wesley had apparently destroyed his family's magic, Sebastian was offering a new painting to protect his home.

Without asking for anything in return.

He hadn't actually ever asked Wesley for anything, not even to unlock his handcuffs.

Wesley glanced back at Jade. "Well, if it's Sebastian's gift, is he ever coming back to give it to me, or do I just, I don't know, thank the astral plane or that floating teapot?"

Jade pursed her lips, again looking in what Wesley presumed was her unseeable man's direction. "Ah," she said awkwardly. "I still don't know where Sebastian is, but it seems your footman is now standing by your front door."

Wesley's stomach gave a sharp twist. *He* looked at the empty wall again, and gritted his teeth. "Excuse me."

He quickly stood from his chair. His brisk steps took him down the hall to the front door, but the foyer was empty save for a glum-faced Ned.

"Where's Sebastian?" said Wesley, his stomach strangely leaden and heavy.

Ned pointed at the front door.

Oh, for fuck's sake. "Did he say where he was going?"

Ned shook his head. "Cook was making breakfast too," he said, with an obnoxious and unnecessarily dramatic sigh. "Poor Elsie's probably going to cry again when she hears she missed him."

Wesley yanked open the front door.

"My lord, your coat!"

Wesley ignored Ned's call as he took the steps down to the walk. He strode to the curb—

But the only person to be seen was seventy-one-year-old Lady Pennington, in a smart green coat and matching hat, a flowered umbrella in one hand and her ridiculous dog's pink leash in the other.

"Well met, Fine," she said cheerfully, and Powderpuff yipped.

Wesley stood at the edge of the road for a moment, the misty rain dampening his hair and face.

Of course Sebastian has gone, his mind pointed out. *You called him a paranormal bully. That doe-eyed softie who let you put a gun between his eyes but couldn't bear it pointed at a dog. He isn't going to stay if he thinks he frightens you, and you made sure that's what he thinks.*

You're simply reaping what you sowed, Wesley. Wasn't it what you wanted?

Jaw tight, Wesley turned around and went back inside.

Jade was talking to the air as he returned to the morning room.

"—if he's willing, it's our best plan—" She broke it off when she saw Wesley. "He left, then?" She sighed. "He really can't bear to make you nervous, not when you don't have magic."

"And I don't suppose he stopped to think, for a single second, that if he actually made me *nervous* I would never have brought him to my home."

He crossed the room, to where the covered painting was propped on a velvet chair near the bookshelves. "Miss Robbins," he said, finding a polite voice for Jade because perhaps magic was real but so was the Fine lineage and he would *not* fray completely at the seams, "will you tell me about this painting, please?"

Jade folded her hands on the table. "I mentioned Sebastian's cousin, Isabel de Leon, is a paranormal painter," she said, as if the bloody sugar cubes weren't floating through the air while her teaspoon stirred itself. "Her paintings only work on other paranormals. They can do marvelous things, like make anyone with magic forget they were looking for you."

"Is that what the painting of Barcelona was doing?" Wesley asked. "The one I—well. Perhaps you already know."

"I do," she said neutrally, because of course Wesley had upended a bottle of turpentine over a paranormal painting, and of course she somehow knew. "This painting is a bit more dangerous. Its presence will not only hide your home from magic, it can apparently trap a paranormal in their own mind, making them very difficult to bring back."

The cloth hiding the painting appeared quite thick. "What happens if I look at it?"

"You see a lovely painting and nothing more," said Jade softly. "The de Leons have a legacy of their own, you see. Their magic is only dangerous to other paranormals."

Wesley snorted. "I'm afraid my joints would disagree."

Jade made a soft half laugh. "Fair enough. Sebastian can't do you any lasting harm, but I imagine his magic hits auras hard enough anyway. Now you see why I told you he was dangerous."

I might also understand why you called him a marshmallow. Wesley stared at the cloth for another moment, then reached for the corner. He waited until Jade was carefully staring in the opposite direction as he pulled back the edge of the drop cloth.

Bright turquoise ocean stared back at him, rolling up on creamy sand under a cloudless blue sky. Palm trees lined the beach, their brown trunks topped with broad green leaves. A row of straight houses bracketed the road, one with a Model T in front, and an old stone fort sat up on a green hill, overlooking the sea.

Wesley stared in surprise. "Where is this? A fairy-tale place, some sort of tropical Avalon for paranormals?"

"I haven't actually seen the painting, you understand," Jade said, sounding amused. "But Sebastian said it's San Juan."

Puerto Rico. Wesley stared for a longer moment. It felt oddly intimate, as when he'd seen the glimpses of Sebastian's skin, a peek into a man who still felt like a mystery. "He's from this island?"

"I don't think he's been back for a long time," Jade said quietly. "But it was where he spent his childhood. And I believe he's very fond of that painting, so if you could, perhaps—"

"I'm not going to destroy his precious painting of his childhood home." Wesley tugged the cover over the painting and abruptly turned back to Jade. "Pardon my language, Miss Robbins, but what the devil is the story behind Sebastian de Leon? He calls himself a villain, a scoundrel, says I need to forget him so that I can stay safe. I'd say that's a load of rot and I've never met a softer touch, but I heard him kidnap a man and he doesn't deny it—in fact, he tells me I'm *too nice* to get *mixed up in his world*. Too *nice*. Me! Have you ever heard anything so ridiculous?"

Jade made a soft noise that seemed part laugh and part grudging sympathy. "Did Sebastian give you any actual details about his past?"

"Of course not, only that he's terribly dangerous," Wesley said testily. "I imagine the young lads and la-

dies fond of the old yellowback novels and penny dread-
fuls find him unbearably sexy." He, of course, was a
grown man, not a youth sneaking pulp magazines, and
was clearly above that sort of rubbish.

Clearly.

The teacup lifted itself, and Jade plucked it out of the
air with a careless sort of ease that came from habit, like
she served herself tea telekinetically every day. "Well,
it's a bit more complicated than that, but yes. Sebastian
is, in fact, a very dangerous man with a past that few
can stomach."

"I may not have magic, but you'd be surprised what
I can stomach." Some of Wesley's own past was decidedly not for the faint of heart. "Please, go on."

She leaned forward. "Not all magic is good."

"What does that mean?" Wesley said, matching her
more serious tone.

"Sebastian's family has guarded a set of dangerous
enchanted items since the Spanish Inquisition, to keep
the nonmagical safe. But the Earl of Blanshard stole the
lock to these relics from the de Leons."

"A thief and a murderer, apparently," said Wesley.

Jade nodded grimly. "A telepath offered a chance at
finding the magical lock again, but in return Sebastian
was enslaved by blood magic for nearly three years."

Blood magic. Just the phrase sent an unpleasant
shudder down Wesley's spine.

"Sebastian's mind remained his own," Jade went on
quietly, "but his body and magic were under the control
of a paranormal known as the Puppeteer, forced into
service for the telepath."

As it had been the night before, the words were so
far out of reality that Wesley's brain simply refused to
process them.

"He was a prisoner of war?" he finally said, trying to understand.

"That's an apt analogy," she agreed.

"And is Sebastian free now?"

Jade nodded once. "The Puppeteer was killed in May. Sebastian doesn't talk about any of it."

Wesley distantly realized he had clenched his fists. He forced them to relax, sitting on the edge of the settee next to the painting. "I realize I've known about this magic business for only hours, but surely that's not something any person, even a paranormal, simply shrugs off?"

Jade's eyebrows went up. "That's sympathetic of you."

God, everyone was always so unflatteringly surprised that he was capable of sympathy. He'd be insulted, if he wasn't, well, himself. "Shell shock is real," Wesley said stiffly. "I had soldiers who were captured and kept prisoner behind enemy lines. Suffering like that leaves many kinds of scars." He shook his head. "He should be convalescing in the countryside. Breathing fresh air, riding horses, that sort of thing."

"I agree." Jade looked as ill at ease as Wesley felt. "But does he strike you as a man who will take time for himself while a paranormal murderer is loose in London?"

Considering that Sebastian had saved Wesley's life despite Wesley nearly snapping his arm the day before? Probably not.

His gaze darted, unbidden, to the now-empty wall where Sebastian had stood. A paranormal prisoner of war. If someone had just fucking said that's what he was—

Jade did try to tell you. Maybe next time you ought to listen to the telekinetic, bootlegging ex-spy.

Wesley rubbed his face.

Jade crossed her legs. "Will you recount for us exactly what happened last night?"

Us. Because Mr. Zhang was still around somewhere on the astral plane. Because this was the mad world Wesley had somehow fallen into.

He went over everything that had happened, all of Mercier's words carved into his mind verbatim.

Jade looked grim as he finished. "It seems Jack Mercier and Lord Blanshard are working together."

A paranormal earl, yes, that was exactly what Wesley wanted to learn existed. "Mercier's basically a human match, I saw that much for myself. What's Blanshard's magic?"

Jade winced. "Have you ever read *Dracula*?"

"You're not serious," Wesley said, aghast. "Blanshard has fangs—"

"No—well, *probably* not, I suppose there is precedent, but that's a story for another time," said Jade. "But four bodies have been found recently, all inexplicably shriveled, like they've been drained of life. It matches the murder method from a story in Sebastian's family, about a paranormal who ate the auras of the nonmagical."

"He ate," Wesley slowly repeated, "their *auras*."

Jade nodded. "Sebastian's family called that paranormal *the Vampire*. Magical abilities always come back around in the paranormal world, and it seems as if Blanshard also has this vampire magic. And now," she added, "you're apparently his target."

Wesley tightened his jaw. "Mercier said I brought this on myself, whining to the earl about Sebastian."

Jade set down her tea. "It does seem that all of the victims have had at least a superficial connection to magic, without being magic themselves."

"So I basically printed an invitation when I bloody went and announced to the earl that I had just encountered a paranormal." Wesley pursed his lips. "I don't regret it. I'd far rather Blanshard and Mercier come for me than a defenseless maid in Kilburn."

"We'd rather he didn't come for anyone without magic," Jade said wryly, "but I do appreciate your courage."

Vampire paranormals and human matches. Wesley was going to need another cup of tea to deal with this. "Mercier also said his job was to get more magic into my aura. What does that mean?"

"Paranormals have magic where the nonmagical have auras," said Jade. "But sometimes, our magic can linger in an aura. When Sebastian knocked you down, for example, you might have had a trace of magic in your aura afterward. It's generally fleeting, like sand on the skin at the beach, blown away by the next breeze."

"Then I had Mercier's fire magic in my aura for a moment, before Sebastian's magic came along?" Wesley resisted the urge to touch the bandages on his forearms. He would have met a terrible end last night, if Sebastian hadn't shown up.

Jade nodded. "Both their magic will be gone now. The only exception I know of is Arthur and Rory, who've made things a bit more permanent. Don't underestimate Rory," she advised. "He's actually an exceptionally powerful paranormal and you went and kissed his boyfriend. You're lucky all he did was yell at you."

There were not enough cups of tea in the world to deal with this morning.

"If Mercier was purposefully putting magic in your aura, perhaps that's what Blanshard wanted, which is a troubling thought. And now Blanshard might be coming back for you." She steepled her fingers. "This new painting can protect your home. But it would be safest if you left town."

"You want me to run like a coward?" Wesley said sharply. "No. I don't care one whit what anyone's magic might be—if any paranormal so much as thinks about coming here and endangering a single one of my staff—"

"Your staff is who I'm worrying about," she said pointedly. "I don't want you to *run*, I want you to set a false trail that leads Blanshard and Mercier away from London."

Wesley folded his arms. "What do you suggest?"

Jade leaned forward to rest her chin on her fingers. "How do you feel about cats?" she said and, incongruously, she had a tiny hint of a smile.

Sebastian went from Kensington to Liverpool Street Station and then home, to put new food and water out for the strays and then for a desperately needed shower and change of clothes.

He was using what he could see of his reflection in the window to tie his tie when Zhang's astral projection appeared in the middle of the room.

"Sebastian, if you're here, come down and unlock your door and let me in. And no, you're not allowed to run away," he added dryly.

Sebastian huffed but went downstairs. Zhang was waiting at the alley door, arms folded.

"I didn't *run away*," Sebastian protested, which was only a half lie, as he opened the door wide and moved to the side. "I left because I scare Lord Fine. Every time he's around me, he's afraid."

"You certainly give him feelings, but I don't think it's fear," Zhang said cryptically, as he came inside.

Back up in his room, Sebastian gestured to the stove and his tins of instant coffee, sugar, and powdered milk. "Coffee?"

"Tea?" Zhang said hopefully.

Sebastian wrinkled his nose.

Zhang sighed. "Coffee, then. Plain."

They sat together with their mugs at the tiny table a few moments later. "Zhang is your family name, yes? Why is Jade the only one who calls you by your given name?"

Zhang hesitated, then said, "Because growing up, people changed *Jianwei* to *John*."

"Ah," Sebastian said, in understanding. "My brother Mateo is always *Matthew* in America, whether he wants to be or not."

"It was easier to have people say Zhang. But Jade asked me how to say Jianwei, and then she asked me to help her say it right." Zhang picked up his cup, mouth curved in the smitten sort of smile that he seemed to always have around Jade. "She actually still can't pronounce it perfectly," he admitted, "but I like the way she says it."

Lord Fine's sardonic English accent rolled through Sebastian's mind. *So, Sebastian, are you a faery or a witch?*

Sebastian could, possibly, relate.

"Jade is still with Lord Fine," Zhang went on, as they split the last of a loaf of white bread. "He's agreed to hang the painting of San Juan in his home. For what it's worth, I don't think he'll destroy this one. He actually seems a little embarrassed about the turpentine."

"It's not his fault. He didn't know." Sebastian dipped his bread in his coffee. "He's new to all of this."

"Sometimes it's so obvious you come from a family that protects the nonmagical." Zhang sat back in the chair. "Is there anything you can add about last night that Lord Fine wouldn't know?"

"Mercier was using magic to keep the alley silenced—alchemy, perhaps, or a potion. It formed a cage around Lord Fine where no sound escaped." Sebastian had been lucky to find Lord Fine. "It was old magic, though. Strong. I was using my magic to sweep for any traces of magic that might lead me to Lord Fine, and it was strong enough I found it."

Sebastian frowned. "Mercier's magic is also stronger than it was when we were with Baron Zeppler. He has something new boosting his power now—not a relic, not that powerful, but I almost couldn't stop him."

"Always nice to hear the jerk who controls fire can make more of it," Zhang said dryly.

If Sebastian hadn't managed to put out Mercier's flames—but no. He always had to find enough magic to counter others' magic. The alternative was unthinkable. "What if they come back after Lord Fine?"

"Jade and I have an idea," Zhang said cagily. "But I don't know what either of you will think."

Sebastian raised his eyebrows. "Should I be nervous?" he asked, as he bit into coffee-soaked bread.

Zhang smiled weakly. "Depends on whether you've ever secretly dreamed of bunkering in the English countryside with a viscount."

Sebastian blinked.

"You hid from us in Manhattan," Zhang said. "Can you hide Lord Fine now?"

"Well, yes," said Sebastian. "But he won't agree. He doesn't like me."

"He'll agree, and he doesn't like anyone."

"No, he *really* doesn't like me," said Sebastian.

"Right," Zhang said skeptically. "That's why instead of leaving you in the alley last night, he carried you to his home."

"To his home where I woke up handcuffed to his bed."

"Handcuffed…to his bed?"

"Yes."

Zhang bit his lip, almost like he was trying not to smile. "I'm sorry," he said sincerely. "But that does nothing to convince me he doesn't like you."

Sebastian rolled his eyes.

"Last night Lord Fine saw with his own eyes that you can protect him," said Zhang. "He'll go with you. He can't stay in London—his staff would be in danger and his cook has a young daughter."

Sebastian winced. "You're right, he can't stay here. But—"

"Are you saying you won't protect this innocent non-magical viscount?"

Sebastian gave him a dirty look over his coffee. "Of course I'm not saying that."

"So do you need me to help you pack?"

Sebastian sighed. "Where are we going?"

"Yorkshire."

"Yorkshire? But Lord Blanshard has a manor there."

"I saw the body in York," Zhang said, more quietly, "but neither Jade nor I can pick up traces of magic like you can. We hoped maybe you could learn something at the murder scene, maybe figure out how they're doing this without witnesses."

"But wouldn't York put Lord Fine in more danger?"

"Mercier is here, in London, and it sounds like Blanshard is too," said Zhang. "The San Juan painting will be hung at Fine's townhouse here, to keep the staff safe. Lord Fine is currently setting a false trail to another of his homes in the Lake District. He has his own Yorkshire manor, which he said is empty. Seems he hasn't been back to it since Blanshard's party in 1922."

"But what about Molly's boarding house?"

"The murder scene is still too busy for you to get close without knocking all of the nonmagical to the ground. Jade and I will keep investigating, and then meet you in York in a day or two."

Sebastian folded his arms. "Who's going to feed the strays if I go?"

"Jade even thought of that," Zhang said, sounding amused. "The cook's daughter is eleven and adores animals. Lord Fine has apparently never allowed pets in the basement before, but under the circumstances, Jade convinced him to make an exception. Elsie will care for any cats we bring her. She's over the moon."

"That's very sweet," Sebastian grudgingly admitted. It was a nice thought, his strays finding a home with a kind little girl and making her happy.

Zhang leaned forward. "I know you knew the maid who was killed, but you can't help her now. You can help Lord Fine. Will you say yes?"

Sebastian chewed on his lip. Of course he was going to go with Lord Fine. Mercier had tried to kill him already, and they might come back after him.

Sebastian could hide Lord Fine; all he had to do was keep close enough that the whirlpool effect of his tattoo could hide them both.

Close enough that if a former British Army captain

still slept battlefield-light, he might catch Sebastian if he woke trapped in a blood terror.

Sebastian quickly picked up his coffee. Zhang had said they were staying in a country manor; surely there would be a servant's room close to Lord Fine where Sebastian could sleep and not risk waking him. Why would Lord Fine even agree to this plan? He didn't like or trust Sebastian. The blood terrors weren't going to be an issue.

The blood terrors should never have been an issue in the first place, his mind needled him. *With your magic, you should have been over them long ago. Now Mercier is back, and a nonmagical viscount is in danger, and all you are is a ghost of yourself, broken and fractured—*

"Of course I'll go with him," Sebastian said, bringing the coffee to his lips to hide an unsteady hand. "Just tell me where and when to meet him."

Chapter Eight

A few hours later, Sebastian was standing on a train platform in King's Cross, hands in his coat pockets, his rucksack on the floor next to him.

Zhang had seemed confident Lord Fine would go along with the plan, but Sebastian frankly didn't expect him to.

You're certainly giving him feelings, Zhang had said, *but I don't think it's fear.*

Of course it was fear. What else would Lord Fine be feeling around him?

A new train pulled up, the blast of air whipping around the underground station. Then the train doors opened, and there was Lord Fine. That morning, at the side of the bed, Lord Fine's shirtsleeves had been rolled up and he'd worn no jacket or robe. Now he was impeccably dressed in a charcoal three-piece suit and a blue tie around his stiff, high collar, topped with a tall hat. In one hand, he held a walking stick, a black coat draped over his arm, and in his other hand he was carrying his own suitcase. He walked with a very straight spine like he was marching onto a battlefield.

Sebastian's heart did a funny twist in his chest. Lord Fine had known about magic for less than a day and nearly been killed by it. Now he was walking into the company of a paranormal he barely knew. Whatever else he was, the man had courage.

"Your lordship," he called softly, purposefully not using Lord Fine's name.

Lord Fine turned immediately in his direction. *I'll never forget the sound of your voice,* he had said, and apparently meant it.

Sebastian flushed slightly, but held up a hand in greeting. "I was not sure you would come."

Lord Fine's mouth thinned. He strode purposefully up to Sebastian, who had to steel himself not to draw back.

Lord Fine set his suitcase down with an abrupt gesture. "Before we go anywhere, you and I are going to get something straight."

Sebastian swallowed, putting his hands up in a gesture of surrender. "I won't use my magic on you again, I promise."

"What?" Lord Fine looked like Sebastian had just promised to lick the station floor. "Don't be ridiculous. I most certainly expect you will use your magic on me again if it's necessary, as I would far rather have those watery limbs you create than be on fucking fire."

Oh, Sebastian's mouth formed. He lowered his hands, slow and confused. "Then what did you want to get straight between us?"

"That I misspoke this morning," said Lord Fine crisply. "You've apparently been protecting my home with art and clandestine visits since May. And now your magic saved my life last night—which is not a sentence I ever expected to hear myself say—and I don't know if this is a fae bargain or paranormal *noblesse oblige,* but regardless, I should have told you I was grateful, not—well, the things I said."

That was also not at all what Sebastian had ever expected to hear Lord Fine say. "You didn't say anything I haven't thought myself," he said, surprise making him a little too honest.

"Don't be absurd," Lord Fine said crossly. "Only a mendacious wretch would have called you a bully." And before Sebastian could object to Lord Fine insulting himself, he added, "You really are just a dangerous marshmallow."

"A dangerous *what*?" This close, their height difference was enough that Sebastian had to tilt his head back to see Lord Fine from under his cap. "I'm not sure if I should say thank you."

Lord Fine lifted his nose. "Fortunately one of us has manners and already said thank you."

"You didn't actually say thank you," Sebastian pointed out. "You said you *should* have said thank you."

"I'm sure that was close enough."

Sebastian rolled his eyes, but incongruously, he felt a little better. Lord Fine wasn't acting scared of him, at least. Perhaps this wouldn't be complete torture for the other man. "Would you like me to carry your suitcase?"

"No," Lord Fine said snappishly, like he'd been insulted. "You already have your own bag to carry."

"Well, yes, but—"

"But what? I'm a lord, not a princess."

"There once was a Spanish princess with paranormal super strength," Sebastian said. "She probably carried her own bags. I bet Jade could carry her own bags with her mind."

"Don't be cute," Lord Fine said, then quickly added, "*Get* cute. Don't *get* cute with me, no one is saying anything about you *being* cute. Look." He picked up his suitcase. "I don't need to be handled with kid gloves, is what I'm saying. It's bad enough that I'm suddenly in a world where everyone has magic and I don't; at least treat me like a capable man."

He looked a little vulnerable as he said it, and that did something funny to Sebastian's heart. "I think you are very capable. You had me in handcuffs only hours ago, yes?"

Lord Fine straightened up. "I did do that, didn't I? I could have shot you."

"You don't have to sound so happy about that," Sebastian said dryly.

Something almost like a grudging smile played on Lord Fine's mouth. "It's not as if it did me any good. You didn't care until I aimed that gun at Powderpuff."

"I suppose this is the part where you tell me you played me for a fool," Sebastian said, "and you wouldn't really have shot your neighbor's dog?"

"And why would I tell you what you want to hear?" Sebastian folded his arms.

"What I would or wouldn't have done is irrelevant," Lord Fine said. "You're the one who let a Maltese expose your secrets. Christ, you never would have survived the war."

Sebastian *had* survived the war, but he said, "You have to tell me you wouldn't hurt a dog," instead of correcting Lord Fine, because this was what mattered. "Lord Fine, you took in my stray cats."

"I did no such thing. My cook's daughter took them in. She's a ridiculously soft and sentimental creature; you two would get along swimmingly."

"You agreed she could have them."

"Well—look, she's only eleven, and she's been *sad* recently because I—ugh, all right, if you're going to make those ridiculous eyes at me until you hear it

spelled out," Lord Fine said testily. "Yes, I was bluffing about Powderpuff. That is all the concession you're
going to get and I make no promises about what else I
might or might not shoot, but your cats will live a happy,
spoilt life in Mrs. Harrick's kitchen. Miss Elsie squealed
so loud when she saw them, she almost brought the
house down."

"Really?" Sebastian brightened. "Did she name them
yet?"

Lord Fine pinched the bridge of his nose. "It doesn't
matter."

"Why wouldn't it matter?"

"Because they're cats! I don't give a fucking toss
for people's names; what do I care what the felines are
called? You seem to think I'm going to stand here and
tell you things just because you want to hear them, but
I assure you that I will not be so easily persuaded."

Sebastian stuck his hands in his pockets again. "Are
they cute names?"

"For fuck's sake." Lord Fine narrowed his eyes. "She
named them Crumpet and Flan," he said tartly, then
pointed at Sebastian. "Not another word out of you. I
don't want to hear if you think that's obnoxiously precious, and I expect you to stop pouting now. Can we
carry on? I thought we were on the two o'clock."

They boarded the train fifteen minutes later, where
Sebastian had bought tickets for adjoining compart-
ments in first class. As he set his rucksack on the plush
seat in his own compartment, Lord Fine appeared in
his sliding doors.

"We're not sharing?" he said, one hand on the door,
watching Sebastian with an unreadable expression. "I
understood we have to keep a certain proximity for that
tattoo of yours to work for me too."

"This is close enough," Sebastian promised. "You can lock your own door, yes? I assumed you would want the privacy."

Lord Fine's eyes narrowed. "And why did you assume that?"

Because you didn't sleep at all last night because of me, and I thought you would want to sleep without fear. "Because—"

"I feel certain you wouldn't dare say it's because you still assume I'm afraid of you," Lord Fine went on, light and dangerous. "Not when I've just told you to treat me like a competent man."

"Oh." Sebastian floundered. "Um. Because you are... tall?"

"Tall."

Sebastian smiled weakly. "You need space to stretch out?"

Lord Fine rolled his eyes, and pulled the wooden doors shut with a very final jerk.

In his own compartment, Wesley shut the curtains on his internal sliding door, blocking out the train's hall, then snuck his cigarettes out of his coat and smoked two in a row, letting the smoke float out the train window as they pulled out of the station.

So. Magic was real.

Wesley probably should have been alarmed, or angry, to discover that all this time there had been a clandestine supernatural world under his nose, and he'd never known. But it was—interesting. The most interesting thing that had happened to him in an age. The other people he knew were content to attend parties, or wear pretty clothes, but here Jade, Mr. Zhang, and Sebastian were, apparently hunting down paranormal murderers.

And now Wesley was part of it.

It was absolute lunacy, of course. But as the train picked up speed, Wesley felt the vibration in his heart, like the leaden stone in his breast was capable of—not feelings, of course, but purpose, at least. He'd choose the risks that came with trying to stop paranormals like Mercier and the Earl of Blanshard over sitting useless and ever more bitter at home. Nothing like a magical attempt on one's life to get the blood stirring.

He glanced at the wooden wall that separated him from Sebastian in the next compartment.

There was admittedly more than one thing stirring his blood these days. And as it turned out, the handsome bastard next door wasn't a criminal at all, but a man who'd gone through hell yet still lit up when he talked about kittens.

Still, handsome or not, criminal or hero, Sebastian had bloody well better treat him like a full partner and not a useless sot, or he'd quickly discover just how competent Wesley actually was.

In fact, Wesley had quite a number of skills he'd like to show off to Sebastian. After all, at the manor they'd have privacy and a very large bed—

And that was Wesley's mind once again barreling down its singular track with more speed than the train.

He rang the attendant and instructed he was not to be disturbed. He settled into the upholstered couch, rested his head against the window, and promptly fell into a light sleep, the kind he'd taught himself during the war—restful, but awake enough to keep dreams away and stay aware of the noise around him.

He woke fully as the conductor called out their stop in York, and a soft knock came on his door.

Wesley reached forward and pulled aside the curtain,

and there was Sebastian, framed by the glass door. The man had a good tailor, whether he shopped on Saville Row or in Spain or bloody Avalon, because Wesley was still not convinced he wasn't a witch. His long wool coat was heavier than Wesley wore for fall, but its close fit accented the lean lines of Sebastian's body, and the soft brown, paired with the plaid flat cap and warm scarf, complemented the autumn shades of his eyes and hair.

He was so obnoxiously attractive, and just as obnoxiously certain Wesley was afraid of him. The man never needed to know how Wesley's body now *relaxed* at the sight, as if some part of him—almost certainly the atavistic part that didn't want to be on *fucking fire*—now permanently associated Sebastian with safety.

They got a taxi at the station for the hour's drive to the village. "Up from London, eh?" the cab driver said, as they drove down narrow, bumpy country roads. "We're getting murders here like we're a big city like yours. They still haven't caught the blighter that did that poor fellow in the Shambles in."

Wesley opened his mouth, an irritable *I'm not paying you to talk* on the tip of his tongue. But his gaze stole sideways. Sebastian looked sad, and tired, and like he felt personally responsible for some nonmagical bloke pushing up the daisies in York. Perhaps that's what happened when one had a family legacy: the weight stayed on one's shoulders regardless.

Maybe, against all odds, he and Sebastian had something in common.

Wesley bit his reply back, settling against the seat instead and letting Sebastian engage in pointless chatter with the driver about the weather (rainy), the day (gray), and the city of York (old). He normally only entertained complete silence on a car ride—or, if he were being truly honest, the sound of his own voice—but listening to Sebastian's soft accent and warm words was, against all odds, not entirely off-putting.

Wesley had them dropped off on the village's outskirts, because for all Sebastian could hide them from magic, he couldn't hide them from gossip, and no one needed to know the master of the manor was visiting. It was only about a mile to the gates, and Sebastian had agreed they should walk.

Long grass brushed Wesley's shins as they trekked in the road's green shoulder next to the short stone wall that bordered the farm next to the manor. The same green grass covered the small rolling hills of the farm, and Wesley couldn't stop himself from automatically looking them over.

The lambs are in the barn, you sentimental twit, he chastised himself. *If there even are any lambs to be seen in the fall.*

He wanted another cigarette, but he gritted his teeth and left the pack in his pocket. There would be imported cigars in the manor; he could pretend he wanted one, not needed it.

"Zhang said we would be staying at a manor of yours?" Sebastian said, making it a question.

"Shepherd Hall," Wesley said, answering automatically as his feelings continued to jumble. "The first Viscount Fine had it built on the ruins of an abbey. Fair warning, I don't visit often—" *ever* "—so the electricity's been turned off."

"Does it have a fireplace?"

The painting of San Juan came to Wesley's mind, the bright sun over the cream-colored sand, palm trees, and turquoise ocean. "Several fireplaces," he said dryly. "We'll be perfectly warm, stop worrying."

"I wasn't *worrying*."

A clear lie from the thin-blooded tropical flower. And obviously not endearing at all. "I'm not sure what the status of supplies is, but I have a car in the manor's garage that we can sneak out without alerting the whole village that someone is staying at the manor."

"A car?" Sebastian repeated, and Wesley was pretty sure he heard a note of genuine enthusiasm. "Will your groundskeeper not notice us, though?"

Wesley's throat tightened. "Mr. Fitzgerald passed away last spring. The land around us is tended by farmers, but there's no one at Shepherd Hall right now."

A butler, Wesley could manage without, but an estate like Shepherd Hall needed a groundskeeper. He braced himself for the inevitable: *it's been six months, why the hell haven't you replaced him?*

"Oh," Sebastian said, more gently. "I am sorry for your loss."

"I—why would you say that?" Wesley said in surprise, the words tumbling out. "He was only a groundskeeper."

"But aren't we here because you care for your staff?"

"Well—I mean, I certainly don't want any of them immolated—"

"And this is a lovely countryside," Sebastian said. "Gardeners are treasures, yes? They care for the plants and flowers, and make things beautiful for the rest of us to enjoy."

Wesley's gaze stole to the hills of the farm, barely visible in the dim light, and he didn't respond.

They pulled out torches when it got too dark to see— flashlights, Sebastian insisted on calling them, because he had a Spanish father but was still hopelessly American—and found their way over the river bridge and up to the manor's stone and iron gates. Wesley unlocked the padlock, locking up behind them.

A light rain had begun, dotting Wesley's neck as they trudged up the driveway, gravel crunching under their feet. It was in many ways a relief to arrive at night, when he wouldn't have to see the state of the manor's neglected gardens.

The driveway was another quarter-mile, but eventually they passed the copse of short but thick trees that framed the end of the driveway, and stepped onto the drive that circled the hedges and giant fountain in front of the manor. Wesley could almost see the ghosts of the cars that had brought the guests to his mother's funeral, could almost hear their voices drifting over the grounds.

He gritted his teeth. There was a reason he didn't come to Yorkshire.

Sebastian shone his torch beam onto the fountain with its carved stone rams, then over to the stately archway over the manor's heavy wooden front door, now partially overgrown with ivy that swayed in the night's breeze. Beyond the beam would be another stone archway leading around the side of the manor, where the servants' wing jutted out, and then to the gardens beyond.

"Qué casa linda," Sebastian murmured, then glanced at Wesley. "What a pretty home."

"Yes, well," Wesley said brusquely, "more importantly, it's got lots of whiskey."

He had just unlocked the door when Sebastian moved in front of him. "Let me go in first."

"Why the hell—"

"We hope Blanshard will follow your false trail to the Lake District, but he knows about this manor, doesn't he?" Sebastian's voice wasn't much more than a whisper. "If there is magic here, let me stop it before it hits you."

"I *am* armed, you know," Wesley said testily.

"You brought your revolver?"

"I was nearly murdered by a human match last night, of course I brought it. However much magic is in something, I suspect I can still stop it with a bullet."

"But I can take it down with a thought and no death," said Sebastian. "Let me go first. After all, I am here as your bodyguard, yes?"

Wesley's *bodyguard*. This looker. The very idea sounded exactly like the type of yellowback novel or penny dreadful Wesley absolutely and most certainly had never read.

"Fine," he said, his own whisper a little too high. "But do remember I can shoot things, won't you?"

He stepped behind Sebastian into the foyer, and then into the great hall. The room was eerily quiet in the way abandoned houses often were, as if the dust muffled everything in the same way as newly fallen snow. No moonlight came through the heavy velvet drapes, shut tight to the world, and the air was musty and uncomfortably still from months without movement.

"Are we good?" he murmured to Sebastian.

"I think so." Sebastian was shining his torch around the room, from the covered paintings to the covered furniture. "But we should stay careful."

They left their hats on the hat stand in the foyer. Their footsteps were too loud on the marble as they crossed to the wide, curved staircase tucked into the corner.

"Normally I'd offer you a guest suite of your own," Wesley said, as they climbed to the first floor. "But they're in another wing."

"Oh." Sebastian chewed on his lip. "That would be too far for the magic, yes. But I don't need a suite of my own, I can sleep anywhere."

Wesley could too, although it wasn't a fact he advertised. There were standards one must demand, after all, and he didn't want Sebastian judging him. "We're staying in the master's chambers," he said, as they reached the chambers' door.

Wesley had only stayed in here twice; first when he'd unexpectedly become lord of this manor, and then when he'd come up for Blanshard's godforsaken party. Still, the sitting area was exactly as he remembered: a man-height fireplace flanked by a burgundy settee and two high-backed chairs set around a black walnut table, and a selection of trophies of his father's hunts: a buck's head on the wall, a stuffed fox, a tiger rug on the floor.

He heard Sebastian swallow audibly.

"Oh, come on," said Wesley, leading the way in. "Where did you think I learned how to shoot, by *magic*?"

"I was trying not to think about it at all," Sebastian muttered behind his back.

"Christ, you're as bad as my mother was. She used to make my father keep everything in the trophy room. First thing he did when she died was redecorate both of their chambers."

Wesley set his torch on an end table, facing upright so the beam could illuminate more of the space. Sebastian was shining his torch around the room, from the giant bed with its gold canopy to the balcony's glass doors to the gilded ceiling.

"So we are...staying together...in just this one room?"

There was a new note in his voice, the first sign

of actual nerves Wesley had ever heard. "You're the one who said we have to stay close so your magic will work," Wesley snapped. "These quarters are private intentionally; there are no other rooms close to this suite, and most of the bedrooms in this home no longer have furniture anyway."

"I didn't—"

"Are you seriously that weak for animals?" Wesley went on, because he had no intention of explaining why he'd started allowing the furniture to be sold. "I mean, all right, we can debate the ethics of safaris, I have read the arguments, but these animals are all quite dead already."

"It's not *that*," Sebastian said. "I just—it's nothing." He set his rucksack on the floor next to the settee.

It obviously wasn't nothing, and now the man was back to treating Wesley like he was made of glass. "Dare I ask why you seem to assume I'm taking the bed?"

"It's your home," said Sebastian.

"Which makes you my guest," Wesley snapped. "If you're giving me the bed because you think I can't handle a settee—"

"You outranked me."

Wesley blinked.

Sebastian gestured at himself. "Corporal," he said. "Medical department."

"You were in the army?" Wesley had learned on the front that the Americans had given Puerto Ricans citizenship and then promptly drafted them. He hadn't put it together that Sebastian had been one of those soldiers. "Why didn't you say something earlier, at the train station? Why did you let me think you hadn't gone?"

"Because we were talking about Powderpuff," Sebastian guilelessly. "I didn't think my history mattered."

Didn't *matter*? He'd let Wesley think he was even softer than he actually was. Did it not even bother him, to be seen as weak?

"I wouldn't have thought a paranormal would enlist," Wesley said.

"Maybe I was an idealist." Sebastian leaned against the high back of the settee. "I was in school in America when we joined the war. My father wasn't happy, told me to come to him in Spain. But I thought I could use my magic in secret, maybe ease the pain for hurt soldiers." He made a face. "I'm not sure how much help I was."

What was he, an actual angel? Wesley would have scoffed, except he'd been in the medical tents and seen the suffering firsthand. Sebastian's magic would have been a godsend.

"I imagine you were quite a bit of help. You pack a far harder punch than a shot of whiskey, which is all the anesthetic most soldiers got." Wesley tilted his head. "So you're, what, thirty?"

"Twenty-seven."

That meant he'd enlisted at eighteen, nineteen at the most. "I assumed you were older," Wesley said, to cover his discombobulation. How was Sebastian not a relentlessly jaded cynic? Wesley had been twenty-one when he went to war, was thirty-two now, and despised nearly everyone and everything.

"Well, now you know, and it is yet another reason to give you the bed, yes, Captain Fine?" The tenseness was back in Sebastian's shoulders. "And I will sleep here. In the same room."

"I was Captain Collins then. And why are you so

wrong-footed over this? Do we need to sleep in a different room? There's a nursery down the hall."

It came out sharp, Wesley's always-harsh voice turning what he'd meant as a tease into mockery. But so what? Wesley had been afraid of the snarling tiger rug as a child, and his father's mocking had pushed him past that. He was doing Sebastian a favor, really, mocking what deserved to be mocked, toughening the soft touch up.

Sebastian had looked away. "It's not the animals," he said, flatly enough that Wesley believed him. "I'm just not a good sleeper."

Now Wesley did scoff. "Is that supposed to be less embarrassing than crying over the animals?"

Sebastian didn't snap back. He didn't even seem rattled by Wesley's jabs, simply turning away and heading over to the fireplace.

Not that he was *trying* to rattle Sebastian. Wesley was a grown man, after all, not a schoolboy pulling the pigtails on a pretty girl. Or a pretty, *magical* boy, in this case.

One who had saved Wesley's life.

Wesley's gaze went from his handsome guest to the fireplace. The healing blisters on his forearms prickled with echoes of remembered pain, a reminder that the previous night would have gone very differently if Sebastian hadn't appeared in that alley.

He's here for you, the little voice in Wesley's head pointed out. *Not for reward, not for status, but out of the goodness of that bleeding heart you just mocked. He came for no reason except to keep you safe, because he has magic and you don't. He doesn't care if you think he's weak because he has nothing to prove: you need his protection but he doesn't need anything from you.*

Good thing too, because you won't give him your gratitude. Or even your manners.

He watched as Sebastian checked the wood box next to the fireplace. They'd both gone to war, but Wesley had spent the years since avoiding parties while Sebastian was enslaved by blood magic because he was trying to protect the nonmagical.

So perhaps he wasn't rattled by mocking because on the long list of *shitty things Sebastian de Leon had had to deal with*, Wesley barely registered.

He was a prisoner of war? Wesley had asked Jade. *That's an apt analogy.*

Wesley's soldiers who'd been captive behind enemy lines hadn't been *good sleepers* when they'd finally been rescued, either.

Wesley's chest burned, hot and uncomfortable. He was mocking a traumatized medic who'd survived years of supernatural torture, who might be suffering a kind of paranormal shell shock, and why? Did he actually believe he should toughen Sebastian up, like his own father had toughened him up? As if it wasn't the height of hubris to think he could toughen a man who had lived through something Wesley's own mind still couldn't comprehend.

Sebastian was now kneeling on the edge of the marble, examining the flume, and abruptly Wesley found himself walking toward him. "Sebastian."

Sebastian glanced up, his expression guarded. Of course he was fucking guarded around Wesley; everything the man had been through recently had hurt him, up to and including Wesley himself.

"I—" Wesley hesitated. He normally didn't entertain the notion of shame; if people disliked his sharp edges, they were free to fuck off and find wealth and status somewhere else. Except Sebastian wasn't going to fuck off, because he wasn't here for those things; he was here to protect Wesley's sorry life and the very least Wesley could do was try to be less miserable than blood magic. Surely even Wesley could manage that?

Sack up, Wes. The man survived torture—he can survive you, and you *can survive an apology.*

Wesley straightened and steeled himself. "I shouldn't have mocked you, whether this evening or this morning. Please accept my apology."

Surprise crossed Sebastian's face, and didn't *that* say worlds about Sebastian's life, that when Wesley had handcuffed him to a bed, he'd only looked resigned, but when Wesley attempted to treat him with a speck of decency the man seemed genuinely lost. "You don't—"

"I do," Wesley said. "I do, in fact, need to say sorry, because that's what one should do when one has been an utter arse." He cleared his throat and hurriedly went on, before Sebastian could speak. "If there's no firewood in the box, there's likely some in one of the other suites, or the kitchens."

"There is wood," said Sebastian. "No matches, though."

"I have matches," Wesley said, because suddenly it seemed ridiculous that he could have ever thought Sebastian would mock him for needing to keep a pack of cheap cigarettes always on hand. That was the kind of thing Wesley himself would have done, not the sweet thing who was gingerly avoiding kneeling on the tiger rug. "I smoke. I mean, I've decided I don't want to anymore, but stopping is devilishly more difficult than starting, isn't it? Do you? Smoke, I mean?" *Christ, Wesley, speak in full sentences, can't you?*

"Sometimes I did in the army." Sebastian sat back

on his heels, looking up at Wesley. "It wasn't an option the past few years."

Because he was trapped under *blood magic*. Right. Wesley reached into his coat pocket for the matchbook. "Here, if you insist on a fire. You do realize it's not particularly cold out?"

"You're right. It's cold *and* wet."

Sebastian reached for the matches, and their hands brushed. Sebastian's fingers were like ice, and Wesley had an unfamiliar urge to wrap them tightly in his own. "You're ruining your reputation as a dangerous rogue, you know," he said, forcing himself to drop his hand. "Apparently you're a delicate orchid who ought to be sheltered in the greenhouse with the other tropical flowers."

And *finally*, his tone came out right, not mocking but the tease he wanted, and he got to watch Sebastian sputter. "I'm not *delicate*."

"Oh yes, that magic business," Wesley said wryly. "I don't suppose you'd consider that for helping me quit the smokes?"

"My *magic*? You are joking, yes?"

"Why would I be?" Wesley said. "I reach for my cigarettes, you knock me on my arse. Dashed good bargain, I'd think."

Sebastian rolled his eyes, but a grudging smile was on his lips. "I am not going to knock you on your *arse*."

Christ, he was fucking adorable. "Why not? I bet you want to, everyone who speaks to me does. I'm the worst person most people have met."

Sebastian smiled, soft and kind of sad. "You are not the worst person *I've* met," he said, sweet and patient. "And the first time you met me, I was literally kidnapping someone. If you want to be the villain of the two of us, I'm sorry, but you'll have to try harder."

Wesley opened his mouth, then closed it. No, Sebastian wasn't going to judge him for addiction, or even for his sharp tongue. Sebastian's judgment was apparently reserved for himself.

"You should take the bed," Wesley said, because abruptly things like army ranks and being lord of the manor didn't matter. What mattered was that he make Sebastian more comfortable.

But Sebastian shook his head. "As we said, I am your bodyguard, yes? I will sleep on the couch and keep you safe from any magic."

Ugh, wasn't that typical. For once in his life, Wesley wanted to be the chivalrous one and Sebastian had to go and effortlessly outshine him.

"It's a big bed. We could share," he said lightly. He never shared his bed to sleep, not even with his lovers. He had a very nice guest room for exactly that reason. Wesley didn't keep men in his space longer than it took to fuck them—not because he disliked touch, but because he enjoyed it *too* much, and it would be too easy to crave as uncontrollably as a cigarette. He had to keep himself in check.

But they'd only be sleeping, and he already craved Sebastian to distraction anyway. It would be exquisite torture to be so close, but he wasn't going to make the man suffer just to spare himself an aching cock.

Except Sebastian's sad smile had returned. "You do not want to sleep next to me," he said, like it had a deeper meaning. "You take the bed. It's my fault you didn't sleep last night."

I'm more likely to blame you if I don't sleep tonight.

Wesley cleared his throat. "There might be some

kerosene lamps in a closet. If you're tending to the fire, I'll take a look."

And the next time he caught Sebastian staring at the settee, quiet and pale, Wesley didn't comment. He wasn't good for much, but he could try not to make things worse, and he could sleep light in case an ex-medic who *wasn't a good sleeper* needed anything during the night.

Wake up, de Leon.

"Sebastian."

Sebastian heard his name from a distance, the roll of the English accent tinted with something almost like concern.

But he couldn't move. The voice was a dream, an illusion of freedom. There was no freedom, only the Puppeteer's control.

This isn't your tropical paradise.

"Sebastian, wake up."

I need your magic.

A hand firmly gripped Sebastian's shoulder. "Sebastian, wake the bloody hell up."

Sebastian's eyes flew open on their own. For a moment, he didn't understand—a face was inches from his own, barely visible in the dark, an incessant drumming was coming from somewhere behind him—

"Come on, keep those pretty eyes open, that's right."

The hand on Sebastian's shoulder was warm and strong, and something in him responded like a falling man clutching a rope. His surroundings came to him in a rush: the butter-soft velvet of the settee beneath his cheek; the fireplace, burned down to only glowing embers now; the drumbeat of rain lashing the windows and glass balcony door.

And Lord Fine gripping his shoulder, waking him up.

And abruptly, the terror let Sebastian go. His limbs reflexively loosened and he sagged into the settee, breathing hard. "Gracias, thank you," he said, the words tumbling out, low and hoarse. "What a welcome sight you are."

Lord Fine made a surprised sound. "Well, that has to be the first time anyone has said that to me," he said, sounding a little hoarse himself. "I'd ask if you're all right, but what a stupid and pointless question that would be."

Sebastian tried to laugh, but it was broken even to his own ears. He rubbed his face with his hand. "I'm sorry I woke you."

"Oh, shut up," Lord Fine said, without bite. He was still holding Sebastian's shoulder, his hand a single point of warmth. If anything, his grip had grown tighter. "You're shaking."

Sebastian was, both from the terror and the cold. He'd stacked the wood high in the fireplace but it hadn't lasted the night, and now the rain's staccato filled the room and the air had the icy edge of the hours past midnight.

"You ridiculous tropical flower." Lord Fine let go of his shoulder then, reaching for something on the floor. "I assume you didn't intend to lose this."

His blanket, the thick wool one Lord Fine had given him off the bed. Sebastian took it, sitting up and pulling it around his shoulders like armor as Lord Fine shifted from the settee to crouch by the fireplace.

"What are you doing?" Sebastian asked, squinting at the dark shape in front of the glowing ashes.

"The better question is why you keep assuming I'm completely useless."

There was the sound of wood stacked on wood, then a small bright flame lit the area as Lord Fine struck a match. He tossed the match into the fireplace, and a fire jumped up with a burst of light and an audible roar.

Sebastian's eyes widened.

"It's lamp oil, relax." Lord Fine moved back to sit on one of the velvet chairs. "You're still shivering. I may not have magic, but I can fix that."

The warmth was already reaching Sebastian's frozen limbs, almost dizzyingly welcome. "It is wonderful," he said, with feeling.

"Good." Lord Fine sat back in the chair. "So what was that I just saw you going through?"

Sebastian blew out a breath. "Nothing. Thank you for waking me, but you should go back to bed."

"And *you* should stop trying to lie to my face," said Lord Fine. "I just found you trapped in some kind of sleeping disturbance. It was as if you were paralyzed. I've never seen a nightmare like it. Yet you seem so completely unsurprised that I'm certain you go through whatever that was on a regular basis."

The bright orange-and-red flames would die down soon, but for now were still dancing high. They sat without speaking for a moment, watching the fire, the rain loud against the glass.

Lord Fine spoke first. "Jade told me some of your past. The blood magic."

Sebastian stiffened.

"I realize I don't fully know the standards of your paranormal world," Lord Fine added, "but that sounded very much like the stuff of nightmares."

Sebastian chewed on his lip. "Not nightmares, exactly," he tentatively admitted. "Well, yes, nightmares too, but these are technically blood terrors."

"Blood. *Terrors*."

"My blood was under another's control. Sometimes, in sleep, the chains come back."

Lord Fine's voice was unsteady as he said, "So you, what? Can't move until your blood remembers you're free?"

I don't know that my blood has ever remembered how to be free. Sebastian didn't say it out loud, just nodded as he watched the fire flicker.

"Well that sounds absolutely wretched," Lord Fine said flatly. "What brings them on?"

Sebastian tried to shrug, the movement jerky. "They come at random, perhaps more often when I get cold during sleep. It's not as bad as it sounds," he lied. "I can usually break the magic with something familiar."

"So does someone stay with you to snap you out of it?"

Sebastian hadn't shared a room with anyone since before the Puppeteer's death. He shook his head.

Lord Fine frowned. "So what have you been doing?"

"Oh, you know," Sebastian said awkwardly. "Using… familiar things."

Lord Fine's eyes narrowed. "Familiar like a painting of your childhood home?"

Sebastian winced. "Well—"

"The painting now hanging in Kensington to keep some nonmagical fellow's home safe?" Lord Fine snapped at him. "Did you give away the very thing you use to break your blood terrors?"

Sebastian pulled the blanket up over the back of his head like a cloak. He wasn't *hiding*, he was just staying warm. "You needed that painting more than I did."

"I wouldn't have if I hadn't destroyed your first one!"

"But you didn't know," Sebastian protested. "You had good reasons not to trust me."

Lord Fine leaned forward, enough so there was now only a couple feet between them. "Stop making excuses for me."

"But—"

"I said *stop it*," Lord Fine said, with the imperiousness of the aristocracy behind him. "I'm not made of glass. If you'll recall, I was in the war too, but *I* wasn't a medic."

Sebastian glanced at him from under the edge of the blanket. "What does that mean?"

"It means everything you saw in your medical tent, I did or ordered done to the other side." Lord Fine's voice was tight. "You don't arm your medics and send them onto the field, and you don't call for a medic to interrogate the man who knows where your captured soldiers are held prisoner but won't talk. Trust me, Sebastian: you don't need to sugarcoat your demons. Not for me."

Oh. Sebastian swallowed. "I'm sorry that happened to all of you," he said quietly.

"Not good memories, no, but you seem to know a thing or two about that," Lord Fine said gruffly. "My point is that I can handle the consequences of my own actions, I can handle your past, and I can handle *you*, particularly because I suspect you're so sweet that if I broke out the handcuffs again, you'd let me use them on you. I swear, you're like something out of a storybook, a fae prince who escaped an evil curse and now martyrs himself for the good of the ungrateful humans, and I refuse to be part of such a fanciful fairy tale."

Sebastian furrowed his brow. "You might be the one being fanciful."

"How dare you." Lord Fine said, though not meanly.

"There's not a drop of fancy in me. I actually see the world for exactly as cold and callous as it is."

He spoke as if that were certain fact—except at that moment, the world *wasn't* cold. Their space had warmed enough that Sebastian could relax his stranglehold on the blanket, letting it fall loose on his shoulders. And the moment didn't feel *callous* either, not when Lord Fine's profile was limned in the flickering glow of the flames he'd built to stop Sebastian's shivering. Not when Lord Fine had seen Sebastian's demons and unflinchingly chased them off. "Not everything in the world is cold and callous."

"Well, maybe not *you*, I suppose," Lord Fine said. "But I most certainly am. So there will be absolutely no more excuses made for me, do you understand?"

"Yes, *sir*," Sebastian muttered.

"Oh, duck, if you're trying to be sarcastic, you should know I love the way that sounds in your voice." Lord Fine had the barest ghost of a smile. "And you should also know by now I'm a remorseless prick who would happily pop those handcuffs back on you until you see things my way."

Sebastian snorted, but a grudging smile of his own was tugging at his mouth. "You don't scare me either, you know."

"Only because you have more heart than sense." Unlike Sebastian in his T-shirt, Lord Fine was dressed in striped silk pajamas that shimmered in the firelight. It had been a long time since Sebastian had spent a night in the company of someone who wasn't dressed to wake at any second. Lord Fine was a handsome man in whatever he wore, but seeing the strong lines of his body dressed for bed projected such a welcome air of steadiness and domesticity that Sebastian was having a hard time looking away.

Lord Fine's eyes were also on him, lingering on Sebastian's throat above the blanket, where his collarbones were probably visible above the T-shirt's collar. "Is that—one of the American army T-shirts?"

Sebastian's skin was almost buzzing under Lord Fine's gaze, or maybe he was just warm from the fire. "It is," he admitted. "I've been told I need to size up."

"Who told you that? I'll have them drawn and quartered. You're wearing the absolute perfect size." Lord Fine abruptly stood up. "Well, come on, then."

"Where?"

"Bed."

"Bed?"

"We're sharing. Like we should have from the bloody start—are you always so stubborn? We'll sleep back to back, like soldiers. Well, to be fair, I always had my own tent, but I feel certain you've done it."

Sebastian's cheeks flushed with sudden heat. That was not a path of memories to go down in front of Lord Fine, especially not when the man was offering to share a bed. "But—"

"Besides, I wake at the slightest noise," Lord Fine went on. "So you'll only make it inconvenient for me if this happens again and I have to cross the room. And you said it's worse when you're cold, so perhaps if you're warmer you won't wake at all."

"But—"

"Sebastian," Lord Fine said testily. "Stop arguing with me and get your arse in the bed."

He held out his hand expectantly.

Sebastian bit his lip. Then he took Lord Fine's hand,

much warmer than his own, and let himself be pulled up to his feet.

The bed was more than big enough for two men, so that they could lie facing in opposite directions and not touch. Lord Fine, whether on accident or on purpose, had maneuvered so Sebastian was on the side with the fireplace, just able to see the orange flames flickering across the room. The bed was still warm, and Sebastian still had the extra blanket on top of him.

When was the last time he was this comfortable?

The heavy rain continued to pelt the window and balcony doors. Sebastian watched the flames, and then sighed quietly. "You must think me a coward."

"Are you daft?" Lord Fine said incredulously. "I mean, I do think you're a posturing fool for not taking me up on my offer in the first place. But a coward? After the torture you went through? No. I think you must have the courage of a lion."

Sebastian automatically wrapped his hand around the tattoo on his wrist.

"Look," Lord Fine went on gruffly. "You know what the war was like. Whatever badness you think you've done, you did it under blood magic. I've done plenty without that excuse."

Sebastian half glanced over his shoulder, seeing only the edge of Lord Fine's back. "Are we actually going to compete over who is the bigger scoundrel?"

"I would win," Lord Fine said decisively. "Because you're an angel, while I'm an actual beast."

Sebastian pursed his lips. "You're really not so bad, you know."

"Ugh, you are such a menace with those rose-colored glasses," said Lord Fine. "I bet you said the same thing about your mangy, rabid strays, and now two of them live in my home."

The corner of Sebastian's mouth turned up.

"Go to sleep," said Lord Fine. "And bloody stay asleep, this time."

Sebastian huffed, but the ever-present knot in his chest was looser. He watched the fire, listening to the rain against the window and feeling the mattress shift as Lord Fine settled.

You're really, really not so bad, he wanted to whisper.

Chapter Nine

Wesley woke to pale light giving the room a silver-gray glow. The rain had stopped during the night, the morning cloudy and cool.

Sebastian was still asleep, burrowed deep under the blankets, and Wesley absolutely did not indulge in a long moment of eying what he could see of that handsome face.

Blood terrors. Christ.

An hour later they went together to the kitchen and foraged in the pantry for tins. Sebastian knew how to light a stove and put a kettle on, but Wesley's searches only turned up chipped mugs and a box of tea so ancient the leaves had paled and lost their scent.

The manor had both a dining room and a morning room, but Sebastian had looked at Wesley with his big pretty eyes and said *the stove makes it warmer in here* and Wesley had heard himself agree to sit at the scored wooden kitchen table like a fucking hall boy. Handsome men were a bloody hazard.

"Blanshard has reduced me to brewed dust for breakfast in my own manor." Wesley picked up his mug with distaste. "If I didn't already want vengeance, this might have done the trick. And why are *you* eating biscuits?"

Sebastian dipped the biscuit straight into an opened

tin of sweetened condensed milk. Like Wesley, he was dressed in country tweeds; unlike Wesley, the casual tans and browns suited Sebastian perfectly. "These are cookies. Biscuits are round fluffy breads."

"No, you've just described scones." Wesley pointed at Sebastian's tin. "That's also nothing but sugar and I saw you stir it into that dirt you claim is instant coffee."

"I could eat this entire can with a spoon," Sebastian said dreamily. "You should try it."

"Absolutely not. All I want is proper tea."

"Now who's being delicate?" Sebastian said innocently.

Ugh, he was downright charming, teasing Wesley. "Put down that stone in your glass greenhouse, Caribbean boy on a Yorkshire moor."

Sebastian grinned and popped the biscuit into his mouth. "We are going to York to investigate. I will buy you a proper tea in town, yes?"

"Hmph." More teasing, perhaps, but Wesley wouldn't mind letting Sebastian buy him drinks. "So what exactly are we going to be looking for today?"

"Traces of magic."

"Traces of what kind of magic?" Wesley asked. "Mercier's? The Earl of Blanshard's?"

"Maybe," said Sebastian. "But they are also murdering people with no witnesses. I am hoping to find some trace that will help us figure out how they are moving without being found."

Wesley reached for a tin of kippers and the can opener. "Miss Robbins said you lot think Blanshard has the power to eat auras."

Sebastian hesitated.

"Sebastian," Wesley said warningly. "No sugarcoating."

Sebastian sighed. "It sounds exactly like the story my family tells."

"What happens in your story? Did your ancestors manage to stop this vampire paranormal?"

"A distant aunt, yes," Sebastian said. "But we don't know exactly how she did it."

"Someone in your family stops a paranormal who eats auras and no one writes that story down?" Wesley said incredulously.

Sebastian winced. "Supposedly tía Casilda was supposed to marry an Englishman as part of some political alliance. But she refused and was disowned."

"But she still came back to stop this vampire, disowned or not." Wesley tilted his head. "Frankly that sounds like something you would do, with your whole *protect the nonmagical* bit."

"It's what we try to do in my family," Sebastian said.

Vampire paranormals and family legends and blood magic, and Sebastian in the thick of it, doing his best to save people without magic. Even a bitter cynic like Wesley was finding it hard not to feel some admiration for the man.

He watched as Sebastian took another biscuit and dipped it in the tin. He licked off sweetened condensed milk, and Wesley abruptly went a little hot under the collar.

Hard not to feel a lot of things for the man.

After breakfast, they got their caps and stepped out through a back door. Wesley carefully kept his eyes on the house, because perhaps he was a coward, but it was daylight now and he simply didn't want to see the state of the untended gardens.

"The garage is just over there," he started.

But Sebastian wasn't looking in the direction of the

garage; he was looking out over the land. "What a beautiful garden."

Wesley turned before he could stop himself.

He stilled. He'd expected a mess, and it certainly wasn't neat. But beneath the gray sky, the hedges were still lush green despite their unmanicured edges. The stone walls up ahead were prettier with the ivy crawling up their sides, and the overgrown plants tumbling over the sides of the stone planters had flowers in shades of pink and violet.

"Oh," he said in surprise. "I thought it would have gone completely to seed."

"Wild is beautiful too." Sebastian pointed at a fountain. "You've even got birds." He glanced at Wesley out of the corner of his eye. "You're not going to shoot him, are you?"

Wesley rolled his eyes. "Well, I don't eat robin, so no. But if he was a partridge or a pheasant, I certainly would, and no amount of pouting on your part will change that."

That earned him a dirty look, which was cute. For all the beauty of the wild garden, Sebastian was still the most beautiful thing to be seen, and Wesley needed a cigarette or he was going to get caught staring. "We might see lambs today, on the drive."

Sebastian glanced over his shoulder. "Really?"

"Thought you'd like that." Wesley pulled out his pack from his coat. It had been laughable to think Sebastian would judge him for his addiction or a preference for cheap tobacco over fine cigars; might as well give the man more of his Yorkshire truths. "I'm donating the manor."

Sebastian blinked in surprise, maybe at the non sequitur, maybe at the idea that Wesley would indulge anything so outrageously soft as charity.

"I never come anymore," Wesley admitted. "Too many ghosts for me, but maybe for others, it could be, I don't know. A hospital, or a school, or an orphanage."

"That would be lovely," Sebastian said, with so much sincerity that the tenseness in Wesley's chest eased. "Children would love to play in this garden."

"I did, once upon a time." Wesley stuck the cigarette between his lips. He struck a match, and cupped his hands around the tip while lighting it. "This whole area used to be Fine land, when Shepherd Hall got its name. But my great-uncle had his own vices and sold some acres off, and now there's a farm next door. The animals used to come to the stone wall that divides the property, and the groundskeeper used to give me treats for them."

"Oh." Sebastian bit his thumb. "Was that your Mr. Fitzgerald who passed in spring?"

He'd remembered. "Yes." Wesley inhaled the acrid smoke. "I'd known Fitz my whole life. He indulged me terribly and my mother encouraged it, traipsing down to feed the animals with me. She particularly loved the lambs." He shook out the match. "My father of course put a stop to all the coddling when she died."

"Coddling." Sebastian sounded skeptical. "How old were you?"

"Six." Wesley gestured carelessly with the cigarette. "Wipe that concerned look off your face. I was the younger son who was never supposed to have to worry about the title, and she did coddle me—you know how mothers are. My father was right to end it, but. Well. Fitz was the last staff member I had who remembered her."

Wesley blew the smoke out in a hard rush. "Anyway.

Now you know why the furniture is missing from many of the rooms, and why I've been ridiculously sentimental and haven't replaced my groundskeeper."

"I don't think anything you've said has been ridiculous," Sebastian said quietly. "It should not be too much to ask of the world that children are cared for and happy."

"Oh, please, I didn't want for anything," Wesley said. "Save your sympathy for those who deserve it."

"I can have sympathy for everyone who has suffered," Sebastian said. "Including six-year-old Lord Fine."

"Try a little for yourself, then."

Sebastian opened his mouth, then closed it. He stuck his hands in his coat pockets, and said, "I hope we see the lambs."

Wesley snorted. "Of course you do."

"I hope we see cows too."

"Cows."

"And goats, and chickens, and piglets. Perhaps there are cats in the barn?"

"I thought we were going to York."

Sebastian shrugged, but he had a small smile of his own. "Did you want me to *knock you on your arse* first?" he said innocently, gesturing at Wesley's cigarette.

Oh, that was so much sexier than it had any right to be, the playful smile, the big doe eyes, the fact that this man had magic and could flatten Wesley with his mind.

Wesley inhaled the vile smoke deeply. "Yes, please."

Sebastian rolled his eyes. "Come show me your car. It is this way, no?"

He set off. Wesley dropped the half-smoked cigarette to the stone and ground it out under his foot, then caught up.

The garage sat apart from the manor itself, big enough for at least four cars, although there was only the one inside. Wesley pulled open the garage door, and the gray light streamed into the space onto the blanket-covered car.

Together, they pulled the blanket off, and Sebastian's eyes lit up.

"Is that a Bentley?" He was walking back toward the car like a magnet.

"Yes," Wesley said, setting the cover aside. "Blue Label tourer, same as I have in London, although I'm not entirely certain this one is going to start."

"I will get her to start," Sebastian promised.

Wesley scoffed lightly. "What, does your magic work on cars?"

"My tío had a Model T in San Juan." Sebastian ran his hand along the passenger door frame—what would have been the driver's door on his American cars—and then over the top of the spare tire mounted on the car's side. "Cars must be brought by boat to Puerto Rico. On islands, we don't take things for granted and I learned to keep ours running. Sometimes, in the army, we found cars in towns, and I'd get those running too."

He was studying the roof, which was folded down at the moment, and then glanced into the backseat. Then he bent over the side of the car, and Wesley had to swallow down the noise that nearly escaped his throat.

Sebastian's voice floated up from the car. "And you have all the driving gear!"

"I have the what now?" Wesley said, voice too high.

"The accessories."

"Oh. I mean, of course I do, help yourself," Wesley

managed to say. He quickly turned away to pull two spare umbrellas out of the stand.

When he turned back, Sebastian had pulled on the leather gloves, and was adjusting a pair of driving goggles on his face. He still wore his cap and his scarf and he looked like he'd just stepped out of a younger Wesley's dreams.

Then, to make it worse, he grinned at Wesley. "How do I look?"

Was Wesley actually supposed to stand this without bending him right back over the car? "Does every bleeding thing you wear suit you perfectly?"

Sebastian froze. "Um—"

"Oh, come off it," said Wesley. "You have to know you're a handsome man. A compliment to your looks is hardly going to make the *Times*; it's like saying the sky is blue."

"But the sky is gray today."

"Do I have to tell you that you're a looker no matter what color the sky?"

Sebastian bit his lip. "You are very good at saying whatever you like without shame."

"Shame is for peasants," said Wesley. "There's no point in being flattered by my words. I despise beautiful people. You're all terribly spoilt because when you want something, everyone's too besotted to tell you no."

Sebastian lifted the goggles up to rest on his forehead, under his flat cap. Then he leaned back against the hood of the car, and his eyes had an edge of mischief that made Wesley's stomach flip. "So if I say that what I very much want is to drive your Bentley, does that mean you will say yes?"

Was—was Wesley being flirted with?

Wesley might have just been flirted with.

But no. No, Wesley would consider how interesting that was at another time. A little flirting was not enough to see him wrapped around the pinky of a handsome man, no matter how sweet.

"Do you even know how to drive on our side of the road?"

Sebastian shrugged innocently. "Maybe a magnanimous lord could teach me?"

Wesley narrowed his eyes.

Sebastian smiled hopefully.

With a loud sigh, Wesley gestured for him to take the driver's seat.

You can't flirt with the British Army captain. No puedes hacerlo, you can't do it.

Sebastian repeated the lecture to himself as he cautiously navigated the Yorkshire country roads. He hadn't *meant* to flirt with Lord Fine. Yes, Lord Fine was strong, and smart, and witty, and he spoke his mind, and he was exactly the kind of man Sebastian sometimes liked, the way he liked some women.

And there had been the moments, last night, and then in the garage, when Lord Fine's eyes were on him with what Sebastian could have sworn was desire—

But even if Lord Fine were interested in men, Sebastian would mess it up. Other men could keep things simple. Transactional, an exchange of pleasure. Not him. Sebastian felt things too hard, wanted things that were too soft. He was here to protect Lord Fine and that was all he would do. There would be no complicating it with attraction.

Lord Fine was gesturing to a stretch of forest. "This land here belongs to Lord Ryland. He had ten children with Lady Ryland, they're basically titled rabbits."

He was turning out to be a surprisingly good passenger. He sat comfortably in his seat and kept up a steady if grumpy narration about the countryside and its history. He wasn't critical of Sebastian's driving, not even when Sebastian had misjudged what a right turn required in England and gone straight into the oncoming lane. Maybe a viscount was used to being driven around, which would suit Sebastian perfectly. He liked to drive, and as it turned out, he also liked listening to Lord Fine in the passenger seat.

It didn't make the man less attractive, though.

The city center of York was surrounded by a thick stone wall and the roads were especially narrow, like horse paths only grudgingly now allowing cars. The rows of shops were interspersed with stone churches, and despite the chilly fall air, pedestrians were everywhere.

Sebastian carefully brought the Bentley down a cobbled street as tight as the oldest parts of San Juan. Lord Fine continued his dialogue as Sebastian looked for a place to park.

"—and don't let yourself get taken in by the buskers, they like to tell the tourists that more misery and suffering happened here than anywhere else, and while in fairness that might be an unembellished truth, they want to regale you with gruesome details in exchange for your money."

Sebastian shuddered. No gracias. "It looks like a very charming city. Listen to those church bells."

Lord Fine rolled his eyes. "I'm sure the streets are full of strays you can feed."

"Ooh, can we—"

"*No.*"

They drove past the towering cathedral with the

beautiful bells. Up close it was even more massive, spanning what looked like a block, its carved stone and graceful arches stretching up into the sky.

"Look at that." Sebastian craned his head to look up at the two rectangular towers that rose up from the church. "Maybe we will have time to stop in."

"What are we, tourists?" Lord Fine said derisively.

"No, but life is uncertain, isn't it? You must take your chances to enjoy beauty when you can, don't you think?"

"Oh." Lord Fine glanced at him out of the corner of his eye, his gaze lingering. "I suppose I hadn't thought of it like that."

Sebastian found a spot not far from the stunning cathedral. As they walked along cobblestones, he reached into his coat pocket and retrieved the *Yorkshire Evening Press* clipping that Jade and Zhang had mailed him.

"According to the newspaper, the body was found near the Shambles," he said, tucking his neck a little deeper into his scarf as the wind cut down their street.

"I know where that is." Unlike Sebastian's hunching, Lord Fine stood very straight as he walked, seemingly unbothered by the cold. "Are we looking for the murder scene?"

"Eventually," Sebastian said. "If what happened to you is the same as what happened here, then I bet no one heard this murder. In London, Mercier used some kind of silencing magic in that alley, that glittering cage around you."

"He did, until you showed up and it vanished." Lord Fine tilted his head. "What exactly did you do to it?"

"Destroyed it."

Lord Fine's eyebrows went up. "You can do that?" he

said curiously. "Is that why you told Mercier his magic might not survive your battle?"

"That was a bluff," Sebastian admitted. "I cannot destroy living magic, the magic tied to another paranormal. But the flames Mercier had made, or the cage he'd made—those I can destroy, if I use enough force."

The streets were lined with little shops and pubs and eateries, in the shadow of the giant church. It was a busy town, people filling the sidewalks and cars squeezing around each other on the narrow roads.

"Maybe before we look for the murder scene, we should talk to the shop owners and market sellers," said Sebastian. "Even if they could not hear anything, maybe someone saw something odd."

Lord Fine frowned. "Why would they talk to us?"

"Why wouldn't they?"

"What, you just walk up to people and they talk to you?"

"Usually."

Lord Fine pursed his lips. "I suppose I'd forgotten that every skirt in England is eager for your time."

"Don't be silly," Sebastian said. "Some people don't like my accent, or my Spanish."

"Some people don't like opera. The world is full of classless philistines."

Sebastian blinked.

"Xenophobia is a waste of time," Lord Fine went on, like he hadn't just paid Sebastian something of a compliment. "Everyone is a foreigner somewhere. Foreigners are just people and all people are universally terrible, so what's the point of disliking foreigners in particular?"

Sebastian side-eyed him. "Qué cínico."

"How cynical?" Lord Fine guessed, correctly. "You

see? People are predictable, whatever the language. It's always the same conversations, about the weather or a particularly good cheese or what a bastard I am. Which is your mother tongue anyway, English or Spanish?"

Sebastian shrugged helplessly. "I was born right after America invaded Puerto Rico and we went from a Spanish colony to an American one. I spoke Spanish at home but the government tried to mandate English at school, and then I went to university in America when I was sixteen." He made a face. "My brother speaks both with almost no hint of the other, and excellent French and Italian too. But I have an accent now even when I speak Spanish, and I never get idioms right."

"Some people like accents," Lord Fine said pointedly. He pursed his lips. "Spain, America, the Caribbean— you move between a lot of worlds. I'm only English."

"Sometimes it feels like the world was only made for people who are one straightforward thing," Sebastian said. "I was a colonizer's kid who got colonized. I'm not exactly Spanish or American, and I've been anchorless from the island so long I don't know if I get to call myself Puerto Rican anymore."

"You don't owe anyone a simple explanation for yourself," said Lord Fine. "You're allowed to be everything you are at once, and if anyone thinks you're too complicated, tell them to fuck off."

Sebastian snorted, but that had made him smile. "I don't really tell people to fuck off."

"That's a shame. I highly recommend it."

That drew a surprised laugh from Sebastian. "Not all people are terrible," he said, with feeling, glancing at Lord Fine from under his flat cap.

"As if I would listen to your Panglossian prattling,"

Lord Fine said. "You think I'm *not so bad*; you're clearly addled."

"You're not bad at *all*," Sebastian protested.

Lord Fine raised his eyebrow. "No?"

"No," Sebastian said emphatically. "You're—" *Smart. Witty. Attractive.* "—um," he stumbled.

"Go on, duck," Lord Fine said, a new note in his voice. "What am I?"

Sebastian bit his lip. "...tall?"

"Tall, again." Lord Fine glanced down, and their eyes met. "Sure, Sebastian," he said, slow and knowing, like he didn't buy it for a single second.

Sebastian stuck his hands in his pockets to hide his shiver.

Soon they were in a market square in a very old part of an already-old city. People were eager to gossip about the murder, but none of them could add anything that wasn't in the paper.

"Horrible murder, but that's Yorkshire for you," an elderly chemist told them. "Didn't you read *Dracula*? Takes place in Whitby, it does. The villages have got all sorts of nasty legends, about witches and beasts. Lords who hunted their own vassals, doing the devil's work for him."

Lord Fine narrowed his eyes. "Just exactly what sort of stories is everyone telling about the lords around here?"

Sebastian took that as their cue to go search the alleys instead.

They walked from the chemist past a tea shop that smelled like baking pies. "A murder takes place in a city center and no one seems to know anything or comes forward with any evidence," Lord Fine observed. "But of course, no one would have had evidence had I been murdered the night before last, despite being a stone's throw from Fenchurch. I was completely alone with that fire paranormal, Jack Mercier."

Sebastian frowned. "The cage seemed to muffle the sound, but I don't know how he ensured he was alone with you. I didn't notice any other magic in the street."

"Even the busiest city streets are empty now and again," said Lord Fine. "Could he have simply timed it right?"

"Why rely on timing when you could use magic?"

"Fair point." Lord Fine considered Sebastian. "Mercier knew you. He knew you'd be at the limits of your magic."

"We were under the same blood magic," Sebastian admitted. "I used to know his limits too."

"He seemed particularly angry to see you," said Lord Fine. "I mean, I assume most baddies would be, since you can apparently douse their magic like a snuffer on a candle. But he called you a *spanner in the works*."

"I suppose I am." Sebastian held up his arm. "It's the same reason I can hide you. If they're using some kind of magic to conceal or plan these murders, it won't work on me."

Lord Fine's gaze was lingering on his wrist, where the edges of the tattoo would be visible to him as swirls of color. "It sounds like we can at least look for the murder site, then, in the Shambles or close by." He set his jaw. "My guess would be an alley where the victim could be isolated and trapped."

A few minutes later, they stood together in the mouth of an alley. "Now what?" Lord Fine said.

"Powerful magic sometimes leaves a residue. I can't feel it standing here, the way a subordinate paranormal would, and I'll never know what kind, but I might be able to feel traces of magic left behind if those traces weaken under my magic." Sebastian made a face. "Of course, that means using my magic, and normally I would recommend you get some distance from me for this part. But you must stay close to avoid magical detection."

Lord Fine's gaze flicked over him. "And what do I do if I'm *close to you*?" he said lightly.

Sebastian winced. "Brace yourself."

Lord Fine rolled his eyes. "I can handle some watery limbs if it means catching the blighters who tried to murder me." He looked at the wall of the alley, and then wrinkled his nose. "Christ, have these walls been washed in a century? Ever? Brick isn't supposed to be slimy."

Sebastian's lips quirked up. "I can give you my handkerchief."

"Fuck off." Lord Fine gingerly rested his fingertips on the alley wall with an air of great reluctance. "There. Braced."

"No, you're not," Sebastian said. "You'll be covered in slime and worse from the cobblestones if you fall."

"I'm not going to fall. Stop coddling me, you know I don't abide it."

"Lord Fine—"

"Any day now, princess."

Sebastian sighed, and then surreptitiously moved within arm's reach of Lord Fine.

He let his magic sweep out over the alley—

And Lord Fine made a strangled noise next to him.

Sebastian lunged for Lord Fine before the other man could hit the ground.

"Oof," he said inelegantly, as he successfully caught

Lord Fine around the ribs but staggered under the sudden deadweight. He scrambled to stop the flow of his own magic as he simultaneously tried to pull Lord Fine back to his feet.

A miscalculation. It was like yanking the tug-of-war rope just as the other side suddenly lets go. Lord Fine regained control of his muscles and pushed himself just as Sebastian pulled him, and their combined strength sent the two of them stumbling like drunks.

Sebastian's back hit the alley wall, his breath leaving him in a rush just as Lord Fine's back smacked into Sebastian's chest. There were only three, maybe four inches of height difference between them, but Lord Fine was heavier than he looked, a solid mass flattening Sebastian against the wall.

"Ugh." Lord Fine's huff sounded more annoyed than hurt. "Is this the part where you insufferably say I told you so?"

"I'd have to be able to breathe first." It wasn't so bad, though, really. Lord Fine was warm and his weight kind of comforting. The bare skin of the back of his neck was under Sebastian's nose, and with every breath he caught masculine soap layered on skin.

"I suppose I'm crushing you terribly, aren't I?" There was a pause, then Lord Fine cleared his throat. "I can't free your lungs if your arms are still around me."

Oops. Sebastian quickly let go.

Lord Fine straightened up, smoothing his suit with a distracted swipe as he turned toward Sebastian. He hadn't stepped away, and they were still very close, close enough Sebastian had to tilt his head back to keep their eyes aligned.

Lord Fine's gaze darted over Sebastian's face. "I suppose I owe you another apology."

A tiny smile formed on Sebastian's lips. "You keep racking up that tally."

Lord Fine snorted. He still hadn't stepped away, which kept Sebastian caught between him and the wall. The market crowd was muted in the distance, the only sound in the alley their quiet breaths and Sebastian's own pulse in his ears, which for some reason was thumping too loudly.

Lord Fine was eying him almost like he could hear Sebastian's heart. "I'm the one who didn't listen, yet you're the one who ended up against the filthy alley wall."

"It's not filthy. A little bit dirty, and London's worse."

"Semantics, and how dare you."

This close, Sebastian was still aware of body heat and the scent of Lord Fine's shaving soap. His usual sneer had eased from his lips; in fact, he had an amused, almost soft smile, like he knew he was being teased and didn't mind, and very suddenly, Sebastian wanted to kiss him.

Oh *no*.

Sebastian swallowed. Lord Fine's gaze dropped to his throat, where his tie suddenly felt too tight and his skin too hot beneath his shirt collar.

You can't kiss him. No man has ever wanted you to kiss them, you know that. Tell him to back up and give you space before he wonders why you haven't.

Sebastian should. It didn't matter that they were still alone in the alley, he needed to make it seem like he wasn't the kind of man who wanted to be pinned to walls by other men. Because if Lord Fine had any idea that Sebastian was aching to stretch up those few inches and close the distance to his lips—

He's a viscount. He's a British Army captain.

Sebastian needed to tell Lord Fine to move. But he didn't.

The moment stretched out, Sebastian's nerves on alert, his skin tingling with their proximity and the craving to be touched.

Footsteps echoed on cobblestones, closer than others had been.

Lord Fine calmly took a step back, giving Sebastian all the personal space he didn't want. "Did you feel anything just now?"

"What?" Sebastian said helplessly.

"Did you feel anything," Lord Fine said, slowly and patronizingly, like Sebastian was an idiot, "with your magic just now?"

Oh.

"Um." Sebastian tried to focus. *Magic.* Of course he was asking about magic; they were here to investigate a murder. "I didn't have time to notice."

"What, like you were busy catching some pigheaded fool who didn't listen to you? Please, what kind of an excuse is that."

Oh no, Lord Fine's rueful smile was back and it was charming. Sebastian quickly averted his eyes from Lord Fine's lips and pushed off the alley wall.

"I can try again," he said, aiming for the kind of teasing tone he would have taken with a friend. Appropriately platonic and not at all like Sebastian had been about to try to kiss him. "If you can."

With a sigh, Lord Fine leaned heavily on the alley wall. He watched with open and unabashed interest as Sebastian stepped to the middle of the alley. Then Sebastian closed his eyes and swept out.

He heard Lord Fine grunt, but from a distance, his concentration on the cobblestones and bricks as his magic swept the alley like a tide rippling out with Sebastian in the center.

But as his magic covered the alley, there was nothing to feel beyond Lord Fine's aura, and Sebastian didn't want to weaken him more than he absolutely had to. He abruptly pulled his magic back into himself and opened his eyes.

Only to find Lord Fine had slid down the wall to the alley floor and was glaring at him.

"'You must brace yourself, Lord Fine,'" he said dryly, mimicking Sebastian's accent. "It didn't help, you absolute arse. You're a sucker punch, a bottle of whiskey masquerading as a man." He huffed. "I wish I was actually angry and not simply fascinated by you."

Sebastian hesitated. "I would not blame you if I made you nervous, you know."

"Don't flatter yourself." Lord Fine got to his feet. "Did you feel anything that time?"

"No. Either there was never anything to feel, or the residuals are gone." Sebastian cleared his throat. "You might want to wait before you take the time to clean yourself off."

Lord Fine, who had been brushing dirt from his jacket, side-eyed him. "Why?" he said suspiciously.

"Because we should check all the alleys." Sebastian gave Lord Fine an apologetic look. "And you're probably going to fall a lot more."

They tried three more alcoves or alleys, each dirtier than the last. Lord Fine grudgingly sat on a stoop before each round, and his nice tweed suit was getting stained.

The Shambles were still full of people, which meant Sebastian had to hold his magic close, keeping a tighter grip on the reins so he wouldn't knock down the crowds.

But he still had to use enough magic to pick up days-old traces of other magic, and the effort of keeping so much magic so tightly contained was wringing him out.

By the time they ducked into a fifth location, the empty courtyard behind an ancient stone church, he was sweating with effort. He waited until Lord Fine got settled, and then carefully swept out through the tiny space with a burst of magic that had him gritting his teeth to keep it controlled.

But this time, there was something to feel.

Sebastian's eyes widened. He walked forward, toward the residual, as poor Lord Fine lolled in his little stone alcove.

"Got something?" Lord Fine slurred.

"I'm not sure." Sebastian was walking forward, toward the alley's dead end. "I'll be quick as I can."

"M'fine," came Lord Fine's thick words. "I mean, s'lunacy, but it'd be nice lunacy if I had a pillow."

There were traces of magic at the dead end at the stone wall. Sebastian could feel it under his own. He brought the tide, like an ocean rolling onto the beach, and something crumpled beneath his magic like a sandcastle under a wave.

But it wasn't alone.

Something had weakened, but there was something else, another kind of magic here. Sebastian crouched down, trying to find the difference. He put his hands over the stones, and reached so deep into himself that his bones ached, and then struck out with his magic again.

And something fought back.

Sebastian jerked his hands away, taking several steps backward as he pulled his magic into himself so abruptly it hurt. He stared at the corner of the courtyard.

"Sebastian." Lord Fine was back on his feet, approaching quickly. "What is it?"

Sebastian pointed at the base of the wall. "There's magic there, but—that isn't right."

Lord Fine frowned. He crouched and swept his finger along the stones of the courtyard, beneath a statute of St. Frances where the rain might not have reached.

"Ashes," he said, as he rubbed his fingers together. "So you're feeling traces of Mercier's magic?"

"Probably." Sebastian's heart was beating too fast.

"But then what's wrong? Besides the obvious, that some poor fellow was magically murdered in this very spot. You look like you've seen a ghost."

"Not a ghost." Sebastian swallowed hard. "A mirror."

"What?"

Sebastian looked up at him. "I need to call Zhang."

There was an inn two blocks over with a phone on the desk. Lord Fine bribed the innkeeper behind the desk to take a smoke break while Sebastian got the operator on the line and was put through to the lobby of the Great Eastern.

Lord Fine leaned against the counter next to him. "How exactly is this going to work? Mr. Zhang and Miss Robbins aren't simply hanging around waiting for our call."

Sebastian relayed his message to the front desk of the hotel, giving the name of the town and the inn. Then he hung up. "Zhang is watching the hotel on the astral plane. He'll see the message and call us here from wherever he is, if he can."

"Magic," Lord Fine muttered.

Three minutes later, the inn's phone rang. Sebastian quickly grabbed it before the innkeeper came running back.

"It's me." Zhang's familiar American accent was on the line. "What did you find?"

Sebastian spoke quietly into the phone, explaining what had happened.

"You picked up magic that felt like *you*," Zhang repeated slowly.

Sebastian glanced up. "I'm your sentry," Lord Fine said. "Talk freely, I'll let you know if someone's coming."

Sebastian gave him a grateful look. "I thought I just heard Lord Fine in the background," said Zhang in his ear, "except whoever that was sounded nice, so clearly I'm hearing things. Explain what you mean, it felt like your own magic."

"There was something new in the alley today, something that wasn't in London. I couldn't weaken it, but not because it was too strong. Because it was like fighting myself."

"Well, that's not good."

"Zhang," Sebastian said. "You're a paranormal scholar, say something more helpful!"

"Give a man a moment to think," Zhang said. "You didn't feel this sensation in London, so maybe it was the victim."

"Is there any reason to think the victim was a paranormal?"

"No," Zhang acknowledged. "So maybe the traces you felt are from Lord Blanshard."

Sebastian frowned. "But that would mean we were wrong about Lord Blanshard, that he doesn't have vampire magic but instead has magic like mine. Except I can't kill anyone."

Zhang hesitated.

"What?" Sebastian said.

"It's just—you can't kill anyone right *now*," said Zhang. "But you can destroy traces of magic, and you can weaken auras."

"So?"

"So we're also missing a relic," said Zhang. "Relics strengthen magic, and the missing brooch relic makes magic work on other paranormals. What would *you* be able to do to magic and auras if you got your hands on the brooch?"

Sebastian frowned. "I don't know," he admitted. "My magic already works on magic—maybe it would do nothing?"

"Somehow I doubt that," Zhang said dryly.

"You don't think Blanshard could have the brooch and *my* magic?" Sebastian curled his hand, the arm with the tattoo. "Zhang, I don't want to think that my magic could do this."

"I know. There might be another explanation, let me work on this. Jade and I are coming up to York tomorrow. Is there a place we can meet you?"

Sebastian asked Lord Fine, who described a restaurant near the train station. He said goodbye to Zhang and hung up the phone, off-kilter like he was standing on the deck of a boat in stormy seas.

Lord Fine looked him up and down. "You look terribly pale again. Have you considered that it's past tea-time and you've used your magic repeatedly while eating nothing but biscuits today?"

Sebastian opened his mouth, then closed it.

"I watched you faint once already and I'm not keen on you driving yourself to it again." Lord Fine straightened up. "Come on. You owe me a proper tea, don't you? Let's find something."

Chapter Ten

Wesley would have liked to take Sebastian to the hotel by the train station now, just the two of them, instead of waiting for Jade and Zhang in the morning. The ground-floor restaurant was elegant, the food was excellent, and it might even have felt a bit like a date to have Sebastian across the table, something Wesley hadn't had in a very long time.

But Sebastian was obviously shaken by his exertions and whatever he'd felt in the alley. So when the inn-keeper pointed them to a pub one block over, Wesley didn't want to take the time to find a better recommendation and dragged Sebastian there instead.

The pub was in the red-bricked ground floor of a two-story building with a peaked roof. Inside was brighter than he'd expected, a bay window letting in gray light as it framed a small courtyard with a few outdoor tables. It was early enough only a few others were inside, a couple men playing darts, a woman talking to the barkeep behind a counter made of small white tiles with a dark wood bar top.

They sat in a wooden booth with brown velvet cushions and a waitress came by to take their order.

But when Sebastian looked up, she visibly startled.

"Oh, you're back!" she said. "I didn't think we'd get to see you again."

Sebastian furrowed his brow.

"You don't remember?" She snorted. "I remember *you*. You were quiet last time, but there aren't men like you around here." She tapped her pencil against her notepad, her expression very keen. "Are you, um. Staying in town?"

"No, he isn't," Wesley said, rather snappishly. "May we give our orders now?"

She gave Wesley a decidedly less keen look, but took their orders.

"I can't take you anywhere," Wesley said, as soon as she'd left.

"But I didn't do anything."

"No, of course you didn't, that's what's so galling," said Wesley. "You just sit there, doing absolutely nothing, and people flock to you like lecherous moths to a sexy flame."

"What's *galling* about that? Besides the questionable metaphor, because you are certainly the first person to call me that."

"It was a *simile*," Wesley said, because it was, and also because it was better than saying, *because I'm one of those lecherous moths and I'm getting territorial*. A territorial lecherous moth, Christ, that *was* a terrible metaphor.

"And why did she think she had seen me before?" Sebastian went on, looking confused again. "I've never been to York before this trip."

"Do you expect an answer more sophisticated than *she's hoping you want in her knickers*?"

"She seemed sincere," Sebastian protested.

Wesley rolled his eyes. "Maybe she mistook you for

another Caribbean boy wandering the Yorkshire moors, I don't know. You owe me a drink and I want something stronger than tea. Go get me an ale."

And try not to get fucked on the way to the bar, he stopped himself from saying out loud, because maybe Wesley was rude and unpleasant but he didn't have to be rude and unpleasant to *Sebastian.* It wasn't his fault he was a sexy flame while Wesley was a territorial lecherous moth.

In short order, they both had drinks and food. Wesley picked up the vinegar for his fried fish and chips, another taste from his army years that he'd acquired alongside cheap cigarettes. He would never have been allowed to eat here in his youth. It was not a meal fit for a gentleman, and he'd be lying if he said he wasn't looking forward to every greasy bite.

Sebastian had gone quiet and lost in his thoughts again in the seat across the booth, his outer coat now off and no jacket beneath. Just the waistcoat and tie, his chin propped in his hand and the edge of his tattoo visible where his shirtsleeve had slid down. The impossibly attractive sod frankly also looked good enough to eat, but he was still too pale, making no move for his fork as he bit his distractingly kissable lips and stared blankly with golden-brown eyes.

Wesley speared a chip with his fork. The waitress had been pretty, and she'd obviously been interested, but Sebastian didn't seem to have even noticed. He'd been only quietly polite, as he usually was with everyone.

Except Wesley was actually getting more than *quietly polite* from Sebastian now, wasn't he? Sebastian had teased him over biscuits at breakfast, kept protesting that Wesley *wasn't bad at all*, had shamelessly charmed his way right into the driver's seat of Wesley's Bentley.

Had been flushed and breathless when Wesley had him boxed in against the bricks in the alley.

No, Sebastian hadn't flirted with the waitress just now, but he might have been flirting with Wesley today. And if Sebastian *was* interested, Wesley would like nothing better than to pin him to the big bed in Shepherd Hall and show him another way they could spend their time in Yorkshire.

Or let Sebastian pin him down with some of that magic. Now there was a thought.

But, on the other hand, Wesley had pulled the man out of a blood terror. Perhaps it wasn't flirtation so much as Sebastian now seeing Wesley as some kind of gallant rescuer. Perhaps it was just a bit of hero worship.

Perhaps he was seconds away from throwing himself into Wesley's arms in heartfelt, clinging gratitude.

Wesley loudly cleared his throat. Sebastian looked at him, startled.

"Just bringing both our minds back to the present." Wesley nodded at Sebastian's untouched plate. "Are there pork pies in Puerto Rico?"

That got Sebastian talking, some of the tension finally leaving him as he told Wesley about some of his childhood favorites, pasteles and mofongo and rice with pigeon peas.

"Intriguing." Wesley cut into his fish with his knife and fork. "I've never had anything like that."

Sebastian was finally eating too. "This is my first pork pie," he said, dipping a piece in the gravy on the side.

"I see what you're doing, trying to be polite about my lack of experience," said Wesley. "Except you've been in England only months, and I'd wager you've gamely tried many of our regional cuisines. Whereas I've lived for years only a stone's throw from London's restaurants, yet I've tried almost nothing."

Sebastian tilted his head. "You can always wake up one morning and decide *today is the day I try something new.*"

"Out of the question," said Wesley. "I don't change."

Sebastian's lips quirked up as he picked up his drink. He'd opted for tonic water, not an ale like Wesley. *Alcohol makes paranormals lose control of their magic,* he'd explained, which sounded either terrifying or intriguing, depending on the paranormal. "You don't change?"

"Never," Wesley said firmly. He sat for a moment, then huffed. "You can see how well that's worked out for me, with my hordes of admirers and lovers."

Sebastian's eyes softened. "No one needs a partner to be a whole person."

"Oh, shut up," Wesley said, although not harshly, because somewhere along the line he'd discovered he didn't want to be harsh with Sebastian. "That's the kind of thing someone says when they could have their pick of partners at any time. I refuse to listen to a handsome man pretend he understands what it's like to want to find someone when no one can tolerate your presence."

Sebastian opened his mouth, probably to protest that he wasn't handsome, which he was, or offer another platitude, which Wesley wouldn't listen to. He held up a hand to cut Sebastian off. "It's for the best. I'm a terrible partner."

"I don't believe that."

Sebastian coming to his defense perversely made Wesley all the more determined to convince him of how awful he was. "The day I heard you in that antiques shop in New York, do you know why I was there?

Because I had sailed all the way to America to try and win a lover back."

"Isn't that a gallant gesture?"

"Maybe from someone else," said Wesley. "But I only wanted them back because they were attractive and fit conveniently into my life. Then I got to New York and discovered my ex-lover had found someone else, someone genuinely in love with them. And I'm happy for them, because they deserve that. I had treated them no better than a quality accessory, or a well-tailored suit, so you see, I'm no good for anyone."

But Sebastian shook his head stubbornly. "Not every man would share his bed to keep another man's demons away."

Wesley huffed. "You're looking at me through your rose-colored glasses again—"

"I'm not," Sebastian said, cutting Wesley off with flattering passion. "You are being mean about yourself when you have been kind to me. You offered me comfort, and you kept my blood terrors away, and I think you're—"

He snapped his mouth shut.

"You think I'm what?" Wesley pressed. "And if you try to say *tall* again, I might have to thrash you."

Sebastian bit his lip.

This would never do. Wesley had to know the sentiments Sebastian kept stopping himself from uttering. "Say it in Spanish, then I won't understand what it means."

Sebastian hesitated, then said, "Creo que eres el brujo, porque cuando estoy contigo, recuerdo como ser libre."

Wesley could stand to hear some more of that warm, velvety language. "That was pretty." He propped his chin on his hand. "Now translate."

"You just said I wouldn't have to!"

"No, I said I wouldn't know what it *meant*," Wesley pointed out. "Which I don't, so now you have to tell me."

Sebastian narrowed his eyes, then gave a short, sharp sigh and averted his gaze. "I said, *I think you're the witch, because when I'm with you, I remember how to be free.*"

Wesley froze.

"And *also*," Sebastian said, still not meeting Wesley's gaze, "you obviously can and have changed, because you see where you can be better now. People are allowed to grow, even viscounts, you know."

Wesley stared for a long moment. And then he leaned forward very suddenly. "You and I must return to the manor."

Sebastian blinked. "Is everything okay?"

No, it isn't. You've just uttered the most romantic words anyone has ever said to me, in a Yorkshire pub over chips.

Wesley picked up his ale. "I have some things I need to take care of."

"Like what?"

Like finding out what you do when the man you've been flirting with flirts back. See if you'd like to give me the chance to take care of you.

Wesley brought the glass to his lips. "Business."

Sebastian furrowed his brows. "Anything I can help with?"

Oh, I have something you could help with, right here in my trousers.

"We'll see," Wesley said lightly.

It was the beginning of twilight as they walked back to the Bentley, and Sebastian was never going to get used to how much earlier the sun set in the fall in northern countries.

"I suppose you think you're driving again," Lord Fine said, as the cathedral loomed in front of them.

Sebastian bit down his lip before he smiled. "Am I?" he said innocently.

"What was I just saying about beautiful people being spoilt because no one tells them *no*?" Lord Fine's gaze traveled over Sebastian, a slow sweep over his body and back up to linger on his lips. "Anything else you want from me?" he said lightly. "I'm clearly going to say yes."

If Lord Fine kept saying he thought Sebastian was handsome, Sebastian was going to have a very hard time remembering why he shouldn't kiss him.

Sebastian glanced up at the cathedral, one of the largest he'd ever seen, stone and stained glass stretching up to the sky. The opening notes of the choir's evensong were drifting out to the street.

He looked over at Lord Fine hopefully.

"When I said *what do you want from me*, the answer I was hoping for wasn't *church*," Lord Fine said sardonically.

"We're not going to church, we're going to see the architecture." Sebastian took a pointed step backward, toward the cathedral, trying to get Lord Fine to follow. "I bet it's very pretty inside."

"It's a church. You already know what's inside—pews and priests."

Sebastian took another step back. "The choir has started."

"I'm sorry, you seem to have confused me with a man who has an ounce of sentiment. Why would I agree to play tourists at York Minster?"

"You're not," Sebastian said. "*I'm* playing the tourist, and *you* have to come with me to stay with the tattoo."

"And the medic uses a tactical maneuver to win the battle, I'm impressed," Lord Fine said, with a grudging smile. "Lead on, then."

He fell into step beside Sebastian as they made their way into the giant cathedral. The roof of the nave stretched far above their heads, the evening light illuminating the stained glass windows and giving the white arches a soft glow. From the quire, the ethereal notes of the chorus echoed through the cavernous space.

"The Five Sisters was restored this summer," Lord Fine murmured, as they approached a grouping of five tall and narrow stained glass windows that rose to high peaks at the top. "It's a memorial now, to the women lost in the war."

Sebastian stood at the windows for a long moment, waiting for the tide of threatening memories to subside. Lord Fine lingered next to him without complaint, his own gaze on the memorial. Maybe Lord Fine wasn't a tourist, but Sebastian didn't believe he was as devoid of feelings as he claimed.

Outside was a small green park with beautiful views of the cathedral in the last of the day's light. Sebastian pointed to one of the towers, where a sleek gray-and-white bird with a curved yellow beak was perched on a gargoyle. "What is that?"

"Peregrine," said Lord Fine, because he probably could see it better than Sebastian. "And even I'll admit falcons are a worthy sight."

Sebastian smiled. "See? It is good we stopped." He then turned to head back to the car.

But Lord Fine cleared his throat. "I keep catching the edges of your tattoo under your sleeve when you move your hands. It's a paranormal tattoo, is that right? It's what keeps us hidden?"

They were mostly alone in the park save for another couple admiring the falcon and a mother and child walking hand in hand toward the street. Sebastian glanced down at his left wrist, and sure enough, his shirtsleeve had rucked up enough to show some of the ink. "Yes. Isabel was able to weave our magic together."

"Does she do a lot of paranormal tattoos?"

Sebastian shook his head. "She does other tattoos, yes, but mine is the only magic one. We were not sure it would work."

"Why risk it, then?"

Sebastian shrugged, as casually as he could. "I was going into the service of a telepath," he said. "It felt worth any risk to protect my mind so he could not read my thoughts."

Sebastian and Isabel hadn't known about the Puppeteer, about the blood magic that could slither its way even past the tattoo. But there would have been nothing they could have done anyway.

"May I see it?" Lord Fine said lightly. "Now, before nightfall? I'd like to know what's keeping me safe."

"Of course." Sebastian reached for his cufflink, and worked the stud out of the hole at his wrist. He began to roll up his sleeve, still palming the cufflink—

Lord Fine caught his wrist. "Devilishly awkward to do yourself, isn't it," he said breezily, as he took over, casually rolling up Sebastian's sleeve for him.

It was such a small, simple touch, but Sebastian seemed to have forgotten to breathe. Surely Lord Fine could feel his pulse in his wrist, a rapid staccato under the warm fingers that brushed his skin with every movement?

Sleeve out of the way, Lord Fine turned Sebastian's arm until it was upright. "So it's an abstract design, then? Swirls of color?"

That was all anyone else ever saw. "Yes," Sebastian started to say.

Except Lord Fine had tilted his head back, getting more distance from the tattoo, and said suddenly, "Oh, it's a lion!"

Sebastian's eyes widened.

"A lion for your name, *de Leon*, like the Latin *leo*, I presume?" Lord Fine went on. "I see him now, the rampant lion—there's the mane, the legs, all of it almost hidden."

"It's supposed to be." Sebastian's voice had gone hoarse. "That's the magic. It hides me, so the lion is—" *supposed to be* "—hidden too."

How could Lord Fine see it?

The magic couldn't be wearing off—could it?

"It's quite a fine work of art." Lord Fine sounded genuinely impressed. "What are these marks around the tattoo?"

Sebastian froze.

When the moment stretched out, Lord Fine looked up, away from the tattoo and into Sebastian's eyes. "They're not part of the tattoo, I can see that now that I see the lion," he said slowly. "They look like burn scars."

Sebastian bit his lip.

"Sebastian," Lord Fine said, still holding his wrist. "You don't have to sugarcoat things for me. What happened to you?"

Another long moment passed, then Sebastian said, very quietly, "The man who had me put under blood magic, the telepath who went by Baron Zeppler. He hated being unable to read my thoughts, so he tried to burn the tattoo off."

Lord Fine's fingers tightened on Sebastian's wrist.

Sebastian had to look away. "I suppose that's not exactly the truth," he said haltingly, watching the couple now walking briskly across the cathedral's small park. "Zeppler promised my family he would help us find the siphon, help us put the relics away before anyone got hurt—a lie, as it turned out. It didn't happen right away, but when he was certain my family had bought his charade, that no one knew of his deception, he dropped the pretense that I was a partner."

Sebastian swallowed. "So the real truth is that *I* tried to burn it off, because the first thing the Puppeteer did when he had my blood was make me pick up the brand myself."

Lord Fine was still gripping Sebastian's forearm too tightly, skin reddening under his fingers, but it was welcome, a point of strength keeping him from dipping too deep into the memories. But he was still never getting past this. He could play at helping solve murders, he could play at protecting a viscount, but at the end of the day, he wasn't like the others. He wasn't whole anymore.

"As I said, I was a villain," Sebastian said, still quiet. "And now I still have blood terrors, and a past that has hurt everyone I've met, and I don't know what I am anymore, except that I'm broken beyond repair."

Lord Fine's gaze was fixed on the scars. "How do you say *I don't believe that* in Spanish?"

"Lord Fine—"

"No, Sebastian. You don't owe me penance for anything that happened under blood magic, and you don't get to say lovely things to me over chips and then expect me to tolerate this slander." Lord Fine wrapped his hand fully around Sebastian's wrist, over the tattoo. "This is not your fault. You suffered a terrible torture, and you need to give yourself time."

Sebastian bit his lip. "But I should be past this already. I literally have the magic to weaken other paranormals' magic. I should be able to break this magic's hold on me."

"Wouldn't it be nice if our minds always behaved exactly how we wanted them to?" Lord Fine said dryly.

Sebastian huffed. He rolled his eyes, but that had put a small, grudging smile on his lips.

"Now, to be clear, my mind does, in fact, behave exactly as I wish," said Lord Fine. "But that's one of the benefits of being a remorseless and unchanging prick." His thumb skimmed Sebastian's inner wrist, light as butterfly wings. "Miss Robbins said the men who did this to you have been dealt with, is that right?"

Sebastian nodded.

"Probably too good a fate, whatever it was." Lord Fine's voice gruff. "You lot should have let me have a go at them."

His warm hand was still wrapped around Sebastian's wrist. "I can't even face my own memories," Sebastian blurted. "How does my past not send you running?"

"Because nothing about you could scare me." Lord Fine released Sebastian's arm with what almost seemed like reluctance, if that wouldn't have been odd. "Come on, let's get back to the car before I decide you're too broody to drive."

"That's not a thing."

"I'll make it a thing."

When they'd made it back to the manor, Sebastian set about building a new fire in the fireplace, next to the

snarling head of the tiger rug that had belonged to Lord
Fine's father. As a child, Sebastian had wished he could
have a lion or a tiger as a pet. What kind of man would
shoot one?

But then, based on Lord Fine's words in the garden
that morning, his father sounded like he'd been a hard
man. Lord Fine seemed to think he was the same.

Sebastian lit a match and held it to the tinder. *He*
didn't think that about Lord Fine. Sebastian wouldn't
have called him soft—he wasn't suicidal—but he wasn't
going to listen to anyone claiming Lord Fine was cold
or callous, not even Lord Fine himself. Sebastian *liked*
him, and not just because he was handsome. His gruff,
straightforward manner was refreshing, and he had the
courage to stare down both their pasts while Sebastian still flinched from his own memories. He hadn't
expected Lord Fine to be so comforting to be around.

His gaze stole to the tattoo on his wrist, where he
could have sworn he still felt the ghost of Lord Fine's
touch.

Lord Fine could see the lion.

Sebastian hadn't expected that either.

He straightened up from the floor just in time to see
Lord Fine setting a bottle and two glasses on the table
between the burgundy high-backed chairs.

"Are we having company?" Sebastian asked curiously.

"Don't be silly." Lord Fine tapped the bottle. "My
father had an excellent collection of whiskey." He gestured at the glasses. "You're my guest, after a fashion.
Join me."

Sebastian's eyebrows went up. "You did hear me at
the pub, when I told you I lose control of my magic if
I drink, yes?"

"Absolutely," Lord Fine said. "Your magic doesn't hurt. Believe me, I'm well aware of that by now. If you want to abstain for yourself, I respect that and I won't push. But don't abstain for me, because I assure you, I'm not worried."

Sebastian let out a surprised huff. "Mira, loco, you spent all day getting knocked down by my magic, and if you get me drunk, I might do it again."

"Sounds like a perfect chaser to me."

Was Sebastian actually considering this? Could he even remember the last time he had shared a table and a relaxing moment with someone he liked? "I thought we came back because you had business."

"Good whiskey is business." Lord Fine tapped the bottle again. "What's wrong? Afraid to show me you're a lightweight?"

If you have a drink, you might actually sleep. You might get through tonight without waking Lord Fine again. Because if you wake, and he's there in the same bed, and your body is still out of your control and moves for him the way it wants...

Sebastian worried his lower lip between his teeth. "I've only ever done it around other paranormals, where we wanted my magic to weaken theirs anyway. I've never had a drink around someone without magic."

Lord Fine popped the cork out of the whiskey bottle. "Then I'd say it's high time one of us poured you one."

Chapter Eleven

Wesley swirled the second shot of whiskey in his glass. They'd put a kerosene lamp on the table. A deck of cards was between them, but they hadn't played, alongside a box of cigars that Wesley hadn't smoked.

He'd shed his jacket, while Sebastian had undone his collar, his tie now hanging loose around his neck. Sebastian still wore the waistcoat that hugged his torso, paired now with rolled-up sleeves that revealed the lion tattoo and the taut muscles of his forearms. His skin had a golden hue in the firelight, the beginnings of shadow on his jaw as he tipped back the rest of his second shot of whiskey.

Wesley wanted to reach across the table and yank him into a kiss.

He swirled the whiskey again instead.

A bit of flirting was one thing, kissing Sebastian quite another. Wesley would eat his hat before he'd believe that Sebastian would react with violence, or call the papers or police the way some men might. But better to be cautious and give them both an easy path to walk away.

Wesley sat the glass down, undrunk. "How's your magical control?"

Sebastian looked like he was concentrating for a long

moment. "Precarious," he finally admitted. "If you want to remain upright, I would avoid surprising me."

Wesley's lips quirked up. "So you have magic where I have an aura. Do you have anything else that's different than the rest of us?"

"Like what?"

"I don't know. Tentacles?"

Sebastian snorted. He was only two shots in, but his eyes already shone in the warm light of the kerosene lamp. "And where would I be hiding these tentacles?"

"I'm sure I don't know that either. Is there a girlfriend or Mrs. de Leon somewhere who can tell me?" Wesley didn't think so—Sebastian had seemed so surprised that Wesley's touch had brought him out of his blood terrors that it seemed unlikely he'd been with anyone else in a long time.

Sure enough, Sebastian gave him a look that said *please*. "You must have guessed by now that there's not."

"I've learned it's still good to check." Wesley leaned back in the high-backed chair. He was just beginning to feel the whiskey himself, his blood mellow, his skin tingling. Or perhaps his nerves were simply hyperaware of the man across the table, because Wesley had been untouched for a long time too. "But I'd wager you're still popular with women."

Sebastian shrugged, eyes downcast in an obnoxiously modest way that Wesley suspected meant *I don't want to brag, but of course I am, I'm popular with everyone because I'm ridiculously fucking sexy.* Or possibly Wesley was projecting his own thoughts.

"I like making women feel good." Sebastian sounded wistful. "Or I used to."

So he did like women. Perhaps Wesley had no chance and was only setting himself for rejection and misery.

Except people attracted to more than one gender did exist. And Sebastian *had* been flirty today, had come to Wesley's defense so passionately at the pub. And the way he looked at Wesley, with warm eyes and smiles; the way he'd said Wesley made him *remember how to be free.*

Ugh, Wesley knew better than to do anything so foolish as hope, but Sebastian toppled his heart's defenses as surely as his magic capsized Wesley's knees.

He traced his finger along the rim of his glass. "Your magic comes useful in bed, then?"

Sebastian scoffed. "Who would want their partner to flatten them with a thought?"

"Oh, you can't be that innocent," said Wesley. "There are people who would not only want it, they would pay through the nose for it. Pair it with a flogger and men would throw their fortunes at you."

Sebastian huffed a laugh. "You're teasing me."

He had a small grin, his eyes still soft and shiny, and he didn't seem at all offended by the implication men would want to sleep with him. Wesley reached for the bottle. "Nonsense, I never tease."

Sebastian propped his hand in his chin. "Rubbish."

"Are you imitating me?" Wesley said, delighted. "With that truly dreadful English accent? That's very cute."

"See?" said Sebastian. "More teasing."

"You think so?" Wesley pulled Sebastian's empty glass toward himself. "I've told you that you're handsome half a dozen times today. Why would I be *teasing* when I call you cute?

Sebastian stilled. The slight shift in the air between

them was a near-tangible thing as his gaze flitted over Wesley.

"To be clear, I don't object to teasing in all circumstances," Wesley went on, as he refilled Sebastian's glass for him. "There's something to be said for taking your time, drawing things out, reducing another person to helpless begging."

Sebastian tilted his head. "Are we still talking about words?"

"Why wouldn't we be?"

"Because this also sounds like something men would pay for."

Wesley's lips quirked up. "Paired with handcuffs, maybe," he said, pushing the glass toward Sebastian's hand.

Sebastian reached for it, and their fingers brushed, sending Wesley's pulse up a beat. "I have never asked why you happened to have a convenient pair of handcuffs in your bedroom."

"Because they come in very useful. Clearly." Were they flirting now? Wesley certainly was, and he wanted to do it forever, as much as he wanted to reach across the table, grab Sebastian by the collar and kiss him senseless. "Of course, with your magic, you wouldn't need to bother with anything as mundane as handcuffs. That's why you'd be the one in demand, though I assume you're plenty in demand without the magic."

Sebastian's tenor was always soft, and now it was like velvet. "Are we still talking about men?"

Wesley's heart rate spiked yet again. "Would you like to be?"

Sebastian took a sip of whiskey and set the glass down. His gaze dropped to Wesley's shoulders, his arms beneath his shirtsleeves. "What I like very much is that you say what you're thinking. You are—what's the idiom—refreshing, the breath of fresh air. Why don't you tell me what you're thinking now, Lord Fine?"

Wesley's title sounded so good in that accent. How much better would his name sound? He brought his own glass to his lips, judging the lip caught between Sebastian's teeth, the flush to his face. Then he took the shot. "I'm wondering if you've ever kissed a man."

Sebastian's gaze dropped to his half-drunk whiskey, and he was quiet for a long moment.

"No," he finally said.

Wesley's heart sank, so much disappointment he felt it all the way to his stomach, a grief that shocked him in its profoundness, as if he'd just lost something far more than a single night.

That was it then. It didn't matter how much Wesley wanted him; Sebastian would never be his.

Wesley quickly tossed back his entire whiskey with an unsteady hand, needing the kick more than he cared about appreciating the taste.

"But I've jerked one off."

Wesley choked. Twenty-year-old whiskey seared his throat and shot like burning fire up into his nose. He coughed so hard he dropped his glass, which sloshed the last bit of liquid onto his lap as he bent over the table and tried to draw a breath.

"Lord Fine!" Sebastian had shot to his feet. "Are you—oh no."

Oh no?

But Wesley's body had turned to water. His liquid limbs abruptly couldn't hold him and he tumbled from the chair. His face smacked the cottage's stone floor a moment later.

"Ouch," he muttered, as his body crumpled into a useless puddle.

"Lord Fine!"

Sebastian was saying his name again, sounding distressed. Wesley squinted from where his head rested sideways on the floor, and saw Sebastian crawling toward him.

"I am so sorry." Sebastian flopped down on his side on the floor next to Wesley, looking with tipsy earnestness into his eyes. "Are you all right?"

Wesley reeked of well-aged whiskey, his nose and throat still burning, his head probably bruised, his limbs useless as a fish on land.

He started to laugh.

"Oh no, I broke you," Sebastian said miserably.

"No, duck, I'm fine," Wesley promised, trying to raise a hand to wave that concern away and giving up when nothing moved. "I'm marvelous, actually. My limbs are all heavy and tingly to match my head—I haven't been this relaxed in an age."

Sebastian was still looking into his eyes, his handsome face barely inches away. "I can't rein the magic in."

"It's all right," Wesley promised again.

Sebastian sighed, letting his head drop. It landed on Wesley's outstretched arm, and Sebastian didn't move away. He didn't seem to have registered that he was using Wesley's arm as a pillow, but it was nice. "I shouldn't have said that."

"You most certainly should have." Wesley had to force his mouth and tongue to form words, but he wasn't letting this go. "And I'm going to need an explanation."

"Well, controlling magic is—um—I suppose it's like having the reins of wild horses, and when you drink, the reins are hard to hold—"

"Not an explanation for *that* part."

Oh, Sebastian's mouth formed.

Wesley tried to lift his head, and gave up. Sebastian was wonderfully close anyway. "Tell me about the man you didn't kiss."

Sebastian bit his lip. "Another soldier, from Georgia," he said, barely a whisper. "We shared a tent. But I did want to kiss Jasper. I tried to, when our hands were on each other."

"What happened?" Wesley said, also whispering.

Sebastian looked like the moment hurt to remember. "He said, 'What the fuck, de Leon, you're not a fucking fairy, are you? I thought you liked women!'"

Wesley's chest clenched.

"And I said *I do,*" said Sebastian, "because I *do.* And then he sucked my cock."

Wesley took a sharp breath through his nose.

"Jasper wanted his mouth on my dick but not my lips on his, and I didn't understand." Sebastian swallowed. "I still don't."

Anger simmered under Wesley's heavy limbs. He'd met more than one Jasper in his day, some of them in difficult positions and deserving of pity, and some of them the worst kind of hypocrites.

"There was another soldier, after Jasper, and a man in Germany once, but I'd learned better than to try to kiss them," Sebastian said, echoes of old wounds in his voice. "And after the war, there were women again, and wanting men hadn't made me stop wanting women. But I've never kissed a man."

Try kissing me, I'll show you what those other men didn't. Wesley opened his mouth.

"Why did your father shoot all these animals?" Sebastian suddenly said. "That poor fox, and the tiger!

The deer, perhaps you needed him for food, but you did not eat the fox or tiger. Why not enjoy them alive?"

Wesley would have beaten his head against the floor, if he could have moved. "Are you drunk enough to babble? After *two* whiskies?"

"I'm not drunk." Sebastian closed his eyes. "And I'm not babbling, I'm *resting* after two whiskies."

Wesley snorted. "Are you." He watched Sebastian for a moment, the way the firelight danced on his profile. "You know, tigers are beasts of prey, not giant house cats. I'm not advocating for safari hunts, you understand, but I did have a valet get eaten by a tiger once." He paused. "Unless—that wasn't more of this *magic* business, was it?"

Sebastian didn't answer. His head had grown heavier on Wesley's arm. "You had best be resting, not falling asleep on me, because your magic is very much awake." Wesley tried to lift his head, but his neck muscles refused. "Sebastian, you paranormal lightweight, do you hear me? *Sebastian.*"

Sebastian took a slow breath and didn't answer.

"You have completely upended my life, you know," he told Sebastian, appalled when it came out almost *fond.* The magic had to wear off at some point, and in the meantime, the floor was hard but the fire was warm. His body was mellow from whiskey and magic, and Sebastian's head was a pleasant weight on his arm.

It's not cuddling when you're magically pinned to the floor, Wesley told himself. He closed his eyes and let himself enjoy the glow.

Sebastian woke with a start, his head fuzzy, confused. He was in a bed, a gold canopy over his head, but the room was dim, and he didn't know where he was—

A warm hand was suddenly on his shoulder, a now-familiar voice pitched low and soft. "Sebastian?"

Lord Fine.

Sebastian's breath left him in a rush. He was in Yorkshire, on the giant bed in Lord Fine's manor. The fire was still crackling, light coming from the kerosene lamp on the table by the settee and chairs. Lord Fine was leaning over him, one knee on the bed, once again dressed in the striped silk pajamas, this time with a pair of glasses balanced on his nose.

"Do you ever sleep?"

Lord Fine's question was rueful, closer to gentle than mean. Sebastian let his head fall back against the pillow and the welcome sight of Lord Fine fill his vision.

"Not really," he admitted, his pulse still uncomfortably high and his chest too tight.

"What was I rescuing you from that time?" Lord Fine hadn't let go of his shoulder. "Blood terrors? Run-of-the-mill nightmares? Prisoner in someone else's dreams—is that a thing, in your paranormal world? Nothing would surprise me anymore."

Sebastian snorted. "Nothing so exciting. I drank too much and got confused." And his mind had too many dark places to revisit when he got confused.

He scrubbed a hand over his face and found himself blurting, too honestly, "I'm sorry you keep having to save me. I'm sorry we didn't meet when I was still whole, before I was shattered into what I am now."

But Lord Fine shook his head. "Maybe we're a pair of proper scoundrels, you and I," he said quietly. "But when I look at you, I don't see fractures. I see battle scars. And they don't scare me off."

Sebastian swallowed. Lord Fine was still above him, steady and strong, and Sebastian had to ball his hands into fists before he pulled him down on top of him. For comfort, to kiss him—any of it, all of it.

He forced himself to sit up instead. Lord Fine's hand slid down as he moved, but he didn't pull it away, resting it now on Sebastian's bicep. He wore the pajamas but Sebastian appeared to be still fully dressed, only his shoes taken off. "I don't remember going to bed."

"Because I put you here," said Lord Fine. "You passed out on the floor after two and a half whiskies, which apparently is also enough to make you forget you're in Yorkshire. There are lightweights, duck, and there's *you*."

Sebastian winced. Good to know he could still find new humiliations, just in case Lord Fine didn't already find him childish enough. He cast for a topic change and blurted, "I like your glasses."

Wait, no, how was it better to awkwardly stumble through compliments?

But Lord Fine touched the frames. "A new necessity. Very few people have seen them; I usually wear a monocle." He pulled the glasses off his face with his free hand and set them on the nightstand. "I was reading in the armchair. It seemed presumptuous to join you."

Sebastian blew out a breath. "I did not mean to presume—"

"You're adorable, thinking I could mean your presumptions and my maidenly virtue," Lord Fine said dryly. "No, it seemed presumptuous on *my* part, to get you drunk and then undress you and join you in bed. I am supposed to be a gentleman, you know."

Lord Fine's pajama shirt was fastened with frog clasps, the silk clinging to his shoulders and arms and a sliver of his chest visible below the collar. His eyes were a deeper blue than usual, reflecting the navy between the pajama's stripes. He was still so close, his hand still on Sebastian's arm, and the moment felt like it was veering in a direction Sebastian might have gone in a good dream.

He flexed his fingers and tightened his fists to keep his hands at his own sides. "I thought we were sharing the bed like soldiers."

"Oh, *were* we?" There was a new note in Lord Fine's voice. "Because you told me interesting stories about you and other soldiers."

Oh *no*.

Sebastian's face flushed hot. "I didn't."

"You did." Lord Fine suddenly shifted, one knee pressing between Sebastian's legs. He leaned in close, and in a low voice that resonated in Sebastian's bones, he said, "But unlike those fools, I know what I want with you."

Before Sebastian could find words, Lord Fine's hand slid over his jaw to tangle his fingers into the short hairs on the back of his head.

"That means I'm going to kiss you now."

Then Lord Fine's lips were on his.

Sebastian's arms sprang up like they'd been freed from chains, and wrapped around Lord Fine's neck. The headboard dug into Sebastian's back, trapped as he was between it and Lord Fine, but he ignored it to pull him deeper into the kiss. Lord Fine's lips became more demanding, his hand tightening in Sebastian's hair as his other hand braced on the headboard.

Then Lord Fine tipped them over, so that Sebastian fell to the bed with Lord Fine's hand still behind his head. Desire spiked through him at the confident manhandling, and he reached back up, wanting Lord Fine's body on top of his.

"Lord Fine—"

"You will damn well call me Wesley when you're kissing me." Lord Fine—*Wesley*—shifted over him, his leg sliding higher between Sebastian's.

"Wesley," Sebastian breathed, his hands cupping the sharp lines of Wesley's jaw, and the other man shivered. "Come here."

Wesley dropped fully onto Sebastian, a little bigger, a little heavier, the perfect weight as he pressed their lips together again. His tongue slipped into Sebastian's mouth, and Sebastian tilted his head back to get more of his kiss, of the scratch of stubble.

He ran his hands down the silk pajama shirt, then slid them up under the tails, finding the warm skin of his back.

"Take this off," he said against Wesley's mouth.

"That would mean I'd have to stop kissing you." Wesley's thigh slid yet another inch higher, brushing Sebastian's cock, and he caught Sebastian's quiet noise with another kiss. "So no."

Sebastian's fingers tightened on his back. "Wesley—"

"But I do like my name in your intoxicating voice."

His skin was so warm under Sebastian's hands. He tugged at Wesley's shirt. *"Off."*

"Still kissing you." Wesley shifted on top of him to kiss his neck, right under his jaw. "Honestly, who do you think I am?" he said, his breath raising more goose bumps on Sebastian's skin. "Some callow nineteen-year-old afraid of your lips? Some fumbling soldier in a tent, rushing to get off before my commanding officer overhears?"

His lips brushed Sebastian's jugular vein. "Maybe those are the men you've had before. But I was the com-

manding officer, and now I'm the lord of this manor. I
will take all the time I want with you."

Oh. That was—oh. "Okay," Sebastian said weakly,
as his hands ran along the ridges of Wesley's spine.

Wesley stretched back up to his mouth and Sebastian surrendered to being kissed, to letting Wesley's lips
soothe old wounds and write over them with pleasure.

They kissed until Sebastian was dizzy, until his lips
tingled and his cock ached. Their legs were hopelessly
tangled together, and Sebastian thought he might go
mad from the pressure of their hard cocks against each
other. He arched up, deliberately moved their hips together, and Wesley sucked in a breath. Sebastian's lips
turned up; of course Wesley wasn't as unaffected as he
pretended to be.

There are people who would want your magic in bed,
Wesley had said, over whiskey. Sebastian hesitated, and
then he pushed up, putting a tiny touch of magic into it,
just enough to momentarily stagger the bigger Wesley
and let Sebastian flip him.

Wesley's back hit the mattress and an even sharper
breath escaped him. His eyes were wide as Sebastian
straddled his hips, which were still covered in the slip-
pery silk of his pajamas.

Sebastian tentatively put his hands on Wesley's chest.
"Was that—"

"Bloody hell." Wesley licked his lips, which had gone
darker pink from the kiss. "More of that, I would beg
for it."

Wesley, begging. Sebastian's fingers tightened in
Wesley's shirt. "Would begging finally get your clothes
off so I can touch you?"

"Christ." Wesley sat up, so Sebastian was almost in

his lap, and their lips were drawn back together like magnets as they worked at each other's clothes.

Wesley got Sebastian's outer shirt off first, and Sebastian was so intent on undoing the frog clasps of Wesley's pajamas that he startled when hands slid up his biceps. "This looks so good on you."

Sebastian shrugged, the movement a little awkward because of Wesley's hands, which were still exploring where the T-shirt clung to his upper arms, shoulders, and chest. "It's just a shirt."

And Sebastian was suddenly pushed down to his back again.

"I thought I was going to go mad last night, the way you look in this thing. I wanted to take you right on the settee." Wesley rucked the fabric up, baring Sebastian's stomach. "Now I can't decide if I want it on or off."

Sebastian tried to say something, but Wesley bent and kissed the newly revealed skin, and all that came out was a strangled groan.

"Oh, but I certainly want more of that sound." Wesley slid the waistband of Sebastian's trousers down over his hips and down his legs, tossing them somewhere off the bed.

Sebastian was breathing hard, suddenly aware he was mostly naked and Wesley was still mostly clothed. And the easy, confident way Wesley handled him—Sebastian was also suddenly abruptly aware of the contrast in how Wesley seemed to know exactly what he was doing and Sebastian…didn't.

Sebastian propped himself half-up on his elbows. "What, um. What exactly did I tell you about my encounters with men?"

Wesley skimmed his hands up Sebastian's legs, stopping a distracting distance above his knees. "If you're trying to figure out how much I know so you can avoid telling me you're a near-virgin with men, it's too late."

"There've *been* men," Sebastian protested. "I just haven't—you know."

"I do know." Wesley's voice was lower, rougher. "And I know they didn't treat you right, but you're in my arms now."

Sebastian swallowed, a pulse of desire and something even wilder running through him.

"I would be lying if I said I'm not dying to fuck you." Wesley crawled back up Sebastian's body, skimming his fingers up Sebastian's thigh, hip, stomach, and ribs as he shifted. "But not tonight. I don't have anything to ease the way."

"I don't care—"

"I do." Wesley kissed him once, on the mouth. "Oh, I know you'd let me try with spit. You'd grit your teeth against the pain, and lie back and think of England—or Spain, or Puerto Rico or America or maybe the fairy realm, I'll never be convinced you're not fae—but that's not how it's going to happen."

"But I want you, Wesley," Sebastian whispered.

Wesley swallowed audibly. "And there's a sentence I'm going to remember for the rest of my life."

He kissed Sebastian again, toppling him off his elbow and back to his back on the bed.

"Another time," he said firmly, like it was settled and he would brook no more arguments. He lay half on top of Sebastian, pinning him. "Think of it as my way of guaranteeing I get to have you twice."

And before Sebastian could argue, Wesley shoved his shorts down and his hand closed around his cock.

Sebastian's eyes rolled back in his head. "De verdad eres el brujo," he said, the words coming in Spanish which was probably for the best, if he was going to say sappy things like—

"Did you just say I'm the witch again? Because I'm so very good at this?" Wesley's face was close enough his breath tickled Sebastian's ear, and he stroked as he talked, wringing a groan from Sebastian's throat. "How flattering."

Sebastian's hands ran down Wesley's back, over his sides, feeling the firm lines of the body underneath the silky long-sleeved pajamas. He had it half-open and he fumbled to work it off Wesley's shoulders, but his fingers were clumsy as pleasure thrummed through him.

"You don't have to sound so smug," he said, but his voice hitched even as he finally got the shirt off, revealing the warm skin he was craving.

"Oh, but I do," Wesley said roughly. "And if you could see yourself right now, the way you look in my bed—you'd understand why I'm going to be insufferable for days. Weeks. To be honest, years from now I will still be bragging."

Sebastian craned his head up to kiss Wesley again. He had once prided himself on kisses that made knees weak, but now, his lips felt as unskilled as his fingers, his breath coming in pants as Wesley once again took control of the kiss.

"What if I kept you here forever?" Wesley whispered, against his lips. "Jerked you off, watched you squirm under me?"

Sebastian wasn't going to last forever. When was the last time someone had touched him like this? Had anyone *ever* touched him quite like this, like they had all the time in the world for him?

Wesley was acting unaffected, but he was rock-hard under the silk pajama pants, his cock pressed tight against Sebastian's hip. Sebastian ran his hands over Wesley's bare chest and back, over his ass, whatever he could reach. As Wesley's tongue invaded his mouth again, Sebastian crammed a hand between their bodies and under the waistband of the pajama pants.

Wesley made a gratifying sound when Sebastian wrapped a hand around his cock. "You sure you remember what to do with that?" he said, his snark a little breathless.

Sebastian tightened his grip, stroked him hard with a twist, and Wesley groaned.

They fell into a rhythm, and it was exactly like Sebastian had done it before, except it was nothing like anything Sebastian had ever done. Wesley stayed on top of him, kept kissing him even as their motions grew jerkier, more desperate. He muttered soft words against Sebastian's mouth between kisses, *you're gorgeous, you feel like heaven, I want to suck your cock but I can't stop kissing you, I'm going to make you come apart,* hazy and electric and overwhelming.

When Sebastian finally came, it lit his entire body. His hand stuttered on Wesley, his movements faltering as pleasure swept him. Wesley kissed him through it, skilled lips on his clumsy mouth, strong hand not stopping or slowing until Sebastian was boneless in his arms.

As Sebastian's body thrummed with aftershocks, he took deep breaths, and looked up into Wesley's handsome face.

When your magic likes someone, the rest of you falls like dominoes.

Isabel's words came back to him, a phrase his brother Mateo often said. It was superstition, not prophecy.

But everything in him liked Wesley.

Wesley was still hard in his hand, and he was look-ing at Sebastian a little uncertainly.

Sebastian ran his hand up Wesley's shaft, slow and deliberate, and Wesley made a desperate noise in the back of his throat.

Not at all as unaffected as he pretended. Sebastian stroked him again. "Your turn to lie back and think of London."

"It's 'think of *England*.'"

Sebastian kissed him once, then pushed him over, using more magic this time. Wesley made that desper-ate, needy noise again as his back hit the mattress, and he looked up at Sebastian with flushed skin and eyes gone deeply blue.

Sebastian grabbed the waistband of the pajama pants that had been in his way. "What if I make you stop thinking?"

Wesley didn't remember falling asleep. But here he was, waking up, with Sebastian curled behind him so their backs were pressed together.

Wesley didn't sleep with men he fucked.

Except.

Except he'd already shared the bed with Sebastian; it was a necessity, after all, because even Wesley's stone heart wasn't going to abandon Sebastian to face his blood terrors alone. Besides, they were just lying next to each other. It wasn't as if they were cuddling.

Even if, for all his perpetual chill, Sebastian was warm against him, steady breaths as calming as music.

Sebastian suddenly rolled over, pressing close to sling his arm over Wesley's ribs. He rested his cheek against Wesley's bare skin, right at the spot where his shoulder blade met the nape of his neck, and sighed contentedly.

Wesley's eyes widened. "What are you doing?" he said, even though it was obvious.

An indistinguishable mumble, blended Spanish and English, came against his skin.

Charming bastard.

Wesley could, of course, simply stand up. Sebastian wasn't using his magic right now, and Wesley was bigger. He was hardly trapped.

He should extract himself and get on with the morning like a sensible fellow.

The new position had put Sebastian's wrist and the hidden lion tattoo near Wesley's face. He eyed the swirls of ink for a long moment, as Sebastian's soft hair tickled his shoulder blade and his arm stayed pleasantly heavy over Wesley's ribs.

And then instead of standing up, he reached for the tattooed wrist.

Sebastian made another soft noise, but he didn't pull away as Wesley's hand touched his skin. The tattoo drew attention to Sebastian's exceptional arms, to muscles that were sleek but defined enough that even small movements showed them off. Wesley had always liked tattoos, from the ones he'd seen on other aristocrats to the glimpses he'd caught on soldiers. He'd never before thought of getting one himself, but Sebastian's lion made him want one.

He traced the rampant lion's outline. It really was an exceptional work of art, regal and fierce. Sebastian had seemed surprised that Wesley had seen it, and to be fair, it *was* well hidden, but it was right here, clear as day once one had spotted it.

"Wesley?"

Sebastian's voice was quiet and tentative. And too late, Wesley realized Sebastian was no longer heavy against him, and the steady rhythm of his breaths had gone quiet. He was awake, and Wesley had been caught enjoying the moment, tracing Sebastian's tattoo like a sap.

Are you actually cuddling me? Please tell me you're not one of those pathetic, needy sots I'll have to cosset like a pet.

The words were on the tip of his tongue. It was the sort of thing Wesley would have said to another lover, if they'd ever tried affection like this—although of course, they wouldn't have, either because Wesley would have already thrown them out to sleep in the guest room, or because they were like Wesley in the first place, full of contempt for any softness.

Stop simpering over me, you sentimental prick. I'm here to fuck you, not indulge you. Get off.

The words suggested themselves to Wesley, scorn that would push Sebastian away—even when every inch of Wesley's skin was delighting in the feel of Sebastian close against him. When the stone in his chest felt a little less heavy with the weight of Sebastian's arm around him. When the last thing he actually wanted to do was hurt Sebastian.

Wesley's gaze drifted from the ink of the tattoo to the burn scars.

Wesley had always seen himself as the exception to the simpering masses. People would get angry over something he said, but that was because the world was full of weak, spineless prats too sensitive to handle the harsh realities that only Wesley was willing to voice aloud.

Except did that actually make him exceptional? Or

was he just making excuses for himself while being rude and cruel, when nothing could be more common than that?

Sebastian, who had survived years of paranormal torture that Wesley's brain still couldn't truly comprehend, and yet still had affection to give to cats and dogs and even a curmudgeon like Wesley—

Maybe that was special.

"Lord Fine?"

Sebastian's voice was even more tentative. The arm around Wesley's waist had tensed, because Sebastian had also been caught cuddling, and Wesley wouldn't be the first man to treat his affection with scorn.

Wesley had warned Sebastian not to look at him through rose-colored glasses. He'd told Sebastian he didn't change. He was a cold man who said predictably cruel things, and no one would be surprised when Wesley froze the warmth between them and became nothing more than one more scar Sebastian had to carry.

His fingers tightened on Sebastian's wrist.

And then he brought the tattooed skin to his lips, and kissed it. "Only *Wesley* now. For you."

Sebastian made a noise of surprise, *good* surprise, as Wesley rolled over, still under Sebastian's arm, and kissed him on the mouth.

"Good morning," he said quietly, sliding his own arm around Sebastian's waist to pull their bodies together, a heaven of skin against skin under the blankets.

Sebastian's eyes were bright, their beautiful brown lit like burnished gold in the silver Yorkshire morning. The waves in his hair were wilder, tousled from sleep and Wesley's greedy hands. His smile was almost shy, but he looked happy, like it was a wonderful thing to wake up to Wesley. "Buenos días."

Maybe *you reap what you sow* wasn't always an omen of misery. Maybe sometimes, if you sowed soft things, like joy and affection, that's what you reaped.

Wesley cupped Sebastian's stubbled jaw. "Do me a favor?"

"Of course," Sebastian said, sweet and sleepy as he let Wesley trace a thumb over his lower lip.

Wesley swallowed. "I always ruin everything," he whispered. "But I don't want to snuff this spark between us before it's even had a chance to burn. So I'm begging you to put your cock in my mouth so that I can't talk."

Sebastian half laughed in surprise, but with a gentle sweetness to it, like he understood. "You're so hard on yourself." He caught Wesley's thumb between his teeth in a soft bite, then let it go. "Your battle scars don't scare me either. Come here."

Then Sebastian pulled him impossibly closer and kissed him, and Wesley lost himself in him.

Chapter Twelve

Sebastian drove the Bentley to the hotel restaurant by the York railway station where they found Jade and Zhang. The four of them sat in the corner by the windows, at a round table with a white tablecloth and china place settings. Jade and Zhang pulled their chairs close together with the familiarity of long-standing lovers, while Sebastian was excruciatingly aware of the inches he and Wesley were carefully keeping between them.

But then the waiter appeared, and Wesley reached over and tapped Sebastian's menu. "They have coffee."

Jade glanced between them curiously. Maybe Wesley was already more familiar with him than Sebastian had realized.

Their orders taken, the waiter disappeared, and across the table, Zhang's astral projection did as well. "I'm waiting for another cable," he said, with his physical body. "Just checking the front desk."

"Via the astral plane?" Wesley asked. "That is really remarkable."

"He is a remarkable man," Jade agreed. She folded her hands on the table. "Sebastian, you said you came across traces of magic in the alley that felt like *you*."

Sebastian nodded, but Wesley frowned and said, "There's no way Blanshard could actually have the same magic as Sebastian, could he? I thought the hypothesis was that he has the same vampire magic as a paranormal some ancient de Leon fought. Which sounds absolutely mad, yes, but *vampire* doesn't sound like Sebastian."

He leaned forward. "I've been on the receiving end of Sebastian's magic more than half a dozen times by now. It hits like a tidal wave. Even if you made his magic more powerful, it's not going to *shrivel* anyone's heart. Forgive me for being unbearably pedantic, but that sounds like bad magic. Sebastian's magic is good."

"I'm not sure anyone would agree with you," Sebastian said, but that had made him smile.

"*I'm* inclined to agree," said Jade, her gaze darting between them again. "But it means we need another explanation for why Sebastian felt a mirror of his magic in that alley. And we still don't have a way to stop Blanshard."

They fell silent as two waiters approached, balancing plates and cups on trays, and waited as the food was served.

When they were relatively alone again, Wesley turned to Sebastian. "You really have no idea how your ancestral aunt stopped that vampire paranormal in your family's story?"

Sebastian made a face. "It's a story, a legend, with a million different endings. Everyone agrees the vampire went on a killing spree in a Spanish village, eating the auras of several people at once. My father says tía Casilda then gave her life to bind the vampire's magic. My uncle says she lived but the binding cost her own magic, but he didn't know what that magic was. And my great-grandmother used to say Casilda fed the vampire his own cojones and moved to Cuba to live out her days on the beach."

"Hmm." Wesley tilted his head. "And you don't know why she was written out of your family?"

Sebastian shook his head. "But I know what I can do, and if I can get close to Blanshard, I will try to stop him."

"That's very heroic," Wesley said dryly. "But I watched you pass out after you fought with Mercier. I'm not saying that as an insult," he added quickly. "You were a hell of a lot more effective against him than I was."

"And your point is taken," said Jade. "Sebastian, you said Mercier's magic was stronger but you didn't think it was due to a relic. If we think Blanshard could have stolen the brooch relic and be using its magic to enhance his, I don't think it's safe for you to try."

"But maybe I can," said Sebastian. "At least some of the stories say my great-aunt did stop the paranormal who was murdering the nonmagical by also draining their auras."

"But you don't know if it cost her magic, or her *life*," said Wesley.

"Blanshard has murdered at least four people," said Sebastian. "Wouldn't stopping him be worth any price?"

"No," Wesley said flatly. "I have no idea why you expect the rest of us to sit idly by and, I don't know, write sonnets or some other waste of time while you nobly sacrifice yourself to magic that could kill you."

"He's right, Sebastian. We need a better plan." Jade hesitated. "There's something you should know about that. It has to do with the cable Zhang is waiting for."

"The cable that just arrived." Zhang's eyelashes fluttered, and a moment later his astral projection abruptly returned to his body. Something in his expression put chills on Sebastian's skin. "After Lord Fine told us about the encounter in the alley, I couldn't stop thinking about the things Mercier said. *'I do, in fact, get away with this. No one comes when you scream.'*"

"Almost as if he believed he knew the future," Jade said quietly.

No.

"It would explain how there have been murders in busy city centers without witnesses," said Zhang. "Because they know in advance, they know exactly when they can strike. And it would explain why Mercier was shocked to see you, Sebastian, because no one, not even your brother, can see your future with magic."

Sebastian's ears were ringing.

"Seers are so rare, but you mentioned your brother is one, and was at the world's fair in Paris this summer," said Jade, "and we know Blanshard was there too."

"I cabled my mom in New York," said Zhang. "Your family's friends went to Oberlin to check on him—and he never came back this term."

"The waitress," Wesley suddenly said. "The one who thought she recognized you in York, near the scene of the murder. Does your brother look like you?"

"Oh God." Sebastian's heart plummeted. "We have to find him. He wouldn't be working with them willingly, he would never—"

"We don't think he's willing," Jade promised grimly.

"And we'll help you find him. He's a seer, Sebastian, they would never kill him. If they have him, he's certainly alive, and they'll keep him that way."

Sebastian clenched his jaw. Under the table and out of sight, Wesley's hand came to rest on his knee.

"I won't promise either of those gents is going to

stay alive if I meet them again," Wesley said dryly, his hand a strong, grounding weight. "They did try to kill me, and I'm afraid I'm not really a *turn the other cheek* kind of man. And I am doubly motivated to help if they may have kidnapped Sebastian's brother. Shall I draw out the floor plan of Blanshard's mansion?"

When Sebastian furrowed his brow, Wesley added, "Well, obviously we're going to search it today, aren't we, for evidence of your brother?"

Sebastian glanced at Jade and Zhang, who were nodding. Despite the anger and fear swirling in his gut, Sebastian felt a pulse of gratitude. He wasn't going to have to do this alone.

"If we head to the village closest to his manor, I can do some reconnaissance," said Zhang. "Lord Fine mentioned Blanshard had a whole room of artifacts; we have to assume he has safeguards in place."

"For all the good it will do him," Sebastian said gruffly. "The only thing I can't weaken is a relic, and no seer, Mateo or otherwise, can see me coming."

"You do make things interesting," Jade said. "Although Jianwei and I will be a bit hamstrung, if it comes to you using your magic."

"What about me?" Wesley said, looking at Sebastian. There was no trace of complaint in his voice, only genuine question. "If you use your magic—which you'll almost certainly have to—I'll be worse than hamstrung, I'll be a useless puddle on the floor. A *liability*. Would you have me wait in the car? I promise I'm not one of those hotheads who doesn't listen and will come rushing after you," he added wryly. "I use my damn brain."

"Let's get there first," said Jade. "We need to know what we're dealing with."

* * *

Sebastian sat in the backseat with Zhang as Wesley drove the Bentley from York to Malton, and then to the tiny village closest to Blanshard's mansion. The top was still down since Sebastian had driven to York that morning, and it was cold as the wind whipped across the car. The others spoke in quiet voices as Sebastian stared out at the soft browns and greens of the gently rolling landscape and tried not to lose his mind.

If Lord Blanshard had his little brother—

Sebastian couldn't think about it, or he'd lose all focus.

The country roads were in need of repair, and the trip took more than an hour. When they finally reached the village, Zhang opted to stay in the car, to be able to search in multiple places across the astral plane at once without drawing too many stares.

Jade pointed at the tiny pub across from the car. "We should see if we can get any gossip from the locals. Who's been at Blanshard Hall, that sort of thing."

"I'll come with you," Wesley said to her. "Your tattoo should be messing with anyone searching for us with magic, yes?"

Sebastian resisted wrapping a hand around his own wrist. Wesley had seen the lion. *Was* his magic still working as it should?

Jade started walking. Wesley lingered a moment next to Sebastian and said, in what was a very sensitive tone—by Wesley standards, at least—"We're going to find him."

Sebastian looked up into Wesley's now-familiar face. "I am grateful," he said quietly, "but the paranormal world is such a dangerous place, especially for a man without magic. It is such a risk to you to help."

"I had a brother too," Wesley said quietly. "Colin was an entitled, insufferable prat who made me look pleasant, and I'd still move the earth if I could have him back. Of course you have my help."

Jade and Wesley disappeared into the pub. Sebastian leaned against the car outside to wait, running his hands over his face. He had to keep calm. It wouldn't help anything if he panicked.

In what felt like an eternity, but what was surely only minutes later, Jade and Wesley returned.

"No one matching your description has been in the pub," Wesley said, "but Jack Mercier has, as recently as two weeks ago."

In the backseat of the convertible Bentley, Zhang's eyes were moving, like he was dreaming. "I can't get onto the grounds of the mansion itself," he said. "The grounds are warded against magic."

"Not for long," Sebastian muttered, through a clenched jaw.

They all climbed back in the car and started out of the village. "Sebastian can get us past any guardian magic, but do we have a plan for getting inside?" Jade asked.

"I say we simply knock," said Wesley, as he turned from one narrow road to the next. "I'm on the guest lists for the earl's parties—for everyone's parties, God help them—and I certainly have every right to show up at Blanshard's door and expect hospitality. His staff will let me in, and it will be easy enough to explain the rest of you. After all, Miss Robbins and Mr. Zhang are, in fact, successful American business owners."

"And what about me?" Sebastian said.

"You had best keep your head down and your hat pulled low," said Wesley. "If you look enough like your brother for the waitress to have been mistaken, the staff might see the resemblance as well. I'll try to be aggravating enough that their eyes stay on me, not you."

Which meant Wesley putting himself even more into the line of fire. Sebastian leaned forward. "I thought you were going to wait in the car, Lord Fine," he said quietly, using Wesley's title in front of Jade and Zhang. "You don't have magic."

"I don't," Wesley said, "but I have a revolver and a vendetta, so don't confuse me with someone helpless."

"I don't think you're helpless," Sebastian protested. "I just—"

"You're just so used to being alone you've forgotten what it's like to have allies." Wesley pulled the Bentley into a tight turn, and sped down the country road.

The daylight was just beginning to fade as Wesley pulled up to the iron gate guarding Blanshard Hall. The gates were closed, secured by a chain with a large and prominent padlock.

Wesley leaned out the window, but there were no staff in sight. He made a face. "Now what? I had assumed Blanshard would keep a gate guard like a civilized man."

"The magical barrier encircles the property's entire perimeter," said Zhang, from the backseat. "I can't cross on the astral plane."

Sebastian leaned forward, so his head rested on folded arms on the back of the front seat. "Tell me when you've braced yourself," he said quietly, just behind Wesley's left ear, sending shivers over the back of Wesley's neck.

Wesley put the parking brake on, just to be safe, and then nodded.

Sebastian's magic swept out from the car like a dam unleashed, with the strength Wesley remembered from the alley in London. He went instantly boneless in the driver's seat, his eyes closing on their own as magic rushed him.

Then abruptly, it stopped. Wesley straightened, opening his eyes and glancing into the backseat.

Sebastian's eyes were set forward. "Zhang, try to cross the barrier on the astral plane now."

Zhang's eyelashes began fluttering, like he was in a dreaming sleep. "Jesus, Sebastian, you obliterated the guardian ring."

"I'm angry," Sebastian said, in a quiet tone that reminded Wesley that for all his sweetness, he could be very dangerous when he chose to be.

Zhang's eyelashes were still moving. "Key is in the guardhouse," he said. "Hanging on the south wall, about five feet above the floor, second hook from the right. Just a little higher. Another inch to the right."

In the passenger seat next to Wesley, Jade's face was set with concentration. A moment later, a key ring with a single large key came floating their way. The key floated out through the bars of the gate and inserted itself into the padlock.

"Oh," Wesley said weakly as the lock opened and the chain fell to the ground. "I suppose this is one way to solve our problem."

The gate swung itself open for the Bentley. Wesley drove them along the graceful drive for a quarter mile before the trees cleared and the manor loomed in front of him. The sprawling, gothic structure was exactly as he remembered from three years prior, the endless row of arched windows, the peaked roof above the wide front stairs and the dome with the turret on top.

As Wesley pulled the car between the front door and the giant fountain, a white man in a butler's long tails and gloves was hurrying toward them, old-fashioned even by Wesley's curmudgeonly standards.

He leaned over the doorframe as the man approached.

"Excuse me," the butler started, "but how did you get in? And who are—"

"The Viscount Fine," Wesley interrupted, ignoring his first question. "Where the hell is Blanshard? I need to speak to him at once."

The butler wrung his hands. "I'm sorry, sir, but the earl is in London."

"What?" Wesley snapped, like he was surprised. "When I've come all this way? How outrageous."

"My lord—"

"This entire appointment is his fault," Wesley went on, which was perfectly true, "and now you're telling me he doesn't intend to show? I came up from London myself for this. Am I to sit in his driveway with my American associates until he can be bothered to take a train?"

The butler winced. "I'm sure this is a misunderstanding," he said, a little desperately. "Please come in and enjoy the earl's hospitality while I sort everything out."

He opened Wesley's door as a footman came hurrying over to get Jade's door for her, and then the backseat. Wesley was relieved to see Sebastian behaving like a man with some sense, not calling attention to himself and his likely resemblance to his brother with his head ducked and his cap pulled low.

Their group of four was escorted into the foyer and then into a chilly parlor with no fire in the grate. "Apologies, we'll see to it," the butler promised, looking very harried.

"This is highly irregular," Wesley said, in his curtest tone. "Take me to the phone. I'm going to call the earl myself."

"I'll join you," Zhang said, which Wesley now knew probably meant he'd get Zhang's body while his astral projection gallivanted off with the paranormals.

"We'll wait here," Jade said, her sweet voice completely at odds with Wesley's sharp tones. "We've surprised you terribly today. If the earl is out, perhaps you're short-staffed? It's all right if we need to wait."

The butler shot her a grateful look. "That's very understanding of you, miss."

"I'm afraid I'm not nearly so understanding," Wesley cut in. "The phone. Now."

"Of course, sir." The butler's smile looked rather plastered to his face as he led Wesley and Zhang out of the parlor.

Sebastian frowned as the door closed behind Wesley and Zhang's physical body.

"I'm with him," Zhang's astral projection promised. "The servants will certainly be calling or telegramming the earl themselves to tell him Lord Fine is here, but we're safe enough to separate for now. The manor is very leanly staffed and most of them are in another wing, in the kitchen."

"Lord Fine's map had the trophy room one floor up," said Jade. "Let's start there."

They slipped out of the parlor and walked on silent feet down a long carpeted hall lined with portraits.

"Blond man in a ruffled cravat. Blond man in breeches. Blond man in a waistcoat." Jade eyed the portraits. "Was there not one single Blanshard ancestor with even a wife? How did today's Earl of Blanshard come to exist?"

"Maid's coming," said Zhang's projection.

Sebastian and Jade ducked behind velvet drapery twice as tall as a man. The window was open, and Sebastian could hear the autumn breeze rustling the hedges outside.

When the maid had hurried past and disappeared at the end of the hall, they slipped back out and found the stairs Wesley had described.

"I think I found the trophy room, but I can't project into it," Zhang's projection said, floating backward in front of them as Sebastian and Jade climbed the stairs. "He's got more magic guarding the door." He glanced at Sebastian. "At least, for now."

A couple halls over, and they were at the door Wesley had marked on his makeshift napkin map at the restaurant in York. Sebastian stepped in front. He put his hand over the doorknob and closed his eyes. "Zhang—"

"Leaving now." Zhang's astral projection vanished.

Sebastian took a breath, and swept out with his magic. He distantly heard a soft hiss from Jade at his side as her telekinesis weakened beneath his magic, but his attention was focused on the magic traps that disintegrated under his sweep, like a house of cards toppling in a strong wind, or snapping like guitar strings tuned too tightly.

When the sensation of other magic was gone, save for Jade's bobbing beneath the surface, Sebastian pulled his magic back into himself and opened his eyes.

"Goodness." Jade lifted her hand, and the tassel for the drapes down the hall danced like she was tugging on them. "It's working again as normal now, but it's as if I'm wearing lead cuffs when you're using your magic.

Could you ever permanently bind another paranormal, so they can't use their powers at all?"

"I've never tried," Sebastian admitted. "Mateo wanted me to try for him, so he wouldn't have to see the future anymore, but we hadn't figured out how. And then Baron Zeppler came calling, and—well. You know."

Jade touched his arm, gentle but strong. "We do know," she promised.

He put a hand on the doorknob—and it wouldn't turn.

He furrowed his brow. "That's not magic, it's just a lock," Jade said, sounding amused. She raised her hand again, staring at the doorknob in concentration, and then a moment later he heard the soft click of the lock releasing.

Sebastian went through first. He stood in the middle of the room and took a breath through his nose.

"My word." Jade was on his right, her voice gone awed but also tense.

The room was as large as a library, with pedestals set every few feet. Each pedestal was topped with an item in a glass case, like they'd entered some kind of paranormal museum.

Jade walked forward. "Are all of these magical items that he stole?"

The air beside her flickered, and Zhang's astral projection returned. "I don't think so," he said. "I think these are mostly genuine antiques, with a paranormal item here and there because Blanshard can't resist showing off his trophies in plain sight. From the astral plane, I can see only some of the cases are made with leaded glass."

Blanshard had stolen from people across the globe. Sebastian could see jewelry, a nautical compass, fig-

urines. Thumb screws, ugh, how awful. And Mateo
might be somewhere around here.

"We can't leave the paranormal items here," Sebastian said, even as his eyes were scanning the room for
any clues about his brother.

Jade's steady hand was on his arm again. "We won't,"
she promised. "But your brother is our priority too."

The room's ceiling was gilded around the edges and
painted with a scene of wolves chasing rabbits and stags.
And *people*. Sebastian's frown deepened.

Zhang's astral projection floated up just below the
mural, studying an area with heavy gilding. "There's
another floor above this one, but I can't get through the
ceiling. This mural is painted with lead paint."

Sebastian looked around. Beyond the pedestals,
bookshelves lined the walls. He strode over to the closest one, his gaze scanning the titles. Most seemed like
the sort of titles one would expect an English aristocrat to keep in their library, until Sebastian found one
he recognized.

"*Una Teoría de la Magia,*" he read aloud. "*A Theory
of Magic.* Blanshard should not have this book."

Jade appeared at his side. She started scanning the
books too, one hand out in front of her like she was
seeking something.

Zhang's projection flickered out of the room again,
probably off to check on the servants or another part
of the manor. Jade stepped down the shelves, hand still
out, as Sebastian read over the titles. The paranormal
books were interspersed with nonmagic books, collections on curse breaking and blood magic threaded between collections of Shakespeare.

And then, a book that made him pause, because he'd

seen it more times than he could count. *Una Genealogía de la Familia De Leon.* His family's genealogy.

Why the hell did the Earl of Blanshard have a copy? Was this because of Mateo?

"Here we go."

Sebastian looked up from his shelf to see Jade standing on her toes to pull at the spine of a book. A moment later, the entire section of bookshelf swung outward, revealing a staircase that curved away and disappeared.

"The one book I couldn't move with telekinesis," she said grimly, "because it was a built-in handle."

"Oh, Jade, thank you." Sebastian hurried forward, where Jade had already moved to the side and was gesturing for him to go ahead.

The light from the library spilled from behind them into the stairwell, and then disappeared as Sebastian rounded the spiral. He crested the stairs into a dark attic space—and saw the body crumpled at the far end of the room.

Chapter Thirteen

The butler had led Wesley and Zhang to a study not far from the ballroom where Wesley had once spent an unenjoyable evening.

"Here's what you're going to do," Wesley instructed the butler. "You're going to go down to your cellar and find the best scotch Blanshard has. You're going to open it, pour me a glass, put it on a tray, and then wait outside this room with my drink until my associate Mr. Zhang and I are finished with our calls. You will see to it that no one disturbs us in the meantime. Do you understand?"

The butler looked like he had a headache, but he smiled weakly. "Of course, sir."

Wesley waited until the door to the study had been firmly shut.

"Jade and Sebastian found the trophy room. It's exactly as you described it, but no sign of Mateo de Leon yet," said Zhang said quietly. "The butler is cursing your name on his way to the kitchens and we're mostly alone. Let's go."

Across the study was a large window that framed the gardens. It was open, letting in the cool September air, and the grounds within view were empty. Wesley and Zhang carefully maneuvered themselves out the window, dropping lightly to the ground. They walked behind the hedges down the length of the house until they were at the window Wesley remembered by the grand staircase.

This one was open as well. Wesley and then Zhang levered themselves back inside through it, pausing a moment behind the giant drapes.

"The hall is empty," Zhang confirmed in a whisper.

"What even *is* the astral plane?" Wesley said, matching his whisper. "Can all of you paranormals access it?"

Zhang shook his head. "Only those of us with walking magic."

"Christ," Wesley muttered. "You lot can't just be magic, you each have to be special too?"

"Aren't you a viscount? Don't you have special rules just for your name?"

"Hmph."

They quickly took the stairs up, their steps muffled by the thick carpets, and then followed the maze-like hallways from Wesley's memories to the trophy room. The door was shut, and Wesley carefully let himself in, only to find the room empty.

With Zhang right behind him, Wesley strode in between the many pedestals, coming to a stop in the middle of the room. He frowned, looking around—

There was a quiet creak, and Wesley promptly crumpled to the floor in an inelegant puddle.

"Oh, I'm so sorry!"

Wesley managed to crack an eye.

One of the bookshelves had swung open like a door, and Jade was on the bottom step. "With Jianwei's projection gone, I didn't realize you were here already," she said.

"Mph," Wesley tried to say. Maybe he'd just take a nap.

But Zhang was grabbing at his arm, forcing him up to sit up. "Did you find Mateo de Leon?"

That was important. Wesley forced his lips to move. "Is he—?"

"Alive, yes," Jade said grimly, "but entirely unresponsive."

"Seb—?" Wesley tried to ask.

"Is in the hidden room with his brother." Jade stepped down into the room, closing the bookshelf behind her, and suddenly Wesley's limbs were steady again.

"Lead paint on the back of the bookshelves," said Zhang. "It's a barrier that blocks the magic upstairs from coming into this room when the door is closed."

"So I assume Sebastian is upstairs using his magic," Wesley said, scrambling up to his feet. "What is Mateo de Leon's condition?"

"Dehydrated and hungry, I suspect," said Jade. "There's food and water in his room, but it's untouched. My guess is staff brings him meals, but he's been completely lost to his seeing and no one's been making sure he eats and drinks since the earl and Mercier went to London. As for his mind, well." She grimaced. "Sebastian's trying to bring him back, and I'm sorry, Lord Fine, but you're not going to be able to stand upright while he does."

"We'll be useful another way." Zhang pulled Wesley's arm, away from the bookshelf and toward the door.

Wesley gestured around the room, at the many pillars that held antiques in glass cases. "You suspect some of these items are paranormal, don't you? What if more of them belong to Sebastian's family—should we not take whatever we can with us?"

"We can't," said Zhang, hurrying toward the door. "We can't use our bare hands to grab a bunch of magical items when we don't know what they do, and that goes double for you since you don't have magic. I'm sure there will be at least one that can kill on contact."

"Charming," Wesley said dryly. "But then what? We can't leave them here."

"We'll come back," Zhang promised. "But people first. Let's find a way to get the others out of here."

Mateo had been nineteen the last time Sebastian saw him. Now he had a wild beard and hair, like he hadn't groomed in days, and Sebastian could never make up for three lost years if he couldn't bring him back. Mateo's magic was choking him, like living vines grown around him to bury him alive.

Sebastian kept his hands on his brother and tried not to panic. Jade had returned, and was kneeling at his side to check Mateo's pulse and pupils.

"Sebastian," she said softly. It couldn't have been pleasant, to have her magic so suppressed by his, but she hadn't complained. "What do you think's happened to him?"

"I think Blanshard and Mercier forced him into the future somehow," Sebastian said tightly. "I've suppressed his magic a thousand times and it's never been this strong before. It's as strong as Mercier's magic was in that alley in London."

"And you, are you all right?" There was a hint of strain in her voice. "Your magic is coming off you very strong too. How long can you keep this up?"

He didn't know. The horses' reins of his magic were straining his control like trying to hang on to a stampede. Magic poured through him so intensely he felt it in his bones, but he gritted his teeth against the pain. If his brother's mind depended on it, he *would* find the strength, like an opera singer pushing their limit on an aria, or a runner's last reserves with the finish line in sight. He reached as deep as he'd done that night in the alley, when he'd seen Lord Fine on fire, pouring all of his magic onto the magic that held Mateo hostage.

And then Mateo's eyelashes fluttered. "Sebastian?"

Sebastian's breath left him in a rush. "Quien pensaste, who did you think," he said, tacking English on for Jade. He pulled his magic back into himself, muscles aching like he'd lifted a boulder. He wiped at his own brow, and it came away damp with sweat.

Mateo blinked blearily up at him. "You're not here, you're a vision."

"Of course I'm here." Sebastian reached behind Mateo's shoulders, to prop him up. "You know I must be here because your magic can't see me."

"But I did see you."

Sebastian's hands faltered. Tired, Mateo was tired and talking nonsense. They had to get him out of here and keep him out of the future, that was what mattered right now.

"Stay with me," he said to Mateo, more a plea than an order.

Mateo nodded once, his eyes fluttering to half-closed.

Sebastian got a few sips of water into Mateo as Jade disappeared down the stairs to reopen the bookcase door. "What did they do to you, Teo?" he said, pretending his own hand wasn't shaky where it held the glass to Mateo's lips.

"Blanshard." Mateo's voice was hoarse from disuse. "He doesn't just drain the auras. He steals them, drinks them down, absorbs their life force into himself to strengthen his own magic. And now, with the brooch, he can pump them into another paranormal. That's what he did to Jack Mercier, and his fire is too strong now."

He looked at Sebastian with glazed eyes. "Blanshard wanted me to see his future. I refused, but he pushed that stolen energy into me and I couldn't stop it. And once my magic was that strong, I couldn't find my way out of the visions. I don't know what I told him while I was lost, Sebi—what if I helped him *kill* people?"

"Oh, Teo." Sebastian's hands tightened on his brother. "It's not your fault," he promised. "I know what it is like to be used as another's tool but it *isn't your fault*, te lo prometo. We're going to keep you out of the future, now, it's going to be okay."

But Mateo's eyes were already falling shut again. Zhang's astral projection popped back into the room. "There's a servants' staircase around the corner that leads to the ground floor," he said. "Lord Fine's gone ahead—he left the stairway window open for us and he's almost at the car. Let's hurry."

Sebastian helped Mateo to his feet, only to find his own limbs weak and shaky. With the help of Jade and her returned telekinesis, they got Mateo down the stairs, and Jade telekinetically shut the bookshelf behind them.

"The stolen items," Sebastian muttered, as they followed Zhang's astral projection out of the trophy room, each with one of Mateo's arms slung over their shoulders. Mateo's feet stumbled, but Jade seemed to catch them with telekinesis every time.

"We'll come back," Jade promised, with anger in her

voice. "Blanshard doesn't get to rob half the paranormal world and keep the spoils."

They navigated the narrow servants' staircase another flight down. Zhang's physical body met them at the open window. "This way, hurry."

They got Mateo through the window, then Zhang switched places with Jade to help Sebastian keep Mateo on his feet. "The staff has discovered we're missing," said Zhang.

Sebastian could hear the rising clamor in the house. Jade ran ahead, and the car doors opened themselves as they staggered toward Wesley's Bentley.

The car was already running. "Paranormals, let's go," Wesley barked, as Sebastian and Zhang hurriedly got the half-conscious Mateo into the backseat. "Chop fucking chop, gents."

The manor's front door opened. "Lord Fine!" the butler shouted, sprinting toward them.

Wesley began to drive, the car doors still open. Jade said something very unladylike as the car doors began slamming themselves shut.

Mateo cracked an eye. "Quien es ese?"

How the hell did Sebastian explain who Wesley was? "Um," he said awkwardly, as Wesley took the Bentley speeding down the drive.

"Miss Robbins—" Wesley started.

"I've got it," Jade said, and Sebastian heard the creaking metal as the gates threw themselves wide open for the car.

"You're a treasure." Wesley tore through the gates, then hung a right so sharp and quick that Zhang swore and Sebastian had to grab the front seat to keep from falling.

Wesley's eyes were on the road, but he said, "Sebastian, are you hurt?"

"I'm okay, thank you, Wesley."

Wesley? Zhang mouthed at Sebastian, one eyebrow up.

Oops. But that explanation could wait for another day.

Wesley said something to Jade, who replied, but Sebastian's attention had returned to Mateo, whose eyes had concerningly closed again. "Ella dice que sí," came the mumble, "y todos están tan felices en su boda."

"Oh no." Sebastian leaned over him, bracing himself. "Teo, stop."

"What's going on?" Zhang asked.

"He's seeing again," said Sebastian. "Probably your future, he can't see mine and you've got your hand on him."

Zhang glanced at where his hand was on Mateo's shoulder, making contact with the bare skin of his neck. "What did he say?"

"She says yes," Sebastian translated distractedly, *"and everyone is so happy at their wedding."*

Zhang made a strangled sound.

Sebastian suddenly realized what he had said. He looked up to see Zhang staring at him.

Jade turned her head. "Everything all right back there?"

Sebastian winced. "Mateo's seeing again," he said, loud enough to be heard over the wind. Then, under his breath, he added weakly, to Zhang, "Congratulations?"

"Tell your brother he owes me a hell of a wedding present," Zhang muttered. Louder, he said, "We need to get him back out of his visions."

Sebastian bit his lip, but then Wesley's voice came from the front seat, "Can anyone else drive?"

"I've started learning," Zhang said hesitantly. "But I haven't exactly practiced on a Bentley."

"Come on, then," Wesley said, as he swerved to the grass at the side of the road. "I can't be behind the wheel if Sebastian needs to use his magic, but you lot just lose your powers." He opened the driver's door.

Zhang opened his own door. "You did hear the part where I'm still learning?"

"Yes, Mr. Zhang," said Wesley. "But even I wouldn't care more for a car than Sebastian's brother's sanity."

Sebastian stared at Wesley gratefully as he and Zhang changed places. As Zhang cautiously pulled the car back onto the country road, Sebastian whispered, "Thank you."

"Shut up," Wesley said, but it was almost gentle. "Go on, then. I'll brace myself."

Sebastian reached for his magic again. It hurt to use, like lifting weights with sore muscles. He gritted his teeth against the ache, until finally Mateo's eyelashes fluttered. "Sebi."

Mateo's voice had a distant, dreamlike quality, too disturbingly like his moments in clairvoyance. "I told you to stay with me," Sebastian said, like his heart wasn't aching as much as his bones.

"I *saw* you."

A shiver of unease went down Sebastian's spine. "You didn't," he said. "You can't see my future because I have Isa's magic in my tattoo."

"I know," Mateo rasped. "But I did."

"Maybe you had a dream about me, not a vision—"

"I know the difference."

"Teo—"

"I saw you in fire." Mateo's eyes were barely open, but from beneath his lashes he was staring straight at Sebastian with awareness. "Alone, surrounded by flames. There was no escape."

Sebastian's blood went cold.

"Not a dream," Mateo said hoarsely. "A vision." He suddenly grabbed Sebastian's arm. "Don't let the vision come true."

Sebastian clasped his hand over his brother's. "I won't."

"Don't be alone. Don't let it come true."

"I *won't*."

Mateo's eyes closed again, his grip on Sebastian's arm loosening.

"Teo, wait—"

But Mateo had gone silent again.

Sebastian gritted his teeth. He was pouring all his magic out, but he was weakening, and it wasn't enough.

His gaze stole to Wesley. His eyes were half-closed, but he was also looking at Sebastian, and he'd likely heard every word.

Blanshard was going to know they'd been at his house by now. He might come for Mateo and Wesley both, and Sebastian needed to keep them both hidden and safe.

But if Blanshard had a relic, Sebastian's magic wouldn't work. If it was still working at all. And if Sebastian couldn't keep Mateo out of the future, they needed to find someone who could.

Or somewhere.

Like a paranormal home in Barcelona, full of Isabel's magic, her subordinate refuge to keep her magic at bay.

The idea beckoned for a long moment. Isabel's townhouse along the Mediterranean. Familiar, full of warmth and sun, by the beach, the boardwalk, and the sea. A home with enough magical traps painted onto the walls that it might stop Sebastian's blood terrors, might bring Mateo out of the future.

But Wesley wasn't going to go to Paris, to see Isabel, or to Barcelona, to her home, and Wesley still needed protection.

Sebastian gritted his teeth again. He had to find more magic. He had to keep them both safe. But if the tattoo's magic was weakening—maybe from years under blood magic—if Mateo could see his future—if they could be found by their enemies—

"Jade?" When she turned her head to look into the backseat, Sebastian held his wrist up. "May I borrow your eyes?"

He pushed his sleeve up, revealing the tattoo. "Can you tell me what you see when you look at my wrist?"

As Zhang turned onto a wider road, Jade tilted her head. "Colors," she said. "Intricately woven together in a sort of an abstract design."

"Anything else?" he said, heart pounding.

She stared for a long moment more. "No," she finally said honestly. "Is there more *to* see?"

"Yes." Sebastian pulled his wrist back, pulling his sleeve into place and straightening his cufflink. "Jade, could my magic be weakening?"

"It hasn't felt weak for one moment today," she said dryly. "I couldn't lift a thimble around you."

He snorted softly.

She shifted in the seat to more fully look at him. "You've been pouring it out with everything you've got for almost an hour. Yes, I can feel that your magic is weak now, but out of your own sheer exhaustion. Is there a reason you think it might be more than that?"

Wesley saw the lion. Mateo thinks he saw my future. What if I can't keep Mateo out of the future, what if I can't keep Wesley safe—

Wesley stirred at that moment—because he was able to stir now, despite Sebastian still trying to use as much magic as he could. Because despite everything, Sebastian was faltering.

Where was he going to find more strength?

The ride passed in a blur for Wesley, but he'd caught snippets of the brothers speaking in the backseat with him, their mix of English and Spanish carried on the wind.

I saw you in fire, Mateo had said to Sebastian, clear as day. Alone, surrounded by flames. There was no escape.

Wesley came fully back to himself in York, enough to direct Zhang through the tight streets until he pulled the car up to the curb across from the railway hotel and parked. As the car's engine eased into quiet, Wesley realized he could hear Sebastian panting like a boxer ten rounds in.

Jade and Zhang exchanged a look, obviously hearing the same thing.

"We're going to check the train schedule," Jade said quietly, as the roof of Wesley's car raised itself, enclosing them in more privacy. "We'll be right back."

The two of them disappeared, leaving Wesley with the de Leon brothers. Mateo did look a lot like Sebastian—a little paler, perhaps, his hair darker and curlier, but with the same sleek build and double-take handsomeness that would have had people turning on the street.

Sebastian slipped down from the backseat into the space behind the passenger's seat. Mateo at least wasn't babbling nonsense at the moment. He was leaning against the side of the car, and looked like he might be sleeping. But Sebastian was still breathing too hard, and when he looked up at Wesley, his eyes were bleary.

"Damn it, Sebastian." Wesley leaned forward. "You can't keep this up anymore than I could sprint for hours unending."

Sebastian winced. "I can try."

"You have to rest. Get your strength back up."

Sebastian shook his head, not in a *no* but in the way people did when they were hopeless and broken. Because even Sebastian's magic at full strength had only brought Mateo part of the way back.

"Right." Wesley sat up straighter. "What's our plan?"

Sebastian swallowed. "I rest for a moment, and then—"

"No, sorry, that's not going to work," Wesley interrupted. "We can't stay in York now that Blanshard will know full well we broke into his home. You can't do this alone. We need another plan."

Sebastian winced. "I have to do it," he said desperately. "There isn't another plan."

"What are you talking about?" said Wesley. "Look, you were breaking your blood terrors with that painting of San Juan, weren't you, the one you gave my house? What if we take him back to Kensington?"

Sebastian closed his eyes. "I don't think it will be enough to keep Mateo out of the future."

"Well, then, what about more of your cousin's paranormal art? Or more of the familiar? Those were the things you were using; why wouldn't they work for your brother?"

"Isabel is in Paris," Sebastian said, in a hoarse whisper. "She might be able to help, yes, but I won't leave you either, Wesley. Lord Blanshard is going to come for you now, and I'm the only one who can keep you hidden—"

"Wait," Wesley interrupted, in an irritated whisper. "Are you telling me you think you can't take your sick brother to your paranormal cousin because it would put *me* in danger?"

Sebastian buried his face in his hands. "If I can just find enough magic—if I can bring Mateo back myself, I can also stay with you—"

"You absolute *nob*." Wesley should shake some damn sense into Sebastian, except part of him now felt aggravatingly soft because the beautiful idiot apparently had not even considered that abandoning Wesley was an option. "You don't have to choose between protecting me or saving your brother or draining yourself to the bone to save us both. I'll come with you, to Paris or wherever you need to take him."

Sebastian's eyes widened. "But that's such a big ask—a big *change*—"

"Then how lucky for me that a handsome man recently informed me even viscounts can change."

Something vulnerable crossed Sebastian's face. And then, hidden in the backseat of the car he grabbed Wesley's tie and pulled him down for a desperate, exhausted kiss so full of affection and gratitude that it lit Wesley all the way into his chest.

The kiss only lasted a heartbeat, too short and private for anyone to have seen. Then Sebastian pulled back and whispered, "You're a saint."

Wesley wanted to grab him right back into his arms.

"Nonsense," he said gruffly, instead. "I'm just another scoundrel."

"Maybe," Sebastian said. "But you make me believe in good again."

"Oh," Wesley said weakly, and touched his still-tingling lips.

Chapter Fourteen

After the paranormals had a discussion that Wesley could barely follow, full of magical terminology and some very grim tones, Jade and Zhang decided to return to Blanshard's manor.

"I hate leaving you three," Jade said, with frustration.

"I hate leaving you two," Sebastian said, just as frustrated. "But we may only have hours left before Blanshard returns. If you and Zhang can get the stolen magical items out of that trophy room, you'll be doing the entire paranormal world a service."

"And you need to get to your cousin, because your brother has no time to lose," Jade said. "We'll send a telegram ahead to Miss de Leon, and then follow to Paris as soon as we can."

"Be careful," said Sebastian.

"You too," echoed Zhang.

Wesley left the Bentley with Zhang and the keys to his manor with Jade, and then managed to get a first-class compartment on the next train to London. The brothers sat together on the same velvet seat like bookends, Mateo in the corner, his head resting against the window, and Sebastian, who couldn't keep using his magic in a full train, fast asleep on the other side since nearly the instant he'd sat down.

As the train pulled away from the station, Wesley rang the porter for a newspaper and a private dinner service for three to be brought as soon as possible to their compartment. Then he pulled their curtains firmly shut, locked the door, and took his own seat across from the de Leon brothers.

He'd been reading his newspaper for only a few minutes when he felt a gaze on him. He looked up, over the paper, to see Mateo watching him through heavy-lidded eyes.

The other man's voice was just audible over the steady rhythm of the train barreling down the tracks. "I still don't know who you are."

So he did talk, not just prophesize. Sebastian had said Mateo was supposed to be at university in America. Wesley could easily picture him on a campus, carrying books, writing notes in the library. Except, of course, the part where he could see the fucking future.

Regardless, he certainly looked young enough to be in school, except without the naiveté Wesley expected of twenty-two-year-olds who hadn't seen war. No, Mateo de Leon looked like he'd seen plenty, and like he didn't trust Wesley one bit.

Sebastian was still sound asleep in the other corner of their seat. Wesley took off his monocle and set his newspaper to the side, addressing Mateo directly. "The Viscount Fine. I'm an acquaintance of your brother's."

Mateo snorted. "An *acquaintance* of my brother's, but you're coming with us all the way to Paris? Try again."

"What reason would I have to lie?"

"The last English aristocrat I met lied to me and more," Mateo said flatly. "So forgive me for needing more than your flimsy pretexts."

"Fair enough," Wesley muttered. More loudly, he said, "I want no harm to come to your brother. Does that satisfy you?"

"Hmph." Mateo shifted his head against the window. "I recognize you, you know. I saw your future."

Wesley raised his eyebrows before he could stop himself.

"I saw that prick Jack Mercier try to burn you alive," Mateo said. "I couldn't see what happened after that, but clearly it didn't work. You don't seem to be a paranormal yourself, though, so how did you escape?"

"Your brother," Wesley said. "Sebastian saved my life that night."

Mateo frowned.

"What?" When Mateo shook his head, Wesley said, "Just spit it out, already. Sebastian trusts me."

Mateo scoffed openly. "That only makes me trust you less. The last time Sebastian thought he could trust someone, we lost him for three years. He's too sweet."

"He *is* too sweet," Wesley agreed. "Meanwhile you're suspicious—that's very good."

"I'm a seer, no one likes me anyway."

Mateo was turning out to be snappish, cynical and protective of Sebastian. Ugh, he was almost tolerable.

Wesley leaned forward. "I don't wish harm on your brother," he said again. "I would, in fact, like to prevent any more harm from ever coming to Sebastian, because I believe he's suffered more than his share."

Mateo eyed him. He had grown paler, and there was a light sheen of sweat on his forehead, like he was once again fighting the magic trying to send his mind into the future.

"Maybe you saw me in the future, but I heard you in the car," Wesley went on. "You said you saw Sebastian's future. I thought that wasn't supposed to be possible with his tattoo."

Mateo gritted his teeth. "I know what I saw."

"I believe you." When Mateo looked at him, Wesley said, "I've only known about magic for a handful of days. What do I know about possible and impossible now? The rules of my life have been completely subverted, so why shouldn't your magic rules have gone off the deep end too?"

Mateo bit his lip, and Wesley realized he already recognized the gesture from when Sebastian did it.

"You said you saw your brother surrounded by flames," Wesley prompted.

"There were voices," Mateo said hoarsely. "Laughter. Revelry. People in danger under the white clock."

Whatever that fortune-telling madness meant. Wesley leaned even closer. "I won't let that happen to him."

Mateo swallowed. His eyelids were dropping again, his head lolling heavy against the window.

"Mr. de Leon," Wesley said quietly. "Please tell me what to do so that future you saw never comes true."

Mateo's eyes had fully closed. "Isabel."

"Your cousin, the painter and tattoo artist? What can she do?"

But Mateo had gone quiet again.

They changed trains at King's Cross, and then again at London Victoria for the last boat train to Dover. There wasn't much privacy to be had on the ferry to Calais, but they did their best, securing a quiet spot near a railing. It was outside, but they had a long bench to themselves along the covered walkway, and Sebastian overheard Wesley throwing his title around so the ferryman would

keep others away. They let Mateo lie down, and Wesley
sat with Sebastian at the other end.

It was dark and cold on the ocean, and the salty wet
air peppered Sebastian's face. Another September rain
had started, pouring down on the water as their boat
crossed the Channel and giving the white-crested waves
a speckled, textured appearance in the ferry lights. Sebastian huddled deeply into his coat and scarf as Wesley touched his pocket.

"What a perfect moment for a cigarette." He glanced
at Sebastian out of the corner of his eye. "You do remember our bargain, don't you? You're supposed to
stop me."

Sebastian made a quiet huff that he hoped wasn't
as broken as he felt. "I don't have enough magic left
to stop you."

Wesley raised his eyebrow. "You can't knock me on
my arse right now?"

Sebastian shook his head. "The tattoo still works."
At least, he hoped it did. "But my own magic is too
exhausted."

And all of his magic hadn't been enough to bring
Mateo's mind all the way back. Sebastian swallowed
down his despair.

Wesley sighed with a dramatic edge. "What is the
point of being a viscount if one still has to do everything oneself?" he said wryly, as he pushed the cigarette pack back into his pocket. "And what's the point
of having a paranormal lover if he doesn't have enough
magic to pin you to the bed?"

Sebastian bit back a smile even as a pleasant shiver
ran down his spine. Wesley had good ideas. "Are you
saying you only want me for my magic?"

"Nothing so shallow, I assure you. I also want you for

your body," Wesley said, and Sebastian had to bite back another smile. "So. You've once again driven yourself to the breaking point and now you're without magic. Helpless and vulnerable."

It was Sebastian's turn to raise his eyebrow. "You don't have magic. If I called you *helpless and vulnerable*, you would be very cross."

"I'd be proper vexed, yes, but I never have magic. Meanwhile you're fae, or a witch, or a paranormal or all the special things you are." A sardonic smile curled on Wesley's lips. "If I were a nice man, I'd be sensitive about it, say something like *this must be hard for you, to not have your usual ability to flatten the world's mere mortals with your mind.* But I'm not a nice man, so what I'm mostly considering is how good you'd look helpless, vulnerable, *and* pinned to a bed."

Another shiver ran over Sebastian's skin. "You could keep going with that thought."

"Now see, if you say something like that, it's going to get you into trouble," Wesley said, a ragged edge to his polished voice. "Trouble I can't do anything about while we're on a public boat. You have to say something like, *I am shocked, Lord Fine, what a wretched scoundrel you are.*"

Sebastian did smile, then. How much easier it was to fight despair, to have hope, when he had Wesley. "What kind of scoundrel would cross the English Channel with me so I can take my brother to get help?"

"Oh." Wesley straightened. "That is what I'm doing, isn't it? That's actually terribly romantic of me—are you absolutely swooning?"

"A bit, yes," Sebastian admitted.

"Really." Wesley nudged him with his shoulder. "That sounds promising."

He didn't pull away after the nudge, and he was warm against Sebastian's side. Sebastian couldn't stop himself from leaning in closer, but Wesley didn't seem to mind.

"I talked to your brother on the train," said Wesley.

"He came out of the visions without me?"

"Briefly," Wesley said. "Why was he able to see a vision of your future? I thought that wasn't supposed to be possible with your tattoo."

Sebastian winced. "It's not." He was quiet a moment, and then he admitted, "Maybe my magic is weakening. Not just in this moment, from exhaustion, but permanently."

"Does that happen?"

"Not usually," Sebastian said, still quiet. "But then, people are not usually under blood magic as long as I was."

"If your magic was any stronger, I suspect it could kill," Wesley said, blunt and honest. "So forgive me if I remain unconvinced. Didn't your brother say Blanshard pumped him full of magic? Maybe that's why he thinks he saw your future."

"Maybe," Sebastian said hesitantly.

"Now *you* sound unconvinced," said Wesley. "What makes you think it could possibly be weakening?"

Sebastian chewed his lip, but what was the point of hiding? He held up his wrist. "No one is supposed to be able to see the lion."

Wesley's gaze flicked down to where Sebastian's coat sleeve covered the tattoo. "But I saw it."

"Yes. And if you were able to see it, maybe my magical protection is weakening." Sebastian tried not to let his emotions show on his face, but it was gutting, the idea of losing his magic and his ability to protect Wesley and keep Mateo sane.

But Wesley frowned. "I don't know if I believe that," he said brusquely. "I heard you show the tattoo to Jade in York, and she couldn't see the lion. Who else has seen it?"

"Oh. Um. Isabel, when she created it."

"And?"

"That's, um. That's it," Sebastian admitted.

Both of Wesley's eyebrows went up. "You mean no one has *ever* seen your lion except me?"

Sebastian shrugged helplessly.

"Well, is there any other explanation for that?" Wesley said.

There was one other possibility. Sebastian hesitated.

"None of that," Wesley warned. "You've had your cock in my mouth, don't tell me you're getting shy on me now."

Sebastian was going to blame it on being tired, that he was confessing this. "I was going to say that maybe it's because you have good eyes." He shrugged, too lightly. "Or that maybe you can see it because, um. Well. Maybe my magic just likes you. That, um. Supposedly that can happen. But maybe—"

"Not so fast, de Leon," Wesley interrupted. "You don't get to say something as outrageous like *maybe my magic just likes you* and think you can blithely carry on without more explanation."

Sebastian made a face. "Magic is hard to explain. It is wild, like the woods, or like your garden in Yorkshire. So often it is dangerous, but then, sometimes, the flowers grow." Then he quickly added, "But this is fanciful stuff paranormals say to explain their own unexplainable powers. You are a farsighted sharpshooter, yes? Perhaps that is why you saw it."

It was a flimsy excuse, considering Wesley's eyesight made it difficult for him to see things up close, and Wesley's expression said he knew it. But all he said, very lightly, was, "Interesting," and then moved to press even more firmly against Sebastian and share his warmth.

After the ferry, there was yet another train from Calais. Sebastian couldn't have used magic if he'd tried, and he tried not to let the loss bother him, but his attempt at sleep was fitful and unsatisfying as their train rumbled on to Paris.

It was fully night as they emerged from the train station and into a taxi. "Where are we going?" Wesley asked, after Sebastian gave the driver an address.

"We have a family apartment in the fifteenth arrondissement, not far from the fair's pavilions." Sebastian was slumped against the taxi door, his exhaustion too overpowering to hide. "It's a safe building," he told Wesley. "We bought it three generations ago and added all sorts of guardian magic. It can't be found by paranormals who don't already know where we live."

The taxi pulled in front of the awning of their building, four stories with terraces on the top floors and carved moldings around every window. Despite the late hour, Paris felt awake. Couples walked hand in hand down the street while friends sipped wine at outdoor tables at the café next door, its warm yellow lights casting a soft glow on the autumn leaves of the tree in the sidewalk.

As they climbed out of the taxi, the doorman opened the building's front door, and Isabel came running out, straight toward Sebastian and Mateo.

A moment later, her arms were around both of them.

"Mateo, lo siento, I would have come for you," she said, her grief echoing Sebastian's own.

If they'd known sooner—

But they hadn't. Sebastian grabbed Wesley's wrist. "Isabel, this is Lord Fine," he said. "He helped me rescue Mateo."

"Miss de Leon," Wesley started to say.

She threw her arms around him and kissed his cheek. Wesley's eyes widened.

"Thank you so much," she said. "Please, come upstairs."

They piled into an elevator, and the operator pulled the doors shut and took them up to the fourth floor—third floor, Sebastian guessed Wesley was going to call it. As they stepped out onto the blue-and-gold carpet laid over the marble floor, an Irish brogue joined them. "Isa, luv, your cousins are nothing but handsome trouble."

"Hello, Molly," Sebastian said weakly.

Molly held out her hand, her sleeves short enough to show the beautiful Celtic harp tattoo on her inner arm. "Look at you stumbling. Come on, in you get."

Moments later, they were all in the apartment's parlor. Sebastian hadn't been back to any of the family homes in three years, and it put a lump in his throat to see a place that looked so wonderfully familiar. The parlor held the same chaise and settee in matched dark wood and golden velvet, and they'd brought bits of Spain and the Caribbean to France in the art around the room, the sculptures and mosaics and paintings. The phonograph in the corner of the room was playing a contradanza, and the glass doors to the balcony were open, letting in occasional snippets of French from the sidewalk café below.

Isabel had turned the dining room into a makeshift studio and piled the large wooden table with familiar art supplies—tubes of paint, a palette, brushes, and her tattoo equipment from America, half pen, half machine. The only things Sebastian didn't recognize in the apartment were the swirls of color painted on the striped wallpaper around the windows and doors.

"I got the telegram from your friends," Isabel said, gesturing to the doors. "I did what I could for tonight, but Sebi, if your magic wasn't enough to keep him out of the future, nothing I can do in a single night will be either."

Molly sat on the edge of the chaise. "Isabel thinks you should take him to her townhouse in Barcelona."

"You should take him tomorrow." Isabel gestured at Wesley as she helped Mateo down onto the settee. "But what of your friend? Would he rather stay here?"

Sebastian hesitated, but Wesley said, "I'm with Sebastian, wherever he goes."

Isabel and Molly exchanged a glance. Sebastian barely had time to feel a pulse of thankful fondness when Isabel said, "He's going to sleep."

"Isa—" Sebastian started.

"No me digas que no lo necesitas, you're falling over," she said, because of course she was going to say *don't tell me you don't need it*. She added, in a softer voice, "There is nothing more you can do right now. I have been in Teo's shoes, lost to my colors. That he's come out of the future at all—that's your doing."

Sebastian swallowed. It was so hard to watch the subordinate paranormals he knew buried under their own magic. He ought to be able to stop it completely, but he'd poured all his magic out, and nothing had helped, and nothing was left.

A hand came to rest on his shoulder. "Perhaps I may be of service, Miss de Leon," Wesley said, in a voice fit for a king's court. "If you'll point me toward a private bedroom, I'll make certain Sebastian is flat on his back straightaway."

Sebastian gave him a narrow-eyed look, but Isabel said, "Thank you, Lord Fine," and pointed past the dining room.

Wesley pointedly pulled on Sebastian's shoulder. Outnumbered, Sebastian gave in and went with him.

Past the dining room, Wesley found a short hall and then a decent-sized bedroom with a writing desk in the corner and two narrow beds side-by-side. It was gently lit by one small lamp on a nightstand, and by the sparkling city lights outside the large window that framed a beautiful view of Paris. The Eiffel Tower rose the highest, lit in the bright colors of the Citroën advertisement, glittering in oranges and yellows against the night sky.

Someone else might have found the sight romantic. Someone who wasn't Wesley, of course.

"I can't believe you've made me come to fucking Paris, and during a bleeding world's fair at that." Wesley held the door open for Sebastian. "I am not one of those saps who gets sentimental over this city. I despise people. I particularly despise tourists. And yet here I am, because of you."

Sebastian gave him a suspicious look. "Are you going to say the bit about how you think everyone gives beautiful people whatever they want so they're all very spoiled?"

"We do and you are." Wesley leaned on the door to shut it firmly behind him. There was even a lock, wasn't that nice. "And I hope what you want is to be in one of these beds with me, because that's what *I* want and I haven't made that a secret. But you look about to keel over."

That got a tired smile, at least. Sebastian sat at the foot of one of the beds and ran his hands through his hair. "I *am* tired," he admitted. "But I do not know if I can sleep. I am—what is the expression, too locked up?"

"Too *keyed* up." And Wesley could think of a few ways to solve that problem. He casually turned the lock on the door as the music from the living room drifted in. "What's this music called?"

"It's a Cuban contradanza," said Sebastian. "The musicians are from Havana."

"Oh."

There must have been something in Wesley's tone, because Sebastian looked up. "Do you not like it?"

"Actually, I like it very much," Wesley said truthfully. "It's just—well. Do you dance?" He shook his head immediately. "A pointless and ridiculous question, ignore—"

"It is not pointless or ridiculous," Sebastian said. "And yes, I do. At least, I did, a long time ago. Why?"

In for a penny, in for a pound, as the saying went. Wesley might as well confess. "Growing up, I was expected to dance with ladies at society events. I'm not like you, you understand, I've never fancied a woman. But I didn't mind an occasional dance, because I knew the steps, and if I felt no desire for the woman in my arms, well, no one could see through my charade. But I always wondered what it would be like to dance with someone you're attracted to."

He stepped closer, nearly to Sebastian's knees. "And now, I'm rather wildly attracted to a man from San Juan, and we're listening to music from Havana in Paris. But all I could ask him to do is waltz."

But Sebastian held his hand out. "You could teach me to waltz, and we'll try it with a contradanza," he said, "and another day, I can teach you what I know, and we can try a rumba to an English march."

Wesley took his hand. In one smooth pull, he had Sebastian on his feet, only inches between them. "This isn't the right time signature for a waltz," he said, even as he pulled Sebastian close, sliding his hands around his waist to feel the muscles of his lower back firm under his palms.

"We'll make it work," Sebastian promised.

His face was nearly touching Wesley's, the first shading of stubble on his jaw. They'd shared a morning shower far away in Yorkshire and the trace scent of his own soap was distracting when it was layered on Sebastian's skin. Standing so close, their height difference once again became obvious, the way Sebastian had to tilt his head back to keep his eyes aligned with Wesley's, the way he fit in Wesley's arms as perfectly as a hand inside a bespoke glove.

"Actually." Wesley slid his hands down from the small of Sebastian's back to his arse, turning his face just enough to brush his lips against Sebastian's temple. "Fuck the dancing. Let's go straight to you flat on your back."

Sebastian let out a surprised laugh as Wesley gave him a pointed shove that tumbled him to the mattress. Wesley followed him down, and their lips met.

Sebastian's exhaustion was so palpable Wesley could taste it. Wesley slowed the kiss, watching Sebastian's eyelashes flutter. His hands were on Wesley's hips, but they weren't moving, weren't pulling desperately at his clothes the way he had the night before.

Ugh, Wesley despised doing the sensitive thing.

"I'm going to make another bargain with you," he said, against Sebastian's lips.

Sebastian looked up, his eyes hazy, giant black pupils ringed with golden-brown. "What bargain?"

"In five minutes, I will do any filthy thing to you that your mind can dream up."

Sebastian's tongue darted out and wet his lips. "I like this bargain. What's the catch?"

Wesley kissed his jaw. "You have to be awake in five minutes."

Sebastian huffed. "Of course I'll be awake."

"Really," Wesley said dryly. "Because your hands are on my arse, but you're so tired that I think you've forgotten."

Sebastian narrowed his eyes.

Before he could move, Wesley rolled off him, onto his back. "Come on, then. Get comfortable. All you have to do to foil my gambit is stay awake."

Sebastian rolled his eyes, but he had a tiny smile as he shifted onto his side, facing Wesley. But then, instead of putting his head on the pillow, he moved into the crook of Wesley's arm, so their bodies were pressed together.

Oh. Look at them. *Cuddling.*

Sebastian was settling against him, closer still. "You're coming for my body heat, aren't you, you tropical orchid," Wesley said, like Sebastian seeking him for comfort was a trifling thing, like it didn't make the stone he called a heart feel too big for his chest. "You're basically just a big shameless cat yourself."

"If you don't want to cuddle, you could always fuck me," Sebastian said innocently.

A pulse of want went through Wesley. He was going to put this brat through the damn bed—at least, once Sebastian was actually awake for it. "Look at you, trying to goad me when you're half-asleep on top of me already," Wesley said. "I'm trying to be *sensitive* right now and it's like wearing a shirt that doesn't fit, so mind your manners and don't make it harder for me. Metaphorically *or* literally."

Sebastian huffed a quiet sort of laugh. His arm was resting on Wesley's chest, his shirtsleeve rucked up high enough that Wesley could see the top of the lion's mane.

The lion that only Wesley could see.

Maybe my magic just likes you, Sebastian had said.

It had to be impossible. No one liked Wesley, and certainly no one's *magic*, and most certainly not the wild and dangerous magic of the gorgeous sweetheart who'd just trustingly curled up against him.

But the thought of it, of being liked by Sebastian's magic, like flowers blooming in the wild of the woods. Of that magic choosing to allow Wesley, and only Wesley, to see the lion hiding in the tattoo—

Wesley quickly cleared his throat, because if he let these thoughts go on, the stone heart in his chest might crack. "Five minutes, and because I'm not interested in fair fights, I'm going to fill those minutes with a historical accounting of all of England's illustrious Viscount Fines. Good luck staying awake."

Sebastian scoffed. "You can't possibly put me to sleep by talking about yourself. You're much too interesting."

Oh. That was nice. "No flirting," Wesley chided. "This

has to be the topic. I can't talk about anything except myself."

Sebastian snorted.

"I'm quite serious," said Wesley. "I am my own entire conversational repertoire."

"I like it." Sebastian's voice was thick with sleepiness. "Me encanta escucharte."

"Excuse me, you don't get to be cute and switch to Spanish, you know I enjoy it and that's cheating."

Sebastian smiled, his eyes mostly closed. "It means *I like listening to you.* Or maybe, *it enchants me to hear you*, but I thought you would find it weird if I said that in English."

"Oh." No, Wesley didn't find it weird, he found it *fucking romantic*, thank you very much, and it wasn't helping his resolve to let Sebastian sleep without Wesley mauling him through the bed.

Wesley glanced at the nightstand, trying to distract himself. "There's a book here, *Ternura*, if I'm saying that right. I think it's in Spanish, but I can butcher your language if you'd like me to read it to you instead."

"No, I want to hear about you." Sebastian's head rested near Wesley's heart, a pleasant weight on Wesley's chest. Why was this so outrageously comfortable? Why did keeping someone else warm make Wesley feel this good? "You're really going to come to Barcelona with me?"

I might be willing to go anywhere with you.

Or I might be willing to stay right here and never move with you.

Oh, Christ, clearly Wesley was tired too if his thoughts were running in intolerably sappy directions. "I will require plenty of shade," he said out loud, trying for a suitably detached tone. "So. Viscount Fines. Our story begins with a wretched man in the seventeenth century, because I come by my own wretchedness very honestly, you know, it's right there in the blood."

There was no response, except Sebastian's soft breathing.

"I would dearly love to say *I told you so*," Wesley said, amused. "Except you're asleep, so I can't even enjoy being right. You should know I'm always right, and you may as well accept that now because—"

Because Wesley didn't want to let him go.

Oh, hell.

He glanced out the window at the night sky, and the orange-lit Eiffel Tower glittered back.

Wesley narrowed his eyes. "Paris is not going to make me sappy and romantic," he informed the tower, but he wrapped his arm around Sebastian anyway.

When Sebastian opened his eyes, it was dawn, the beginnings of light stretching over the rooftops of Paris. His head was still on Wesley's chest, and he lay quiet for a moment, feeling himself breathe, moving his own fingers because he could.

Maybe the blood terrors couldn't get past all of the building's guardian magic.

Or maybe they couldn't get past Wesley, whose arm was draped like a heavy anchor over Sebastian's ribs, and whose heart beat its steady, lulling rhythm under Sebastian's ear.

Wesley had been so confident when his hand was on Sebastian's cock—but then tentative, when his arm was around Sebastian's waist, like touch without sex broke one of the many tenets he used to rule himself. Maybe Wesley was as inexperienced with affection as Sebastian was with men, or maybe, like Sebastian, somewhere in the past there had been rejection and pain. He hadn't let go of Sebastian in sleep, like he wanted the moment to last, because as hard a man as Wesley claimed to be, he was hardest on himself, and maybe he'd forbidden himself from having the softer things he wanted.

But maybe they could start anew together. Wesley had his own demons, but Sebastian had meant it when he said they didn't scare him. Wesley was trying, and his bravery made Sebastian want to be brave too. Maybe Sebastian would never be the same person he was before blood magic, but maybe no one was ever the exact same person they were yesterday and it didn't make him weak to need to heal. Maybe Wesley was right, and he wasn't fractured but battle scarred. Maybe grace could be stronger than shame; maybe he could have a complicated past but still deserve a happy future.

Maybe Wesley would want to be part of that future.

Sebastian winced. Always with the too-soft feelings, and worse now, because he'd never felt quite this soft for someone else before. It was too soon to ask Wesley something like that. Barcelona first, and as quickly as possible.

He slipped out of the bed, leaving Wesley asleep. In the parlor, the glass doors to the terrace were open, letting in the cool breeze and morning light, framing the view of the Eiffel Tower rising up out of the clustered city.

Isabel had taken the chaise while Mateo was asleep on the settee. It stirred memories of their childhood, fighting over the hammock on the rooftop patio in San Juan, Sebastian always bigger but always the one to give in and let Mateo share it with him.

But even in sleep, Mateo was far too pale. His breaths

seemed too shallow, and despite the cool room, his skin was shiny with sweat. Was he seeing the future again?

I saw you in fire. Alone, surrounded by flames. There was no escape.

Sebastian wrapped his hand around the lion. It shouldn't be possible for Mateo to see Sebastian's future.

But Mateo had seemed so certain it wasn't a dream.

Still, dream or vision, what mattered right now wasn't Sebastian's own future but getting Mateo out of the futures that kept pulling him back in. Isabel was right that they should head to her home, and they needed tickets for the soonest train they could catch to Barcelona. Their building was full of generations-old guardian magic; he could get the concierge to help with the tickets without having to leave.

Sebastian left a quick note on the dining table so the others would know where he'd gone and then took the elevator down to the first floor. The concierge desk was empty, but Sebastian approached anyway. Behind the desk was an open door, although no one was directly visible.

"Bonjour?" he called, hoping someone could hear him.

"Je suis au bureau," came the muffled reply, from within the open door. "Entrez."

Sebastian hesitated, but the concierge had said he was in the office and to come in. He came around the desk and stepped in through the open door, and found himself in a short hall with two doors. The second door was open and the room was occupied, but the man had his back to Sebastian, bent over an open filing cabinet.

Sebastian cleared his throat. Reading French was one thing, speaking it was another, but he'd do his best. "Pouvez-vous m'aider à réserver un billet de train…"

But as he spoke, his gaze fell to the floor, to the

shriveled, unmoving body in a black suit, and the words died in his throat.

The concierge straightened and turned around. "No trains today, I'm afraid."

Sebastian's stomach dropped. "Jack?"

Jack Mercier held up a hand, already burning. "It's too late to save the asshole on the floor. So don't try any heroics, or the whole building goes up in flames."

How did he get in? How did he find their building? Sebastian reached for his magic, the now-familiar bone ache of drawing too deep—

Someone clapped a cloth over his nose and mouth from behind, and a sticky-sweet scent filled his nostrils. "I have been waiting an infuriatingly long time for the right de Leon," a smooth British accent said.

Sebastian lashed out with what magic he had but the scent remained. He was forced to draw a breath, and then the world went dark.

Chapter Fifteen

Wesley opened his eyes to find himself alone. The sun was slanting in through the open window, the pale yellow of early morning. Sebastian must have gone to check on his brother. Or perhaps to get Wesley breakfast, wouldn't that be nice, although hopefully the man wasn't foolish enough to go anywhere alone right now.

The Irish girl, Molly, was going into the kitchen as Wesley passed by, an empty glass in hand. "Welcome to Wonderland, your lordship."

He snorted, because that was very much how it all felt. "Are you magic too, Miss…?"

"Finnegan. And no, I'm not." She tilted her head. "But if I've got to live in a world where I know that some people have magic when I don't, I'm glad I'm with the de Leons."

Wesley could certainly appreciate that. He moved out of her way, and then carried on into the dining room, where Sebastian's cousin, Isabel, was standing by the dining table and frowning at a piece of paper in her hand.

"Good morning," he said, making his voice as polite as he could, partly because she was Sebastian's cousin and he wanted to make a good impression, but also partly because she was Sebastian's cousin and even

Wesley wasn't going to purposefully be rude to anyone in a family that was chock-full of magic.

He awkwardly sat on the edge of the chaise. What was the point of such a decadent piece of furniture? Was he supposed to lounge about like a tart?

Could he get Sebastian to lounge about like a tart?

That was a thought that would wait for another time. "Is something the matter?"

"Sebastian," Isabel said flatly. "He's gone to the concierge to get our train tickets. Alone."

"You're joking," Wesley said. "Why would he do something so foolish when we're on the run?"

"This building is protected from magical discovery," said Isabel. "Our family added guardian magic three generations ago. No paranormal should be able to find us, and Sebi *should* be safe if he stayed in the building."

"I'm never that lucky," said Wesley. "When did he leave?"

"I hoped you might know. Did you hear him this morning?"

"No. The man can move as quietly as those cats he dotes on." Under normal circumstances, there would be absolutely no cause for alarm if a twenty-seven-year-old man wasn't immediately where everyone had expected him to be. But as Wesley had observed all the way back in London, nothing in his life had been normal since the moment he'd heard Sebastian's name.

Isabel held out the note, and Wesley took it, giving it a quick read. "It says he's just going downstairs. How long could that possibly take?"

Mateo's bleary voice came from the settee. "He's in danger."

Wesley exchanged a glance with Isabel, and then they both crossed over to the settee. Mateo was lying on his stomach, head down, but his half-lidded eyes had a spark of awareness, like he'd had on the train.

Wesley crouched down next to him. "You're referring to your vision of Sebastian's future."

Isabel had crouched too, her hand covering Mateo's. "Teo, that shouldn't be possible. You should not be able to see Sebastian's future."

"I know," Mateo said. "But I did."

"The younger Mr. de Leon here was apparently pumped full of some nonmagical victim's aura by Blanshard," Wesley said. "Could that have made him able to see past the tattoo?"

Isabel's frown deepened. "I don't think so. My magic works like whirlpools to trap other magic, and the stronger the magic, the more deeply it's stuck. If anything, it should have made it harder for Mateo to see Sebi's future." She squeezed Mateo's hand. "Teo, can you tell us exactly what you saw?"

Mateo closed his eyes. A moment passed, and then he spoke in a dreamy voice that sent chills down Wesley's spine. "Surrounded by flames. There are so many voices around him, revelry outside the windows, among the banners, the gardens, the statues, beneath the white clock that stretches up toward the clouds. People in danger, but he can't escape. The heat burns."

Wesley swallowed.

Isabel had paled. "There is a tall white clock at the tourism pavilion by the Grand Palais."

Wesley's heart began to pound. "You mean the vision happens *here*, in Paris, at the fair? And we've lost track of Sebastian?"

Isabel leapt to her feet. "I will ask Molly to stay with Mateo," she said. "I'm going downstairs to find him."

"I'm coming too."

Downstairs, the lobby was ominously empty. Behind the concierge desk, a door was open, a short hall just visible. Wesley took a step toward it, and Isabel promptly stepped in front of him. "You don't have magic, Lord Fine."

Ugh, she was as bad as Sebastian. "I assure you, I'm neither helpless nor without protection."

"Stay behind me anyway."

She was a paranormal artist, basically a bohemian with magic. What was she going to do, rapidly sketch a picture to keep them safe?

Actually, that was probably quite within the realm of possibility.

Wesley frowned but let her go first. He followed close behind as they checked the first door and found only a closet of coats.

But behind the next door was a body.

Isabel covered her mouth, but Wesley still heard the quiet gasp. The dead man was dressed in a plain black suit and white shirt, like the concierge would have been. His body was crumpled and unnaturally shriveled, like a grape that had become a raisin. Wesley had never seen anything like it, not even during the war.

Out of habit more than any belief the poor bastard could have been alive, Wesley knelt and checked the neck for a pulse. "Dead," he confirmed.

"This is magic," Isabel said grimly. "Bad magic. And Sebastian is nowhere to be seen."

Wesley set his jaw. "World's fair?"

"World's fair," she confirmed, and she sounded as full of dread as he felt.

Wake up, de Leon—I need your magic.

"Wake up, de Leon—I need your magic."

Sebastian's eyes popped open. But his body wouldn't move; he was trapped, immobilized. He fought for control, to shake it off, his body jerking from head to toe—

And he heard the rattling of chains.

Oh. Not a blood terror.

But not good either.

Sebastian peered blearily at his surroundings. He was bound on a floor of cool tiles laid in a black-and-white checkerboard. There were paintings on the wall, of nearly naked bodies in a grove, and at his head was a giant ceramic urn. Blocking most of his vision was a man-height screen of metal, a tall stylized building in the center flanked by giant bronze flowers and disks.

His hands were chained behind him, and he could feel the bite of lead in the cuffs. Beyond the screen were distant voices—men, women, children, the happy chatter of people on holiday. Shimmering all around him was the outline of a cage—the same kind of cage that had been in the alley in London, that had kept Wesley and Mercier silent to the streets beyond.

Reflexively, Sebastian tried to reach for his magic, to dispel the cage. Nothing happened, except the dull needles of his lead handcuffs stabbing into him more sharply.

Black oxfords stepped behind the screen, into his line of vision. Then a white man crouched in front of him—perhaps forty years old, with a thin face and thin blond hair, his chin and nose both small and pointed. He looked like the men in the portraits that lined the wall in Blanshard's Yorkshire manor.

"You're finally awake." Blanshard looked down his nose with cold blue eyes. "I appreciate that I don't have to waste time on threats. You know we're silenced, and that you can do nothing about it. But you wouldn't risk it anyway. You can hear all the voices, so close, but you'd never call for help because you know I might kill them. A veritable hoard of the nonmagical, just meters away, and you wouldn't risk any of them, even to save yourself."

Sebastian's skull buzzed like someone had released angry bees in his brain, and his throat ached from dryness. The voices of the crowd rose and fell, innocents who had no idea what danger they could too easily step in. "Where's Jack?"

"I believe he's gone to find the other paranormals, and their sweet little pavilion where they can share their paranormal art. Your cousin is an artist, is she not? Are those other paranormals her friends?" Blanshard added, conspiratorially, "Between us, I think Mr. Mercier is getting a bit itchy. He never gets to really let go, does he? Burn it all down, like he wants? It's gotten worse since I put the aura in him, like I did in your brother. They're not like me; their magic isn't meant to contain it and has become much too strong now. Your brother, of course, ended up trapped like Theseus in the maze, but even Mr. Mercier needs a place to release his flames."

Sebastian clenched his teeth. "You killed all those people."

"Of course I did. I needed their life forces." Blanshard sat on the floor, like he was getting comfortable. "You look and act so much like her, you know."

"Like who?"

"Your great-great-great-aunt, of course. Casilda."

A new kind of unease began to creep over Sebastian, like spiders on his skin. That couldn't be possible—there was no way—

"You didn't realize?" Blanshard said, a nasty edge to

his voice. "What did you think happened when I consumed someone's life force? Why did you think they called me the Vampire? I absorb someone's life force and it strengthens mine—and adds to it."

The same paranormal, still alive, powered by stolen life forces? "How old are you?" Sebastian said hoarsely.

"One hundred and ninety-three, this year." Blanshard's lip curled. "I really am an earl, you know, the only one in my line to ever have magic. You can't imagine the rush, the power that comes when a young noble discovers they can absorb another's life. I knew I could live forever. And when I killed my father, to take the title, the villagers were so afraid—the Devil's Lord, they called me. Has there ever been another man so exceptional in every way?"

"You take from the less powerful to feed yourself," Sebastian said tightly. "There's nothing noble about that."

Blanshard's eyes narrowed. "You're certainly Casilda's heir. She was beautiful, you know. I was going to marry her, a well-placed alliance within Spain. The access I would have had to your family's knowledge and relics—but then Casilda discovered what my magic was." His jaw tightened. "She refused to go through with the marriage. She clung to your family's proclaimed role as vanguards of those without magic, put it ahead of her duty, and was banished."

Sebastian shook his head. "She would not have been disowned for following the family code of honor."

"They didn't believe her," Blanshard said smugly. "Like the Cassandra of myth, telling truths that were ignored. Whatever the rumors call me, the Vampire, the Devil's Lord—no one wants to accept I'm real."

Sebastian set his jaw. "She still stopped you."

"She *betrayed* me," said Blanshard. "Broke your family's guardianship to steal the brooch relic while I was feasting on the village peasants that were about to be mine. Then she came for me. She tried to kill me, and when that failed, she bound my magic with hers, left me ruined and unable to consume any more auras."

"Then how are you alive?" Sebastian demanded.

"Because every life force I've consumed has become part of me, has lengthened my own life, and even Casilda couldn't change or undo that." Blanshard leaned in. "But the lives I consumed were not *infinite*. They were starting to run out, and I was going to die like a peasant if I couldn't take more. I've been forced to watch your family for generations, waiting for one of you to be born with the magic I needed to undo Casilda's chains."

He looked down his nose at Sebastian. "When Mr. Mercier told me about you, I knew we needed to meet. You thought you were safe, but you couldn't hide from me in a building that I watched your great-great-uncle enchant. You would have been able to destroy any magic I used, but chloroform knocks you out, same as any man. You were just as easy a mark as your brother was this summer. I recognized him as a de Leon straight away, but it wasn't his magic I needed. It was yours."

Sebastian tugged uselessly at his cuffs. "What are you talking about?"

"Magic always comes back around, doesn't it? Powers eventually repeat themselves? It's taken generations, but one of you de Leons *finally* inherited your aunt Casilda's magic."

Sebastian's eyes widened.

"You didn't know you shared her magic?" Blanshard snorted. "Your family thinks it knows everything, but I've known about all of you for longer than any current de Leon has been alive."

Blanshard opened his jacket, enough to reveal the gold-and-pearl brooch pinned to his waistcoat. "Casilda thought abandoning the brooch under the ocean would keep its power in check. After all, if no one possesses it, it can't be stolen, and if it can't be stolen, its magic can't be used. I'm sure she thought your family would have time to get it back, if it was ever found, but no one counted on Baron Zeppler unlocking the brooch by committing murder during its theft. And you didn't count on me."

The unease deepened into dread, settling into Sebastian's stomach.

"This brooch should have unlocked Casilda's binding on me." Blanshard's eyes flashed with anger. "But she was a tenacious bitch, and so is her magic. I can feel it, still in me. I can finally drain a single aura again, I can give that life force to another paranormal, but a relic should give me the power to drain this entire fair at once. I should be able to make an army of my own paranormals, their aura-enhanced magic stronger, loyal like Mercier, or useful, like your brother. But I'm hobbled yet, because the last of Casilda's chains refuse to break."

Blanshard touched one of the pearls on the brooch. "But I'm tenacious too. I've searched for an answer for decades, collected artifacts, watched your family. Then I stole the brooch myself, and I've tried consuming the auras of the mundane who got close to magic. I thought perhaps having the touch of magic in their auras could break my bindings. And when that fool, Lord Fine, told me he'd been in contact with you, I thought he'd have *your* magic in him still."

Sebastian yanked at his cuffs, useless, always useless. "Leave him alone."

"I hardly need him anymore when I have the actual magic itself." Blanshard touched the brooch again. "This relic makes magic work on other paranormals, doesn't it? It once made Baron Zeppler's telepathy work on me. I've been thinking—I can drain auras. What if this brooch now lets me drain magic too?"

Sebastian went still.

"You understand," Blanshard said approvingly. "You inherited Casilda's magic. So when I drain your magic—your life force—I think it's finally going to break the last of her chains."

Blanshard abruptly shoved Sebastian over, and put a hand on his chest, over his heart.

"No—" Sebastian started to say. But then the words became a choked-off scream as fire flooded his body, as if Blanshard had stabbed a dagger into his heart and begun to rip muscle straight from bone.

Blanshard slapped his other hand over Sebastian's mouth and nose. "Quiet. I need to concentrate, and no one can hear you anyway."

Sebastian's body arched with pain. Blanshard's magic felt like poison, stripping his cells, burning blood and leaving a wasteland behind.

"Normally I'd have Mercier torture you first," Blanshard said conversationally, like he wasn't draining Sebastian's life out of him. "It improves the flavor, so to speak. But I'm too eager for my freedom. Because without your dear auntie's chains, I'll be able to drain many auras at once. I'll be able to feed enough that I live forever."

He dug in his hand, his nails points of fresh pain against Sebastian's skin. "So we're going to make this quick."

Wesley had to dodge again as yet another couple came into his personal space. "Ugh, why are there so many *people*."

Isabel was standing on her toes, trying to see over the crowd. "They are here to see the art."

"They're here to waste time being pointless and frivolous."

They'd come in through the entrance at Les Invalides. The avenue up to the Pont Alexandre III Bridge was lined with pavilions on both sides, and up ahead the gilded roof of the Grand Palais rose up above everything else. And everywhere there were fucking people—families with children in tiny yet fashionable clothes, people hauling cameras, street buskers performing, vendors hawking crepes and other foods. Laughter and happy voices filled the air.

Wesley grimaced. "If I were asked to describe hell, it would look like this."

"I see why you are so drawn to Sebastian's sweetness," said Isabel, "because you are very sour."

They passed a pavilion fronted with statues and greenery, and then another pavilion with a tall, round roof like an inverted bowl and two pillars flanking the entrance, topped with bright flowers. *Primavera*, it said on its side. The bridge itself had been turned into a place for shopping, and below, in the Seine River, restaurants floated up against the banks like houseboats.

Isabel pointed up ahead, to the other side of the bridge. "There is the tourism pavilion, just before the Grand Palais and the Porte d'Honneur."

Wesley squinted, and there it was, a narrow, rectangular pillar stretching high, a clock face at the very top. "But you can see that damn clock from all over. Sebastian could be anywhere."

"And there are so many people." Isabel bit her thumb. "There are children here. If Mercier is here—and he has the magic to start fires—"

"Christ." Wesley balled one fist. "Can we get closer— fucking *hell*."

A mime had just bumped into Wesley, his face painted bright white with blue diamonds drawn around his eyes. He bowed apologetically and then began to pantomime—something, Wesley didn't know or care.

"Fuck off, already," he said, which made the mime's eyes go wide and Isabel side-eye him.

"We know Sebastian is—or will be—somewhere near the clock," said Wesley. "Can you draw something that will help us find him?"

Isabel shook her head. "My art confuses other magic, sometimes stops it completely. It won't help us seek—"

"Feu! Feu!"

Oh no. They were searching for a fire paranormal; Wesley could guess what that meant. He and Isabel both pivoted toward the scream as more people began to shout and tourists began to run.

"Feu!" someone shrieked again, over the pounding of feet.

"Fire," Isabel breathed. "And that's where the paranormal exhibit is."

They ran across the street, and Wesley could see smoke rising in the air behind one of the pavilions. "When Mercier set a fire around me in London, he said water wouldn't put it out."

"Because he creates magic flames, and his magic is too strong now." She swallowed. "I think—I think I need to protect the fair."

"What do you mean?"

Isabel pointed again, this time at a patch of pavement with a chalk drawing of the Eiffel Tower. The street artist had disappeared, leaving his hat behind, still sitting in front of the drawing for tips.

"Oh," Wesley said, as his brain finally made the leap from world's fair to de Leon's Wonderland. "The chalk—you can draw something that will help?" he said, as they hurried toward the art.

"I can't put out the flames, but I can contain them." Isabel crouched, and picked up the small box of chalk. "I will cover as much of this area as I can, with art that will stop the fire from spreading." She looked up at him, and there was pain in her eyes. "Sebastian would never forgive me if I didn't."

And all of Wesley's hope vanished. "Because if you're drawing, you can't look for him."

She squeezed her hand around the chalk, her despair nearly tangible.

Stupid, idiotic to ever feel hope.

Except.

Except Sebastian hadn't written Wesley off as too big an arse to be worth saving, not even once deciding he wasn't worth it. Wesley would not give up on Sebastian either.

"*I'll* keep looking," he promised Isabel. "You protect the fair, I will check every pavilion by the clock until I find Sebastian."

"Lord Fine, you *can't*," she said. "We know Sebastian will be surrounded by fire. You will have no protection, and Mercier will roast you alive."

Wesley's gaze stole past her. The mime with the painted face hadn't run away yet, staring wide-eyed at the smoke rising into the sky.

"How fast can you draw?" he said, an idea finally forming.

Chapter Sixteen

The voices came as if from a great distance.

Why isn't he dead? the first one said, impatient and stressed.

He will be, said the second, a posher voice, cold and dismissive.

The first man snorted. *Not soon enough.*

Speed it up then, the second voice said. *I got what I wanted, what do I care about him now? Cremate him alive if you like, I'll be drinking my fill at the gate.*

The fair was in danger. Sebastian needed to get up.

He tried to stand, but his body wouldn't obey. This time, it wasn't a blood terror; it was as if his blood had no life left in it.

Footsteps echoed on the black-and-white marble tile. "You should be dead."

Get up, Sebastian. Get. Up.

Mercier's face filled Sebastian's sight. "Look at you, trying to move. You shouldn't even be breathing."

As if in answer, the lion tattooed on Sebastian's wrist throbbed.

"Perhaps you somehow kept the tiniest spark of life, because you're you and you always have to be *special*," Mercier went on. "But it doesn't matter. You're going to die now, by *my* hand, and trust me, you're going to wish Blanshard had just finished the job."

"Jack," Sebastian breathed. "You need help."

"Blanshard helped," Mercier said coolly. "He figured out how he could steal an aura and use the brooch to put it in mine. Helped me see that I could get past Zeppler, past the Puppeteer, by fully embracing all the beautiful destruction magic can cause."

He leaned forward. "I wonder. Once you're nothing but ash, how far do you think the fire will spread?"

Sebastian swallowed. "Jack, don't."

"Have you seen how busy the fair is?" Mercier continued, with an unsettling sort of glee. "All these pretty buildings, built just to show off. People think they're so important. But everything burns."

Sebastian's voice cracked when he spoke. "I will stop you."

Mercier threw back his head and laughed. "You don't have enough magic to stop a fly. Don't you get it? The brooch lets Lord Blanshard's magic work on other paranormals. You don't have an aura, so he drained your life force and your magic. You're not a paranormal anymore."

No magic?

But the cuffs on his wrists didn't burn anymore where the lead touched his skin. There was nothing to reach for in his blood. The loss seared him, so profound it sent new pain through his already-aching body.

Sebastian forced it away, forced his chin up so he could meet Mercier's eyes. "I will still stop you."

"Oh, I'm Sebastian de Leon," Mercier said, in a mocking imitation of Sebastian's accent. "I'm from my special family with our special legacy to protect all the precious nonmagical from the dangerous paranormals."

And suddenly they were ringed in a tight circle of flame, the heat close enough that Sebastian's skin screamed.

"I've already set one fire to that little paranormal pavilion. You could have put it out, but not anymore. All those people are going to burn, and the ones here as well," Mercier said, in his normal accent again, as the flames began to slowly but surely creep inward. "And the ones that don't will be eaten alive by Lord Blanshard. Your legacy will be that your magic freed the last of his chains and let him loose on the world again."

Mercier stepped backward, through the circle of fire, and stood, unharmed. The flames closed in, forming a tighter and tighter ring around Sebastian. Distantly, he could hear the revelers at the world's fair as his skin broke out in sweat.

He had to stop Mercier. Except the flames were nearly touching him now, so tall he could barely see Mercier's face up above. Just like Mateo's vision, the fire prison from which there was no escape. And Mateo had been able to see the vision, because in the future he'd seen, Sebastian didn't have magic anymore—

The flames suddenly stopped moving.

"Look at this, Sebastian," Mercier said, with dark amusement. "Your friend Lord Fine has come for you."

"Wesley." *No, no no no.* Sebastian tried to sit up. "Don't, Jack. Don't hurt him."

Mercier ignored him, his aura lit in a blaze of flame, too bright in the dim interior of the pavilion. "Back for more, my lord?" he said, sing-songing the title. "You didn't strike me as suicidal."

Wesley's voice came from a few feet away. "I've seen your circus trick already." He sounded *bored.* "Let's see. We're silenced, so no one out in the fair can hear anything we do in here, and you've leaked magic fire everywhere. Haven't you anything new?"

Mercier narrowed his eyes. "You're in so far over your head."

"Am I?" Wesley stepped close enough Sebastian could see him, the flickering fires casting orange on his skin. "Or have you completely misjudged me? You think I'm like Sebastian here, that I'll play by some noble code of honor, but I won't, Mr. Mercier. Your singular chance for survival is to put your fires out and let Sebastian go."

"Wesley," Sebastian croaked, pushing up with his hands and making it into a half-raised position.

Mercier laughed, a cold sound for a man burning hot. "I could let Sebastian go and it wouldn't matter; he wouldn't make it. I'm still going to kill him, but you know what." He raised his hands. "I think first I'm going to make him watch me kill you."

"No!" Fire singed Sebastian's hands as he threw himself forward in a half lunge, half crawl. But he was too late; fire came up so fast and loud Sebastian heard it, like Mercier had doused the room in gasoline, flooding the space with heat as Sebastian's prison knocked him backward and a new fire engulfed Wesley.

"Wesley—"

Wesley stepped out of the fire. His suit was burning, his shirt in tatters, but he was otherwise unharmed, a pensive look on his face and his revolver in hand.

"Stung a bit," he said, and raised the gun.

The shot was deafeningly loud in the pavilion. The shimmering cage around them flickered but stayed intact as Mercier's body hit the floor and the fires around Sebastian and where Wesley had stood went out like a blown match.

Wesley was suddenly kneeling at Sebastian's side. "Are you all right?" he said urgently.

"Wesley—"

"These cuffs—just a moment, let me check Mercier's body for the keys—" Wesley disappeared for a moment, and then his hands were on Sebastian's handcuffs, and a moment later Sebastian's wrists were free.

He forced his head up, reaching for Wesley. "The silencing cage—"

"Can't you put it out?"

"I—I should be able to, but—" *But I can't feel my magic anymore. I think it's gone for good this time.* The words stuck in Sebastian's throat. He wrapped his hand around Wesley's arm and just shook his head.

Wesley's brow furrowed, but he said, "Mercier had set another fire at the paranormal pavilion. Your cousin was drawing as fast as she can to contain it, but I hope the fires have gone out there with Mercier's death."

"You may have saved many lives, then," Sebastian said hoarsely. "I thought you were going to die, I'm so glad you're alive. How—?"

"Isabel wasn't certain it would work." Wesley pushed aside a piece of his burnt shirt. "But apparently I believe in magic and fairy tales now."

Wesley's chest was covered in blue paint. As Sebastian squinted, he realized what he was seeing. "It's an ocean wave that becomes a rampant lion," he said in awe.

"I stole the paint from a mime," Wesley said, almost proudly. "I told your cousin to treat my skin like a blank canvas. Isabel said the water was to counter the fire, and the lion was for protection, like yours."

Sebastian looked up at him in surprise. "But how did you know?"

"Your brother's vision," said Wesley. "I knew I had

to be ready to rescue you from the flames. I wasn't going to stop until I found you." And as Sebastian's heart swelled with a helpless sort of gratitude, Wesley said, "But you didn't answer my question. Are you all right? What have they done to you?"

Feelings threatened to swamp Sebastian, but he couldn't fall apart. Not now. "Blanshard took my magic."

Wesley's grip on him tightened.

Sebastian made himself keep talking. "Blanshard is the same paranormal once known as the Vampire, the very same paranormal my great-great-great-aunt took down. And apparently I inherited her magic, but he's stolen the brooch relic and my magic and unlocked the chains she'd bound him in, and if we don't find him, he's going to drain all the auras he can and murder countless people here at the fair."

"Oh," Wesley said weakly. "Right. Well. I only understood about half of that, but what I did get is that you and I need to stop Blanshard."

"He was eager," said Sebastian. "I'm sure he did not go far. He will be somewhere where he can be close to many people at once."

"But that's this whole fair."

"He told Mercier he would be drinking his fill at the gate."

"Your cousin mentioned the Porte d'Honneur, by the Grand Palais." When Sebastian blinked, Wesley huffed. "I did have a classical education, you know. I studied Latin, I'm not completely useless around your language or others based on it. Let's find Blanshard before anyone finds us and starts asking questions."

Sebastian took a deep breath and forced himself to his feet.

* * *

There were at least a hundred people around the Porte d'Honneur, clustered in tight crowds in front of the regal Grand Palais.

Sebastian's heart was pounding too hard for such a short walk, the ache in his chest sharp and worrying. *You shouldn't even be breathing,* Mercier had said, and it felt like his entire body agreed.

They stopped at the edge of the plaza, finding something almost like privacy behind a kiosk selling hats. Wesley's eyes scanned nonstop, lingering on the entrance to the exhibition, on the observation tower that had been set up for a photographer.

Two more steps forward, and Sebastian was forced to bend at the waist to get enough air into his lungs. The deep breath backfired, causing him to cough, and he fumbled for a handkerchief to cover his mouth.

"Sebastian." Wesley's hand was on his arm again. "What's going on? You said Blanshard took your magic—why are you gasping?"

There was an undercurrent of something in his voice that was almost distress. And Sebastian realized Wesley was staring at the handkerchief, which was now spotted with blood.

Sebastian took another deep gulp of air and admitted, "Because he also took most of my life."

Wesley's grip turned painfully tight.

Sebastian turned up his wrist to show the tattoo. "I think the lion saved me. I think he held on to the spark that's tattooed into my skin."

"Saved you forever?" Wesley said, his voice as tight as the hand on Sebastian's arm. "Or just bought you some time?"

Sebastian swallowed and shook his head. If his lungs were bleeding, if his heart was failing—"I don't know."

Wesley's nostrils flared. He wrapped his left arm around Sebastian's waist, for support, and then went back to scanning the crowd.

Sebastian took a bracing breath. "Stopping Blanshard is what matters—"

"I see him."

Sebastian squinted, following Wesley's finger to the photographer's nest. And there, climbing the ladder, was Lord Blanshard. "He wants above the crowd," Sebastian said in horror. "He's going to try to drain them all at once."

He staggered forward. He didn't have magic, and he could barely move, but Blanshard's magic chains were gone and it was all Sebastian's fault and he couldn't let this happen—

Wesley was faster. He drew the revolver again in one quick motion, and the afternoon sun flashed off the metal as the shot rang out.

Pandemonium erupted around them. Blanshard fell off the ladder as people screamed and fled.

"Come on!" Wesley grabbed Sebastian's arm, helping him run behind kiosks until they reached the photography tower.

Blanshard was nowhere to be seen.

Sebastian's legs collapsed and he hit the ground on hands and knees. His lungs were seized with a fit of coughs, and when he wiped his mouth, his hand came away bloody.

"*Fuck.*" Wesley began turning every which way. "I'm certain the shot was true."

"It was." Lord Blanshard suddenly appeared behind

Wesley. "But you didn't really think you could stop me with a bullet."

Wesley tried to turn, to raise the gun again, but Blanshard put a hand out, and Wesley hit the ground like a puppet whose strings had been cut, the gun clattering uselessly to the ground.

"My magic is full of others' life forces. I am unstoppable, I do not die," Blanshard went on, advancing on Wesley. "And now I've consumed the magic of a de Leon. Look at him dying, Lord Fine. I took everything from him, just like I'll take everything from everyone here. Starting with *you*."

It happened with horrible slowness. Wesley tried to raise his arm again, but Blanshard crouched and plunged his hand into the air over Wesley's heart, and Wesley screamed.

"Wesley!"

And Sebastian's dying blood found the last spark in the lion. He staggered to his feet and threw himself at Blanshard.

He had one chance. If he was going to die, if he was going to be murdered by Blanshard, he was going to steal the brooch and take its magic with him, take the magic to a grave where Blanshard couldn't use it to hurt anyone—couldn't use it to hurt Wesley.

Blanshard's shriek split the air as Sebastian crashed into him. As they hit the pavement together, Sebastian swiped for Blanshard's vest.

His hand came away with the brooch, his grip so tight the pin drove into skin.

And then, everything happened very fast.

Wesley's scream changed to a choked gasp. Blanshard's shriek became a howl.

And magic poured into Sebastian like it was an army

of wild horses and he'd just thrown open the stable. More magic than he'd ever had, a relic's magic, stolen from Blanshard and now returning tenfold.

Blanshard made another animal howl and lunged for Wesley, aiming for his heart, his hands out and hooked like claws. Like he was going to try to bolster himself by taking *Wesley's life*—

The horses dove out of Sebastian's control and straight for Blanshard, a merciless stampede that took no prisoners, that crushed everything in its path. Where once he had felt other paranormals' magic only weaken, Blanshard's magic now disintegrated under Sebastian's magic like dust.

Blanshard screamed. And then he began to crumble, starting with the tips of his fingers that still reached for Wesley, skin and bone and flesh falling like the ash at the end of a cigarette until nothing was left but a suit and a pile of dust.

Sebastian stared.

"Sebastian." Wesley was scrambling to him. "Christ, are you all right?"

"I—" Sebastian's voice cracked. "I wasn't trying to kill him—but he was going to kill everyone here—he was going to kill *you*—"

"And you stopped him."

"I turned him to ash." Sebastian's voice broke again. "*Ash*, Wesley, my magic did that—"

"Good," Wesley said, and pulled Sebastian into a tight hold.

Every inch of Sebastian's skin buzzed like the horses were still stampeding through him. He dimly realized the closest people were scattered all over the ground, while others were still screaming and running frantically round them. "Did I hurt anyone else?"

"Your magic knocked a few people down but they're fine. Everyone's just being dramatic about it," said Wesley. "Let's go, come on."

"Sebastian!" That was Isabel's voice, coming over the crowd. She was sprinting toward them, her arms loaded with cloth. "Vamanos, the French police will be here any second."

Sebastian stared at the ashes already blowing away. "Blanshard—"

"Was a monster," said Wesley. "You just saved dozens of lives, including mine, and frankly having his ashes scattered by the wind is better than that bastard deserves."

Wesley yanked Sebastian up and the three of them began to run.

They made it out through the gate and to the street beyond, where they got a taxi back to the fifteenth arrondissement.

Sebastian was near silent the whole ride. Wesley didn't know what to say—good riddance to Blanshard and Mercier both, as far as he was concerned—but perhaps it was a bit earth-shattering to suddenly turn an ancient paranormal to ash with your mind.

As they drove over the Seine, Wesley hesitantly pressed a little closer into Sebastian's side. Sebastian leaned into him almost immediately, like he was drawing comfort from Wesley's touch.

And maybe it didn't matter that Wesley almost always chose the wrong words, because maybe with Sebastian, he didn't always have to find those elusive *right words* that would make everything better. Maybe he could just be here, which he would gladly do, and maybe that could be enough.

Back in the de Leons' Paris apartment, they sat in a circle in the salon that was still painted with Isabel's art. Isabel and Molly sat snuggled up together like lovebirds on the end of the settee. Mateo was propped up in the corner of the settee, his eyes half-open but aware.

Wesley was perched on the edge of the ridiculously decadent chaise again, and Sebastian was sitting on the floor next to his legs, his back pressed up against the chaise.

"So you have control of a relic now?" Isabel asked.

Sebastian winced. "Can you or Mateo steal it from me, please?"

"Sure, I'll just off Lord Fine first," Isabel said dryly. "You know it takes theft *and* murder."

"How did Sebastian gain control of it then?" Molly asked.

"His own murder," Wesley guessed. "Blanshard had stolen Sebastian's life force, after all, and he was only breathing because of the spark in the lion tattoo."

"I agree," said Isabel. "Stop looking so guilty, Sebi. You would never have committed the murder needed to transfer the brooch's magic. Blanshard tried to kill you and instead gave you the means to kill him. He did this to himself."

"Yes, he did," said Wesley. "Sebastian said the brooch relic makes magic work on other magic, but I thought all de Leon magic already works on other magic. What exactly has it done to Sebastian?"

"It would have strengthened his enervation magic," Isabel said.

"Cranked it up to *destroy*, it sounds like," said Molly.

"Except that doesn't make sense." Sebastian ran a hand through his hair, his elbow bumping Wesley's shin.

"If tía Casilda also had the brooch relic, why could she only bind Blanshard's magic? Why did I destroy it?"

"For the same reason you lived, I'd wager," Wesley said. "You also have the magic of your tattoo."

Sebastian blew out a breath. "I don't want the power to destroy magic. What if I can destroy *auras*?"

"Except you didn't," Wesley said. "There was an entire crowd present and all you did was knock them down. I was right there, and you didn't hurt *me*."

Sebastian still looked shaken. "But destruction like this—it's bad magic."

"Ask Mateo if he thinks it's bad magic," Isabel said quietly.

All of them turned to look at Mateo. His eyes were still half-open, but he hadn't spoken once since they'd returned.

"Ask Mateo if he thinks all magic is good and should be saved, Sebastian," Isabel went on, still quiet. "Ask him if he wants to see the future ever again, or if he wishes there was someone who could bind his magic."

Sebastian swallowed.

Oh, that couldn't be fair, could it? Even Wesley could see this entire conversation made Sebastian ill. But then, if the other option was losing his brother to magic—

"I don't think I should try to touch Teo's magic," Sebastian said hoarsely. "I killed Blanshard."

"No," said Isabel. "You destroyed Blanshard's magic, so he had no way to hold on to all those stolen lives. That is why he died, not because of you. The power to bind or even destroy magic is not the power to kill."

Sebastian winced. "But—"

"Sebastian." Mateo's raspy whisper somehow seemed to echo around the room. "Can you set me free?"

"Dios mío." Sebastian buried his face in his hands. "Teo—"

"Will you try?" Mateo said.

Wesley frowned. "I thought we were going to take you to the magically painted house in Barcelona," he said to Mateo. "Isn't that still an option? Why do we have to put Sebastian through this?"

"You're protective of my brother. I appreciate that," Mateo said thickly. His eyes were glassy behind half-shut lids. "I don't want to ask him for this either. But I'm not going to make it to Barcelona."

Oh no. Wesley didn't want Sebastian to go through this, but he most certainly didn't want him to lose Mateo and be forced to wonder forever if he could have saved his brother.

"Teo, what if you have no magic anymore?" Sebastian said hoarsely.

"It's worth that price," Mateo said, just as hoarsely.

Sebastian blew out a long breath and raised his head. "Everyone else has to leave."

"Sebi—" Isabel started.

"Isa, por favor, no sé que va a pasar," Sebastian said. "You too, please, Molly. I don't know what's going to happen."

Molly grabbed Isabel's hand. "Come on. Let's go so he doesn't have to worry about your magic being caught in his."

"Thank you, Molly," Sebastian said gratefully. "Wesley—"

"The hell I'm leaving," Wesley said flatly. "I was only inches away when your magic saved us all from Blanshard. It's not going to hurt me now."

He got to his feet, leaning down to address Sebastian where he still sat on the floor. "I'll walk the ladies down," Wesley said. "And then I'm coming back to be with you."

Sebastian had only managed to move as far as the floor next to Mateo's settee when he heard the front door open, then close again.

"You can do this, you know," Wesley said lightly, as he took the chair closest to Mateo's head. Mateo's eyes were closed again, his breathing too shallow. "Your great-aunt only bound Blanshard's magic. It logically follows that you can do the same thing."

Sebastian stared somewhere past his brother, his heart pounding uncomfortably fast. The brooch relic was a heavy weight in his pocket, his magic still buzzing in his blood. "Except I did destroy Blanshard's magic. What if destruction is all I'm capable of now?"

"Your blood inherited a lineage of fighting magic that hurts the nonmagical," said Wesley. "Your legacy may be complicated, but perhaps your magic knew what it was doing, destroying Blanshard's evil magic, and you ought to give yourself a little more credit."

Sebastian glanced up at Wesley. "You make it sound like it wasn't my choice," he said. "But Wesley, he was going to kill you. I wanted to stop him. And now I'm not sure I can use my magic as anything but a weapon, but I would do it again to save you."

Wesley's expression flickered for a moment, the smallest flash of something vulnerable. Then he reached down, and snagged Sebastian's wrist, the one with the tattoo. He turned it over, so the tattoo was facing up. "Whatever has happened to your magic, I can still see your lion."

Sebastian swallowed. "Really?"

"Yes," said Wesley. "And I'm the only one he lets see him, so I'm afraid I'm going to insist you find more faith in him, because really, in a way, he's mine."

The tension in Sebastian's chest eased the barest amount. Nothing could fight his despair like Wesley. "But I have to stay in control," he said, barely more than a whisper, "and I have not had full control of myself for years. I don't know if I believe I can keep enough control on my magic to do this."

"Sebastian," Wesley said, also quiet. "Have more faith in yourself as well. If you can make a scoundrel like me believe in magic, you can do anything. You can bring your brother all the way home."

Sebastian bit his lip. With Wesley's hand still on his wrist, he reached for his magic—and then he reached for Mateo.

Clear the vines but don't raze the jungle, he told himself. *Break the chains, don't break Mateo.*

Magic thrummed through him just below his skin. This was madness. It was asking the ocean to fill a glass of water, asking a stampede to gently pull your carriage—

Wesley's fingers tightened around the lion tattoo. Wesley, who believed Sebastian could do this. Sebastian closed his eyes and swept out with his magic.

"Oh," Wesley said, in surprise, but *good* surprise, like he'd just seen something wonderful.

Sebastian kept his eyes closed, kept his focus on Mateo's living magic, warped by the aura pumped into it, choking Mateo with its unnatural strength.

Sleep, not destroy. Put Teo's magic to sleep—

Mateo gasped.

Sebastian's eyes popped open—and Mateo's eyes were wide too. His hands had gone to his heart.

Sebastian's own heart leapt to his throat. "Did—did I—"

"No." Mateo was breathing hard, but he was starting to smile. "No, it's not completely gone. It's like—it's like you put out the fire, but left a candle. You didn't extinguish the flame."

He slung one arm around Sebastian's neck, and Sebastian made a choked laugh as he was suddenly yanked into a half hug. "Jesus," Mateo breathed. "I don't ever want to see the goddamn future again."

Sebastian hugged him back, hard, words sticking in his tight throat. "You're okay?" he managed to say.

"I will be," Mateo promised, his voice firm and best of all, completely himself.

Relief rushed Sebastian, leaving him weak and almost shaky. Mateo was going to be all right.

With one arm still around Sebastian's neck, Mateo pointed at Wesley with his free hand. "Where did you find this aristocrat, he's a treasure. And also an asshole, have you ever said something nice in your life?" he said to Wesley.

Wesley's lip curled in a tiny smile. "I get the impression you're not one to talk. I hear you don't like anything."

"I bet you don't like anything but my *brother*."

Sebastian covered his face. Well, that answered the question of whether the others had figured out he and Wesley were more than just friends.

Mateo let go, and Sebastian let himself finally relax. He sprawled boneless on the floor with his back against the settee, the voices of the other two washing comfortingly over him. It was wonderful to hear them both. It would be nice if Wesley and Mateo got along. It would make things easier in Barcelona—

Except if his magic was tamed, Mateo didn't need to go to Barcelona now. And if Blanshard and Mercier were gone, Wesley didn't need Sebastian's protection anymore.

There was no reason for the three of them to make the trip, and no reason for Wesley to stay.

As Mateo and Wesley bickered good-naturedly like kindred jaded souls, Sebastian glanced down at his lion tattoo.

There was no reason for Wesley to stay—but Sebastian didn't want him to go.

They found Isabel and Molly just outside, hovering under a tree by the café next door. When she saw Mateo, Isabel squealed so loudly it drew looks from all the outdoor tables.

She hugged Mateo, and Sebastian of course, and then she threw her arms around Wesley's ribs.

Wesley's eyes widened at the sudden affection. "Oh—ah—"

"Thank you," Isabel said.

"I appreciate the sentiment, but I didn't actually do anything—" Wesley started.

"You walked through fire to save Sebastian's life," she said dryly.

"Well—I mean, that was simply trusting your art—"

"And you didn't just save him today." Isabel stretched up on her toes to whisper in Wesley's ear. "You brought Sebastian back when no one could reach him. He smiles more around you than he has for so long."

Oh, Christ. Wesley was not equipped to experience *feelings*, this was completely unacceptable. Luckily Is-

abel let go to hug Mateo again, sparing Wesley the in-
dignity of being sappy over Sebastian's family saying
sentimental rubbish like *he smiles more around you.*

Isabel made some calls inside the café, and the next
thing Wesley knew, there was apparently an army of
paranormal artists on their way to the flat.

"I saved what I could from the fire at the paranormal exhibit," Isabel was saying to Molly. "Things like
dresses, weavings, a tapestry. I want to give them back
to the artists, and they all want to meet you. Adela wants
to hear all of your thoughts on Art Deco."

Ugh, Wesley couldn't stand *normal* bohemians—
was he going to have to spend an evening with paranormal ones?

Sebastian turned to Mateo. "Are you staying?"

Mateo shrugged. "If I don't have to worry about
magic knocking me over? I might. Molly and I can play
cards if the others get too artsy."

Sebastian snagged Wesley's sleeve. "Come with
me?" he said, making it a question, as if Wesley was
ever going to say *no* to him.

The streets smelled of autumn as they walked, of
turning leaves and baking bread. They passed a kiosk
at the corner, taller than Wesley himself and papered
over with adverts for clothes and every kind of show.
Parisians and tourists still filled the walkways, but the
endless parade of people didn't bother him half so much
when he had Sebastian leading him through the streets
of Paris.

"Where are we going?" Wesley asked.

"The first hotel with a vacancy." Sebastian shot him
a small grin. "Unless you wanted to stay in the apartment full of paranormal bohemians and my family?"

"Don't you even." Wesley used an oncoming gaggle

of flappers as an excuse to press against Sebastian's side. "There are too many people, you know. We're never going to find a room."

"I will find us one," Sebastian promised, with flattering determination.

And he did, despite Wesley's pessimism—maybe with magic, obviously that was going to be Wesley's explanation for everything now—in a five-story, cream-colored building with wrought-iron smoking balconies and a gray roof.

Wesley followed Sebastian up carpeted stairs to their first-floor room. "Are you sure that brooch didn't mess with your head?" he said, as Sebastian unlocked the door. "Blanshard and Mercier are gone, your brother is improved, and I'm not in danger anymore. Surely you've realized that you don't have to keep putting up with me?"

It came out gruffer, more vulnerable than Wesley had meant. But all of Sebastian's reasons for staying with Wesley were gone now. There was no reason for Sebastian not to tell Wesley to take a boat train back to London tonight, where all this paranormal lunacy would be over. Where nothing in Wesley's life would ever be magical again.

Except Sebastian had taken his hand and was pulling him into the hotel room. "Get in here," he said, like he *wanted* Wesley with him.

A second later, their door was shut and locked. Wesley found himself pushed up against the wall, Sebastian fitting himself between Wesley's legs, his head tilted back so they could look into each other's eyes. Christ, he made Wesley breathless.

"You came for me, at the fair," Sebastian whispered, as Wesley's arms encircled him in an automatic sort of way. "You knew there would be fire, and you didn't know if Isa's magic would keep you safe. You came anyway."

"Of course I did," Wesley said, still gruff. "But you did hear the part where that's all over, didn't you? The part where you don't have to put up with me anymore?" he said, like he wasn't holding Sebastian tight, refusing to let him go. "You could find someone nice, not a scoundrel like me."

Sebastian bit his lip. "Is that what *you* want?" he said, looking up at Wesley. "You don't need me anymore. Do you want a nice man, not a scoundrel like *me*?"

"How dare you." Wesley pulled him closer, so their bodies were flush. "No, I don't want a *nice man*. If I haven't made it obvious enough—I want *you*."

Sebastian kissed him.

Fuck, his lips, the taste of his mouth. It lit Wesley up like a signal flare, reducing his thoughts to only the man in his arms. He pushed Sebastian over, so he was the one with his back on the wall, and Sebastian's throaty sound of pleasure went straight to his cock.

"And I don't care what kind of scoundrel you think you are; you've never scared me, you know that," Wesley said into his mouth. He pushed his leg between Sebastian's, pushed him more firmly into the wall, and drew another sound of pleasure. "Until today, when you almost fucking died. Don't ever do that again, do you understand?"

"You either." Sebastian threw his arms around Wesley's neck and pulled him down for a deeper kiss.

They kissed until Wesley's lips buzzed, until he finally pulled away, breathing hard and achingly stiff in his trousers. "I would happily have you on the wall or the floor, but is there a bed in here? I haven't managed to look at anything but you."

Sebastian's eyes were the golden-brown of whiskey in the room's dim light. "You do know you're very hand-some yourself, yes?"

"Flatterer." Wesley cupped Sebastian's jaw and ran his thumb over his lips, now deeper pink and shiny from their kiss. "There are so many things I desper-ately want to do to you that I can't decide where to start. Do I drop to my knees? Toss you down on the bed I assume is in here somewhere? So many choices, and I want them all."

Sebastian tilted his head and kissed Wesley's thumb. "I grabbed something off the dining table before we left the apartment, from Isa's art supplies."

And then he was squirming to get his hand between them, twisting his body to get into his own pocket be-fore bringing his hand back up to hold a small tube of petroleum jelly in front of Wesley's face.

"I say you toss me down on the bed."

Wesley was already hard, but a fresh bolt of desire ricocheted out from his stomach, like lightning up his spine, fire down his limbs. He used the hand on Se-bastian's jaw to tilt his head back, then took his lips in a kiss so long and deep it left both of them panting.

Sebastian finally pulled insistently at Wesley's hips, and they staggered their way off the wall into the room with their lips still locked. They fumbled at each other's clothes as they kissed, their hats dropped uncaringly in one place, their jackets and waistcoats discarded in heaps on the rug. Sebastian was stripped to his T-shirt, Wesley's trousers undone, by the time they bumped into the decent-sized bed filling most of the hotel room.

They tumbled down together, Wesley on top, Sebastian on his back.

Wesley found Sebastian's hand, wrapping his palm around the tube of petroleum jelly and enclosing cool fingers in his own warmer ones. "And did you have a plan for this?"

Sebastian's gaze had turned hazy with need, his skin flushed. He licked his lips, and Wesley wanted to kiss him all over again. "Um, no plan," he admitted, a little sheepishly. "I kind of hoped I could throw it at you and you'd know what to do and, um. Take over."

"Fuck," Wesley muttered. "Say all the things that drive me mad, why don't you."

Wesley had never believed in fairy tales, true love or other childish nonsense. But with Sebastian, magic was real.

Maybe all of it could be real.

He deliberately pinned Sebastian's hands to the bed, on either side of his head, in an echo of the handcuffs he'd put on Sebastian only days before, and the small, sharp breath was like music to Wesley's ears. Held down as he was, in only the T-shirt, the rampant lion on the inside of Sebastian's wrist was perfectly visible to Wesley's eyes.

"And there's the lion," Wesley said.

Sebastian smiled, happy and almost shy. "Still?"

"He's right here. All mine." Wesley used his hand to turn Sebastian's wrist to one side then the other, admiring the tattoo. "And I still can't believe I'm the only one your magic lets see the lion. You don't want to know what that does to me."

Sebastian squeezed his hands where they held his own. "Show me," he said, half a plea, as he stretched up to kiss Wesley again.

They made short work of the last of each other's clothes, stripping down to bare skin that warmed like fire everywhere Sebastian's skin touched his. They were both already hard, and it took all of Wesley's self-control not to give in to the need to simply get them both off immediately. But he forced himself to wait, to distract Sebastian with kisses as he worked the lid off the tube.

Sebastian wasn't a virgin, Wesley knew that, but he hadn't done this with a man before. Wesley was self-aware enough to recognize the possessiveness burning his chest, the determination to make it so good Sebastian would never want anyone else.

He kissed Sebastian until he was boneless, the tension melted from his body. His own cock ached with need, but he ignored it, his mouth on Sebastian's throat as he took his time working him open with slick fingers.

They hadn't bothered to turn the lamp on, and the room was lit only by the gray twilight outside of their window, slowly deepening into a night tinged with the yellow glow of the street lamps. But it was enough light to see Sebastian's face, to make sure those pretty eyes were screwed shut with pleasure, not pain, and that Wesley kept it that way.

The more Wesley worked him over, the more Sebastian's grace vanished, until his hands were fumbling with clumsy desperation on Wesley's shoulders and back. "Wes, please."

"Beg all you want, you'll get nowhere. I'm a terrible man without an ounce of mercy and I'll only enjoy it." Wesley crooked his fingers inside Sebastian just to feel the bite of nails on his shoulders, just to hear the half groan, half whine in his throat. "And this turnabout is fair play, duck. All those times you've had me helpless under your magic and now I've got you the same way."

Sebastian arched, rubbing his body against Wesley's hard prick, and Wesley swallowed the needy sound that nearly escaped his own throat, because for all his talk he was barely hanging on to the need to show them *both* mercy.

When he finally pushed inside Sebastian, Wesley saw stars. Sebastian buried his face in Wesley's neck, his grip going so tight on Wesley's shoulders and back that he'd hopefully have marks the next day.

"That's—big," he said hoarsely, making Wesley shiver with pleasure as teeth grazed skin.

"Thank you."

Sebastian huffed a laugh, and this was new to Wesley, the wonder of sharing laughter while your bodies were joined. "You're so *smug.*"

"I've got *you*, of course I'm smug." Wesley rocked his hips, the smallest motion, and Sebastian made a sound that spiked Wesley's desire even higher. "Talk to me, darling, I want you to feel good. What's going through your head?"

Sebastian's face was still pressed to Wesley's neck, his breathy whisper hot on Wesley's skin. "I'm lucky, so lucky to have you, you're bright and vivid as a new tattoo. I think you're inking yourself over all my bad memories so now I only see you."

Oh, that was *unfair*, that was enough to make Wesley think his heart *wasn't* made of stone. Stone couldn't beat this fast, could it? Feel this warm, this happy in his chest?

Wesley moved his hips again, slow and deeper, sweet torture for them both. "Well, you've made me believe in fairy tales, you arse," he said, voice unsteady. "Because I got a fairy tale when I got you."

When he wrapped a hand around Sebastian's cock, it

drew panted words in his two languages. Wesley pushed his own overwhelming need to the side and kept his attention on Sebastian, on making Sebastian's tension climb, on drawing more sounds of pleasure, on the desperate noises and flexing muscles, on hazy eyes and flushed skin.

"You're going to come apart in my arms any second, aren't you?" Wesley said into his ear. He moved his hips to drive that tiniest bit deeper inside, and Sebastian closed his eyes with a groan. "Just for me, like your lion is just for me."

Wesley sped his hand up, and Sebastian did come apart, in a full-body shudder under Wesley. Wesley kissed him to swallow the sounds before they escaped the room, and finally let himself follow Sebastian into bliss.

He came back to his senses, sweaty and breathing hard, his forehead against Sebastian's shoulder and one of Sebastian's arms heavy around his waist. Sebastian's eyes were closed, and he didn't seem like he was capable of moving, so Wesley kissed his collarbone and rolled off him, then put a hand on Sebastian's shoulder and pulled him onto his side too, so they lay face-to-face on the same pillow.

"All right there?" Wesley said, as he let himself lightly stroke his hand up and down Sebastian's side just because he still wanted to touch him.

"Yeah." Sebastian's hair was sticking to his forehead, his waves tousled and wilder. He was smiling softly, almost like he was tipsy. "Wesley?"

"What, sweetheart?" The endearment slipped out, but that was hardly his fault; what could be sweeter than bliss-drunk Sebastian?

Sebastian took a deep breath. "I know you have no

more reasons to need me," he whispered. "But I don't want you to go. Can we—stay together?"

Wesley stared at him. And then he broke into a smile, a real one, big enough that it hurt the muscles unused to such a ridiculous expression. "I must be an incredible shag if you're asking me that, because clearly I've fucked all the good sense out of your head."

Sebastian shook his head fondly. "You helped me feel like maybe I can finally be *me* again," he said. "And if I'm really free to go after the life I want, all I want is *you*."

"Me." Wesley was the lucky one, and he owed the love-struck poets of the world an apology because they hadn't been exaggerating after all. He slid his arm around Sebastian. "You obviously don't know what's good for you if you're giving me a chance to keep you. If I were a nice man, I'd let you come to your senses."

Sebastian's lips quirked up. "I'm glad you're a scoundrel, then."

That made Wesley snort. "I'll certainly never wear your rose-colored glasses. But I will admit there is one tiny place in this godforsaken world that isn't cold and miserable, and that's the corner you light up."

Sebastian's smile was like the sun. "Is that a yes?" he said hopefully.

Wesley tightened his arm, pulling their bodies together, and kissed him deep enough to steal both their breaths as Sebastian's arm wrapped around Wesley's neck, his hand on the back of his head to tug him in even closer.

Wesley was finally forced to draw back to inhale, but he kept their foreheads together and his arm around Sebastian.

"Yes," Wesley whispered, as they breathed the same

air. "I would follow you to Barcelona, or London, or anywhere you need or want to go."

Sebastian hadn't let go of him either. "If you stay with me, there might be a lot of magic."

"I'll be thoroughly enchanted either way," said Wesley, and went back in for another kiss.

Epilogue

Two weeks later

The sky glowed in countless shades of orange, yellow, and red as the sun set out in front of the ship. The October evening was chilly but tolerable as the breeze rolled over the first-class sundeck.

Wesley settled back against the cushions of his deck chair. Sebastian was on the deck chair next to him, of course bundled up like he was on his way to the Arctic. Mateo refused to even set foot on the deck, hiding in the warm cabin instead, so Wesley should probably be impressed Sebastian was outside at all.

"I still can't believe you talked me into chaperoning your brother back to his university in America."

"He's excited to get back to his science, and Oberlin is nice," Sebastian said. "It's a pretty train to Ohio from New York, and it makes my family feel better to know Teo's not alone."

"You convinced me to agree to magic *and* America. You really are dangerously cute." Wesley waved at a passing steward. "Miss Robbins's last cable said she'd like to see us in New York. Do you think she told anyone we're coming?"

Sebastian made a face. "I don't know whether to hope she did or she didn't."

The steward stopped at Wesley's deck chair. "Sir?"

Wesley gestured at himself and Sebastian. "Whiskey for me, and something hot for the island gentleman."

"Coffee, please?" Sebastian said hopefully. The steward nodded and disappeared.

Wesley looked back out at the sky. "There are lots of ships that travel from New York to the Caribbean," he said casually. "Just pointing that out. If, you know, we were looking for somewhere to go after we finish minding your brother."

"Don't let Teo hear you say that out loud." Sebastian glanced at Wesley from under his cap. "An Englishman might be very hot on a tropical island."

"Not in the winter, surely? It might even be..." Wesley sighed. *"Pleasant,"* he grudgingly admitted. "I hear it's possible for people to enjoy things like beaches and beautiful scenery."

Sebastian was starting to smile. "I haven't been back to San Juan in so long. It would be like a fairy tale to get to go again."

Wesley looked from the sunset to the handsome man next to him, the one who smiled when he saw him.

"Yes, well," Wesley said, with a small smile of his own. "Maybe fairy tales aren't all bad."

* * * * *

Loved Proper Scoundrels?
*To find more of Allie's books or join her email list,
visit her website at www.allietherin.com.*

Acknowledgments

My sincerest thanks to so many:

Always to C, who makes me believe in good;

To my sister, who gives the most amazing support;

To my family and friends, who bring me joy;

To my book friends, who put up with my angst in their DMs;

To my agent, Laura Zats, for her counsel;

To my editor, Mackenzie Walton, a superhero with a keyboard;

To everyone at Carina Press, Kerri, Stephanie, Ronan, and the art, marketing, and production teams;

And to T, the brightest star made real.

About the Author

Allie Therin is a writer and avid reader of sci-fi, fantasy, and romance. She also is, or has been, a bookseller, an attorney, a parks & rec assistant, a boom operator, and a barista for one (embarrassing) day. Allie grew up in a tiny Pacific Northwest town with more bears than people, although the bears sadly would not practice Spanish with her.

Allie loves to hear from readers! Find all the ways to connect with her at her website, allietherin.com.

*To save Manhattan, they'll have to
save each other first...*

Keep reading for an excerpt from
Spellbound *by Allie Therin!*

Chapter One

The antique watch was a fraud. Not crafted by some eighteenth-century Swiss fella on a mountain but by a surly doll in a dank room, swilling gin and tap water.

Rory reached deeper into the watch's past.

The flapper with the cloche hat and black bob sets the gin on the rickety table and bends close to the gooseneck lamp. There's a folded newspaper on her table, beneath an ashtray, a gold-plated bronze chain, and a fake crystal watch face. She clamps her cigarette between her teeth, lipstick staining the paper, and pinches a speck of cheap quartz in her tweezers as the passing train shakes the paneled walls—

"Any luck?"

Rory's eyes popped open. For a moment, he saw double: the counterfeiter with her black bob and red lips overlaid on Mrs. Brodigan's gray bun and green eyes.

Then he blinked, and the vision of the pocket watch's creation cleared, leaving only familiar Mrs. Brodigan and the homey back office of the antiques appraisal shop. "That watch was handmade, all right." He tossed it on the side table that flanked his ratty armchair. "Handmade in 1924 right here in New York."

"Blast." Mrs. Brodigan sat at the rolltop desk. "You

didn't see the Swiss watchmaker honing his craft in a mountain hamlet?"

"Saw a girl honing her forgery skills in a dingy room on the J Line." He sank into the chair, mouth dry and body stiff from scrying the watch too long. His glasses slid down his nose and he pushed them back into place, still not used to the feel of the round, all-black frames. "Date was on the counterfeiter's newspaper. That watch is six months old, tops. It belonged to some fancy British captain fighting the French about as much as it belonged to King Tut."

Mrs. Brodigan clucked her tongue. "Mr. McIntyre isn't going to be happy to hear it. But people come to us for truth, and truth they shall have." She broke into a kind smile, the crow's feet at the corners of her eyes crinkling. "What we give them of the truth, at any rate."

Rory, whose fingers still tingled from the aftermath of scrying, snorted. Brodigan's Appraisals looked like the Real McCoy, a Hell's Kitchen hole-in-the-wall with shelves of antiques and some microscopes, loupes, and calipers for show. No one needed to know their appraisal actually came from a scrawny blond fella in glasses who hid in the back and scried antiques' histories with his mind.

Mrs. Brodigan clasped her hands. "Well, I have something else for you, if you're up for it."

"Yeah?" He picked up his canteen from the side table and took a long sip. "Whatcha got? New job?"

But Mrs. Brodigan hesitated. "Why don't I show you?" She got to her feet. "It's a bit unusual."

Oh no. Rory didn't do unusual. "Not interested!" he called after her, as she disappeared through the open pocket doors of the office.

"Perhaps not, but the last time I decided that for you, you sulked for three days."

Rory gave her retreating figure a dirty look from under the brim of his newsboy cap. Then, with a huff, he peeled himself out of his armchair. He clutched his canteen as he wove his way around Mrs. Brodigan's rolltop desk and into the main shop. Twilight had fallen, and outside the shop's large window, the lamppost illuminated the dirty snow piled on the sidewalks and the passersby as they huddled into their coats. Every now and then a head would turn toward the shop, glancing at the faded letters of its name in the window and Mrs. Brodigan's handwritten sign taped below: *Select antiques for sale. No weapon appraisals.*

Mrs. Brodigan was at the counter with the ancient cash register, retrieving a small archival box. He pointed. "That the job? What's weird about a box?"

She frowned. "I really do hesitate to tell you. Considering the hour, and the hours you've already put in this week, and with you still so young—"

"I'm *twenty*," he muttered as he took another sip.

"—but as you keep telling me, you're old enough to make your own decisions, especially when the patron's willing to pay double."

Rory sloshed the canteen, spilling water over his chin and hand. His desperately needed new glasses had cost him everything he'd saved, and rent was due on the fifth. "What's the catch?" he said, wiping his mouth with his sleeve.

"Mr. Kenzie's in a terrible rush and wants any forgeries found by breakfast." She made a face. "And it's rather a lot of letters."

"I can do it," Rory said.

"Yes, dear, because you're as magical as the *sidhe*,

but Mr. Kenzie doesn't know that, does he? It's a very difficult request."

"That's why he's paying *double*," said Rory. "Couldn't you use the dough too?" He tried to keep the question soft and casual. He suspected her late husband's medical bills were still around, but he was the last person who'd want to make the wound of that death hurt fresh.

"I wouldn't risk you to pay any debt," she said firmly. "Mr. Kenzie is under the impression I have a laboratory. It wouldn't do for him to start poking around, asking how we worked so fast."

Rory might've caved at that, but what if he lost his room? Even once he'd scrounged up the cash for a new pad, he'd have to start over, find another place secure enough. Buy new locks. "He's not gonna ask. Rich jerks think they deserve the impossible. Never ask or care 'bout the person at the bottom who's gotta do the work."

"Now that's a bit of unfair. Mr. Kenzie was terribly apologetic—"

"But he *is* some rich high hat, right?"

She sighed. "A congressman's son," she admitted. "So perhaps he is used to getting what he wants, when he wants it." Her eyes were on Rory, a little sad. "And I suppose he's unlikely to discover you. You try so hard to stay unnoticed."

Rory wrapped his arms tight around himself. "That's how it's gotta be. And since no one knows 'bout me, I can do a job like this for him."

"Your house locks the doors at ten—"

"If I can't scry the letters by then, I'll go home," he lied. The shop would be cold, but there were worse places to sleep than the armchair. She still looked reluctant, so he added, "I'm really not a boy anymore."

"Spoken *exactly* like a little boy." But her shoulders

relaxed and her smile crinkled her crow's feet again. "All right, lad, I promised I wouldn't coddle you anymore. I told you about the job so you could make the call and I'll let you make it."

Yes. "I call it good." Rory set the canteen next to the cash register and took the box from her. It was a beautiful piece and pleasantly heavy, solid mahogany he'd bet, with intricate vines carved along all the edges and a fierce bear in the center of the lid. "The box too?"

She shook her head. "Just the letters inside."

He traced the bear's carved fur, feeling the ridges beneath his finger, then opened the box. "*All* of them?" He stared at the stack, which reached the top of the box. "By *breakfast*?"

"If it's too much—"

"Everything's Jake." Because yes, it was enough letters to fill a whole night in the shop, but he'd be spending *all* his nights here if he couldn't make rent. He closed the box with a snap. "See you in the morning."

But Mrs. Brodigan still looked troubled. "It's a lot, dear, and work doesn't need to become another excuse for you to always be alone."

Rory huffed. "Better than blowing all my scratch going out when no one wants a short guy in glasses anyway."

"Nonsense—"

"*Nonsense* is exactly what comes outta my mouth half the time and I don't need anyone else to hear it." He folded his arms. "Scryers aren't good company, Mrs. B."

She sighed. "I like you just fine, dear, even when you're a storm cloud." She smiled at Rory's scowl. "I'll close up," she said, and with a pat on his arm left him to it.

Rory pulled the office's pocket door shut behind him,

muffling the sound of Mrs. Brodigan's familiar steps as she puttered around the shop. He set his newsboy cap on the side table, freeing his shaggy curls before he tucked his legs up under him in the armchair and considered the box.

Ritzy. But then, this was some political big-timer paying double for a rush job, so he was gonna be ritzy too. Rory ought to scry the box and see what all he could learn about *terribly apologetic* Mr. Kenzie—

Except they'd only been asked to appraise the letters and it wouldn't be fair play. So with a last admiring glance at the bear, he opened the box again.

Geez, there had to be two dozen letters. No envelopes either, just ancient pieces of folded paper, yellowed with age and spotted where the ink had run. He picked up the top one and unfolded it. Signed by a Frederick Douglass and dated April 1856, it looked authentic enough—but then, Rory had seen some good forgeries come through the antiques shop in the last four years.

He set the box on his ancient footstool that once must have been a very nice match for a completely different chair. He settled into his seat and carefully set the pads of his fingers on top of the letter's handwriting.

Scrying was like turning a radio dial, searching for just the right notch until suddenly the signal came in clear, static transformed to music. It was always so easy to welcome the music in—

Not always so easy to turn the radio back off. Rory tried not to think about that as he closed his eyes and let the magic sweep him into the letter's past.

The man in the bowler hat sits at a desk in a room that smells like fish. A phonograph lazily spins in the corner, scratching out Margaret Young's "Hard-Hearted Hannah." The man sticks his tongue between

his teeth as he dips his fountain pen in the inkwell.
Carefully, he puts the nib to a piece of yellowed paper
and scratches out an "1856" in the top right corner.

He lifts his head and considers the paper. After a
moment, he sets the pen down, dabs his finger in water,
and deliberately smears the wet ink on the six. He wipes
his finger on an ink-stained towel folded on the corner
of the desk and picks up his pen—

Well, *that* letter was as real as a wooden nickel. Did
Kenzie already suspect he had a forgery? Was that why
he'd come to Brodigan's in the first place?

A distant jingle startled Rory, the sound of the front
door's bell ringing behind Mrs. Brodigan as she left for
the night. He glanced at the clock and groaned. It was
hard to keep track of present time when he scried, and
he'd let himself get distracted and spent longer than he'd
meant watching the vision of that letter's past.

He set the forgery on his side table and reached back
into the box, withdrawing the second letter off the stack.
He unfolded it to find it was also signed by Frederick
Douglass, this time dated October 1855.

Huh.

He emptied the box of all its letters and found them
all signed by Frederick Douglass, all dated between
1855 and 1857, some duplicates of each other. He spread
the letters across his lap, the chair, and the footstool,
and pursed his lips.

There was no way all twenty-two of the letters were
going to be real. Had this sap bought an entire lot of
dodgy historic letters, hoping to get lucky? But why
would a congressman's son need to pay double for some
Hell's Kitchen shop to rush-appraise the lot?

Rory ground his teeth. This was weird and he didn't
like weird—he liked safe and predictable.

But he also liked having a roof over his head, and he still had twenty-one letters to scry. He rubbed his eyes behind the glasses. He'd leave the mysteries to people who could afford to care about them and just be grateful he'd make February's rent.

But as he picked up another letter, he couldn't shake the heavy suspicion that something about this job smelled wrong. Mr. Kenzie had said he wanted any forgeries found by breakfast.

What *wasn't* he saying?

Don't miss Spellbound *by Allie Therin,*
available wherever books are sold.

www.CarinaPress.com